AMERICAN DRAGON

Brandon Bagwell

American Dragon—A Novel

2019 First Printing

© 2019 Brandon Bagwell

ISBN-13: 978-1-7337942-0-6

Library of Congress Control Number: 2019905334

Published by Pill Press Books

For M—
You were the blood in my syringe.

CONTENTS

LETTER OF CAUTION

THANK YOU FOR COMING with me on this most dangerous journey.

I will do my best to ensure no harm will come to you.

American Dragon is a very special story to me. The character of Chris was heavily influenced by my experiences with the drug community and from my experience as a steroid cook. Those who have known me for a long time may remember the crazy phone calls and urgent requests I had to beg of you once I knew I was heading to jail for the first time in my thirties. To those who have served as my proxies during this time, I thank you again for ensuring my affairs were in order during my time of incarceration.

To those who have known me less long, my criminal past is merely a foggy rumor. It appears and disappears in conversation, usually accompanied by whispered phrases and spoken in hushed voices. "I heard he is a felon," one said. "How can a drug cook work around people?" another would add.

Many simply concluded, "He lost his soul to drugs, and is too stupid to even realize it."

Going into writing has been therapeutic for me. It has been my way to quietly feed the beast that is a God complex. Indeed, nothing compares to selling drugs (even using them has made me grow weary and tired), and nothing short of creating narratives of complex worlds made of unseen people and forbidden knowledge comes close. It is the closest to the rush I can come without going back to my more clandestine and covert ways.

Sometimes, I like to think I've won. My steroid lab was called American Dragon, and there is no coincidence that this tale of fiction is named after that at least. It is also true that individuals in various states have asked me what happened to it, or if it's still around. I tell them the answer is sadly no. Any bottles you may find in the shadows and corners of hole-in-the-wall gyms are mere echoes, and their reverberations are growing ever so slightly into nothingness every time they change hands. Still, by naming my novel after it, I have been able to reinvigorate—nee, immortalize—what was once an idea by a man consumed by fire in a way that is safe, healthy, and repeatable.

For me at least.

I say "for me" because I cannot promise you will come out as unscathed as I. No, I'm not suggesting you start a drug lab or go to the far reaches of the world to peddle such wares. But I am suggesting that some of the elements in this book may, at certain times, ring a little too true to you. It is my hope that you find yourself, to some degree, in each of the characters. This includes some at the highest reaches of self-actualization and the deepest pits of addiction.

Self-reflection, after all, can be a very traumatic thing.

This is my first novel, and I can guarantee that there will be more. But I can say, without a doubt, that none will have behind them so much of my personal history on the pages. I likely won't ever write "myself" in a book again, not just because I have disavowed that previous life but because it was traumatic. The veil of fiction is thin and no amount of fabrication seems to offer meaningful protection from that.

Many writers will edit and revise and re-edit and re-revise drafts for years. I couldn't, for many reasons, several of which

I can't explain in this letter. While it was cathartic to express my past on the written page, it was also damned difficult to say goodbye to so many people I helped create, and their characters as well.

I told my editor that the ink on the pages may be dry but, for some, the wounds may just be coming open with its publication. Widespread, national release was agreed upon as the only viable solution to ensure all stakeholders could get the message they needed. Still, fresh pus and old blood may yet come out to haunt me, and it is my hope that by fictionalizing large parts of the book I can protect the egos, jobs, careers, and lives of those involved with affairs that may have occurred, potentially in real places, during only possibly hypothesized events.

Still, I have spoken too much and said too little. As you read *American Dragon*, know that the book and writing will improve, purposefully, as the characters and as you yourself do. If at any point in time you find yourself reflecting on your own actions, I encourage you to put the book down and contemplate them in quiet solitude. Lock the doors, from the outside if necessary, to prevent the monster from getting out. If you are still unable to stop considering doing awesome and terrible things, as many in here do, I implore you to pick the book back up and see where it lands them.

"What kind of person would . . . ?" is a dangerous question to ask when you are in such a mood, and I hope that what you find in the back of the book is something you enjoy. I found myself, and it will stay with me for a very, very a long time.

I hope what you find treats you well, as it should be a reflection of yourself. If it doesn't, I am sorry.

Because I am powerless to help you.

ACKNOWLEDGMENTS

I HAVE ENJOYED MANY UPS and downs during this roller coaster called life, and at each turn, I always took roll call. *American Dragon* would not have been possible if it weren't for the countless individuals who supported me along the way.

Firstly, I have to thank my father. As a writer yourself, I hope you can appreciate the art even if the subject matter is a bit grisly. But then again, you wrote murder mysteries, so compared to murder, drug manufacturing isn't so bad, right?

To my dearest Leandra: words cannot express how much you mean to me, and yet words are all I have. No matter what happens, I will always answer your "moop moops."

Thanks also go to my fraternity brother, Stephen Loftus-Mercer, for being the first to encourage me to put my thoughts to paper.

To my other fraternity brother, Caleb Robertson. Your patience is appreciated so much. You put up with me at my worst and challenged me to be my best.

To Nate Bossea, thank you for giving me the confidence to compete in bodybuilding. Without you I wouldn't have met so many wonderful people in my life.

To Chris M.F. Thompson, for showing me that all of us is stronger than any of us.

To Tanner Shinn, for taking the time to listen to me when I needed to vent.

To Nick Dewey, for reminding me to find the good in any situation.

To my lead editor, Jessica Swift, thank you. If you weren't holding my hand through the roughest parts of the process, I would have surely thrown them in the air and given up.

Thanks go to Sara Dismukes, my wonderful graphic artist, who designed the chilling and enticing cover.

Thanks to Christa Bolain for catching my mistakes, of which there were many.

I'd also like to thank the inmates and staff at Cleveland County Detention Center, for creative input and suggestions during my time in the hole.

To my countless test readers, of which only a few could be featured on the back, thank you for your kind words and advice along the way.

Special thanks go to Folsom Street Events and the entire city of San Francisco. Without events like Dore Alley (Up Your Alley Fair) and Folsom Street Fair, so many men and women wouldn't have sex-positive atmospheres in which to explore themselves.

Similarly, special thanks go to Phoenix Rising, Apothecary, Tramps, Diversity Center of Oklahoma, and all the other members of the OKC Thirty-Ninth Street "gayborhood" district for providing LGBTQ individuals a place they can call home.

To Kelly Kipgen, for helping me understand one of the key themes of the book—substance problems oftentimes have roots in other places.

And, of course, to "Ryan."

ONE

I T WAS FUCKING SLOW.

No one told me how thick the oil was. Despite my obsessive and meticulous research into thousands of bodybuilding forums, none of the countless posts had prepared me for this moment. My fiendish obsession had taught me the intricacies of diet, training, and even how to put together the perfect steroid cycle. Still, nothing in my collection of rapidly consumed knowledge mentioned getting fucking high-gauge needles so I could draw the shit out of the bottle.

It was over four years ago. God, I was such a rookie then. Everything I knew I read in a book or online. I think back to that version of me and realize how many obvious mistakes I made. There were so many "unknown unknowns" to deal with. But deciding to juice was a major step for me, and taking that first step was exhilarating as hell even though it frustrated me to no end to be missing this seemingly minor tool I could have so desperately used.

I paced angrily back and forth in my garage gym, nearly frothing at the mouth. After waiting for almost two months for the steroids to arrive from overseas, I was beyond eager to feel the testosterone flow through my veins. My eagerness manifested as stress against the syringe plunger, where tiny indentations had formed on my fingertips as they fought to fill the barrel with oil faster. I was enamored by the cottonseed oil, too dense for the meager twenty-five gauge needle which suspended pure masculinity in it.

Three bottles of testosterone cypionate, a handful of one milliliter syringes, and some Dianabol to kickstart the cycle were all part of the standard first-time user's kit. I had also opted to include the post-cycle therapy, and thus had Clomid on hand for when my cycle would be complete. I even added some testosterone freebase (TNE, they called it). I speculated my cycle would net me the guaranteed twenty pounds of muscle earlier than it could have if I left it off.

I was tired of being natural. Well, that's what I told myself at least. In reality, I was tired of waiting. Waiting to be happy with my body, or for some great power to will it into perfection. In high school, I was obese, but that was well behind me by then. To be honest, I got started in the gym to kill that guy. I hated him for being unpopular. Unloved. I was an egotist with nothing to be proud of, and a physique was as good a goal as any. After a few years of training and making some headway, I enjoyed being seen as someone who was fit though I still wasn't satisfied with myself. I had spent as many hours in the gym as my professional career could allow, but no matter how many hours I spent reading, lifting, and preparing my meals, I wasn't satisfied with the rate at which the results came. "Progress, not perfection," I heard the older lifters say, but I didn't care about them. No one did. It was the Age of Instagram after all. If I couldn't be as ripped as the gay porn actors I regularly jerked off to, what was the point of even showing up?

Fuck being fit. Freaks get the re-tweets.

And why shouldn't I start using steroids right away if that was my goal? I was twenty-four years old then, 170 pounds, and twelve percent body fat. Not world class, but I met all the bro-science requirements to start juicing. I had no trophies or medals. At my best, I was good, not great. Maybe if I had better genetics or had been athletic when I was younger I wouldn't need the drugs. But who can pick their parents or go back in time?

Drugs were the perfect answer for people like me.

Instead of playing sports, my teen years were spent brooding in front of a computer, learning the ins and outs of a silicon era yet to be. How much time did I lose learning BASIC or C++, while the jocks played rugby or wrestled on the mats? How foolish could I have been, developing my mind while potential dating partners swiped left or right based upon facial features and muscular structures? I was angry at myself. I had wasted the one chance at adolescence I would ever have, and with it any chance to be one of the athletes I lusted after.

Fuck past decisions. Fuck being picked last for gym class. Fuck genetics. I, like God, refused to play with dice. Hormones weren't going to keep me from being what I wanted to be.

Muscular. Masculine. Powerful.

These were the attributes I saw on the Internet. The attributes society associates with successful men. And they were what I coveted as a homosexual. The only way for someone like me to get there was take control of biology away from Him through these drugs. I'd treat myself better than God did anyway.

There was no reason I couldn't become a model. Or a bodybuilder. Or any of the countless male body types that aroused me. I didn't need a coach or an overpriced personal trainer. I had done my homework and figured it all out.

It's true, you know, what they say about jocks—football players, wrestlers, doesn't matter—each is as stupid as a box of bricks, without exception. Most of them couldn't tell you anything about what's going on in the world, much less how they got such a marvelous physique. They were just winners in a genetic lottery. A lottery I had lost.

There were advantages to being an intelligent meathead. I just had to leverage them to outperform my competition.

They knew nothing of chemistry, biology, or physiology like I did. In this regard, I was better than them. Yet they were always more desirable than I'd ever be. At least bodybuilders took the time to learn what they were doing, and that difference was what attracted me to bodybuilding, both as a sport and a lifestyle. So I followed in their footsteps and became a willing acolyte. I devoured every bit of knowledge I could on nutrition, diet, and training regimens. From blog posts to medical journals, no source was left untouched.

Bodybuilding was a sport that felt like science. It was pure athleticism without the distraction of a game or a ball. My competition wasn't limited to a football field or wrestling mat. It was the whole damned world. The rules of engagement were as old as humanity itself, with the primary one being to outperform your competition. There were no yellow flags or foul lines. My priorities were clear. What I lost in time I would make up for with tenacity. Tenacity and drugs. I resolved to train smarter than my competition.

I would leverage economics and take advantage of the fact I could afford better drugs than the guy at home in his mother's basement. He spent his time playing sports instead of studying, so of course he should lose out. I was the better man. By extension, I should become the more confident one. The one in control.

I stared back at the syringe. So many thoughts and feelings were flooding my mind. Drop by agonizingly slow drop the oil filled the barrel. It took what seemed like an eternity before it approached full. It was my initiation, my first time.

My self-doubts and ignorance returned with a rush. I found myself muttering.

"How exactly should one breathe before they stick themselves in the leg with a one-and-a-half-inch long needle? God, I hope I don't hit that nerve. Which one is it? The one that goes down the side of the leg, or the top? Fuck. Okay, sit down. Where's that video again? Thank God for transgender people posting their therapy videos online. Oh, hey, this doctor posted a better video still. Will I grow in my legs because that's where I do my shot?"

Fuck.

A streak of pain blasted through my body as the needle pierced the skin, though it quickly subsided. The further penetration into the meat of my quad was painless, but my hand quivered with every bit I pushed the needle deeper. I was convinced this was playing hell with my muscles.

"God . . . Is this happening? Maybe I shouldn't go in all the way to be safe. What the fuck does *aspirating* mean? Oh, like breathing, got it. No blood in the syringe is good. Well, that and who likes looking at blood anyway? Fuck it, here goes."

Despite the pain, I got hard. The idea of being filled with quintessential masculinity was overwhelming. I began to push the oil into my body. It was slow, though steady. I was such an eager student. An uneducated novice. After you do your first shot you're never natural again, and I was thrilled to cross that threshold. I envisioned the oil pumping my quads up in size. All I wanted in the world was to feel that oil inside me. I wanted to belong to the brotherhood of freaks and chemical bodybuilders.

And I got exactly what I wanted.

"Just a little bit more oil to go. I'm going to love this training session I can tell. I feel so huge already!"

I felt the plunger hit the end of the barrel. Even the discomfort of removing the needle too quickly didn't stop me from shooting my load.

All over the rubberized floor.

My leg muscles tensed slightly when I came. In the needle's place was a small droplet of blood dripping down my leg.

I capped the needle quickly, threw the syringe to the side, then walked a few steps. I sensed the distinct taste and smell of pine needles. It was the newfound flavor of masculinity. I marveled at these new sensations and the slippery puddle of jizz on the floor.

"That was . . . unexpected," I said, licking my lips.

While I knew some drugs could leave a weird taste in your mouth, I didn't think steroids would be one of them. From the research I've done in the years since this first experience with a needle, few ever describe it the same way. Anecdotally, tastes and smells are as unique as the individual bodybuilders themselves.

Hobbling to the kitchen, I grabbed a paper towel to wipe the blood off my leg and my sperm off the floor.

Feeling ever so alive, I took the time for obligatory self-worship in the mirror. Naked and still bleeding down my leg, I rotated through all of the classic bodybuilding poses. Rear triceps. The lat spread. The side chest. Each gave me a chance to validate my newly discovered superiority and manhood. I took the time to examine each body part and allowed my imagination and excitement to swell with possibilities. Finally, I savored my relative size in the front double bicep pose, as my arms were my best feature. Short, military-style, buzz cut hair gave me an edgy look that allowed me to pass as somewhat older.

I resigned to pick up some weight. I curled a few warm-up sets with the mismatched pair of dumbbells I had, imagining the work my tendons and muscle fibers must be doing under the skin to make such motion a reality. Feeling confident with a slight pump, I put the dumbbells down and went to the bench press in the corner of my gym. Its cushion was worn from the previous owner and offered little support to whoever used it. The plates sure felt lighter, though to this day I am unsure how much of that was the drugs or my excitement. Either way, I added an extra plate to the bench press and went on to torture myself for being too small—a torture marked with heavy grunting and half-reps which further fueled my testosterone-aided ambitions.

For the rest of the night, the clatter of plates echoed in my gym as bars were loaded and cable machine handles were swapped out with increased frequency. Feeling perfectly in control of my body and destiny, and armed with some no-name knockoff foreign steroid bottles, I knew that the perfect body was just a matter of time away.

Well, time and drugs, anyway.

TWO

FOUR YEARS AFTER MY first foray into the world of chemical bodybuilding, the rewards of my usage were beyond description. In the same amount of time it takes someone with a bachelor's degree to become a doctor, I had gone up nearly three chest sizes and put two and a half inches on my arms. Bodybuilding was an all-consuming obsession, and while most doctors had patients to practice on, I mostly just had myself.

I say mostly. As I progressed, it didn't take long for me to realize that there was power to buying in bulk. Sources were hard to come by at first, but the so-called Dark Web ran deep and anonymous sellers always seemed to have steroids available. To minimize legal risk, I made few purchases but kept them large enough to be ahead of my consumption. The sellers noticed. What started as a few complimentary bottles here or there slowly turned into a stash. As my horde grew, so did my dosages, but eventually even that became large enough I ended up with spare bottles and no idea what to do with them.

Outside of the gym and buying drugs, I continued to gain experience through academic books, journals, and logging my own reactions to various chems. I began to see myself as a Dr. Jekyll/Mr. Hyde-type character, constantly trying to perfect the right cocktail to maximize results.

Even armed with all the raw knowledge I could find, my self-practice taught me things I never would have imagined.

The most subtle of which was by far the most rewarding. The positive effects that steroids had on my social and professional life were nearly incalculable.

My coworkers, friends, and even random strangers began to respect me.

Online blogs and anonymous forum posts cautioned that, after a certain point of chemical augmentation, rewards would come only with the criticism and inherent disgust reserved for those who juice. Having not rued that day, I was fearless that this respect came without a price. I was fortunate enough to be perceived as a man of strong build and character who owed his success to good genes and a merciless work ethic instead of being looked at as a physical beast fueled by chemical desires.

When you work in IT, the first thing you learn is that a job done well means remaining unseen. When bridges, roads, airplanes, and the other artifacts of traditional engineering start to become unsafe, you want them to look unsafe. Designers have the goal that potential users think to themselves, "You know what, that looks like a bad idea, and for reasons of personal safety, I am not going to go anywhere near that!" Computers, however, don't usually cause the loss of life or limb. Even when things are at their worst, it's just difficult to give the same impression of impending doom when things go poorly. So, whether by grand design or serendipity, computers (and the requisite workforce which enables their function) are unassuming. A total shitstorm can be going on in the background and, of course, you can't pull up a bullhorn and scream, "Everybody! Quit sending e-mail!"

Bland. Whether a good day or bad, the people who gave me this respect all were bland.

None of that seemed to match me now. Cheap khakis and a polo, the normal daily attire of my coworkers, just didn't show off the over two hundred pound, ninety-two percent lean body mass beast I'd become. Dark designer jeans and skin conforming clothes became my uniform, and I seemed to be just as ready for a nightclub as for an office meeting. While considered outside the dress code, no one said a word to me.

I even grew a mohawk, which I occasionally colored for added roughness. It gave me an edgy masculine look, which I took every opportunity to accentuate.

Where my attire was varied, my diet certainly wasn't. Four servings of chicken a day and nearly a dozen eggs for breakfast was my own brand of blandness. For carbs, it was plain oatmeal and flavorless rice. But I didn't care. At that point, I was all in. Food's importance was defined by its function, not its form, and certainly not its taste. Chicken's value was determined by its protein content, not its level of spice. Meal prep was each Sunday, and that sometimes included making white fish. By Thursday, a beautiful layer of fish gel coated the bottom of countless plasticware containers. In what most individuals called fish goo, I saw only fish oil, essential fats, amino acids, and carbohydrates in a perfect combination specific to attaining my training goals.

If eating dog food was going to add an extra ten pounds of muscle to my frame, you can bet your ass I'd be sitting in my cubicle with a spoon inside a can of Alpo, smiling with every bite.

Carrying around a man-purse full of food everywhere was hardly convenient. Sure, I got some laughs. I had to figure out exactly how I was going to shower with two-a-days in the gym, but it was not an unaccomplishable task when I put myself to it. Eventually virtually everyone commented on how much it must suck to eat the same meals over and over again. I perfected replacing their criticism with my ego.

"Doesn't suck as much as only bench pressing two plates."

Inevitably, regardless of the insults, they'd ask how they could follow suit and get my results.

So I'd tell them about my blandness and how it compared to theirs. I told them to step up their style and eat better. I told them to hit the gym consistently and to weigh their food instead of super sizing it. I told them every bit of truth except the one I injected on a regular basis.

I never told anyone steroids were a requirement to get to my level.

Some took the advice I gave and attempted to emulate me. There were the dumbasses who'd just follow me around, getting fat despite eating what I ate, all the while failing to realize I burned off those calories by deadlifting 500 pounds once a week. There were also the idiots who thought cardio was the holy grail of abs (and it is, if you want to be 130 pounds and featured on the front cover of *National Geographic*). But to achieve my look, the formula was deceptively simple, despite my partially true way of presenting the knowledge I had acquired.

Eat big. Lift big. Dose big.

Of course, I couldn't tell people to start sticking themselves. I had taken the time to build the knowledge and dedication through the years to understand the long-term consequences of my choices. But I couldn't trust an eager and jealous coworker to do the same. I had to be truthful, but not honest. Instead, I gave advice on macronutrients and explained what I ate and why. I talked about legal over-the-counter supplements from Vitamin Shoppe and offered my opinions on why one brand was better than the other.

For all things technical and computer-related, I was an open book and would deeply dive into the most arbitrary questions they would ask. But when it came to the body, I was trapped by the truth, and forced to reconcile the desire to give quality advice while first doing no harm. Well, not permanent harm at least. So, as with every bodybuilder, steroids became the forbidden topic.

Everyone at some point came up to me talking about their goals and how to achieve them. My regular feedings meant I occupied the break room and constantly hogged the microwave at work. Occasionally, I'd get practically gang-banged by a flock of people, each with their own goals. Too many of them had the suspicious story that they "knew a guy" who could bench fifty pounds more than I could, or was fifteen pounds more muscular than me. I chalked most of it up to nerds playing a numbers game, and their trying to seem relevant to the obvious alpha male in the room.

One day a pack of hard-gainers from the finance team were gathered around me. It was like watching hyenas near a lion try to be big and intimidating. Hard-gainers, by my definition, weighed less than I warmed-up with on a bench press. This group just wanted to grow.

I was in a particularly friendly mood and giving advice to one of them, while holding court with the rest. He was scrawny, and his shampoo likely had more vitamins in it than his diet did. I was covering the basics of nutrition with him and the rest of the class as another man, named Dylan, walked in the room to use the microwave.

"You're likely not getting enough meat in your diet. And I don't mean that stuff they sell at Burger King," I explained. "To start, do you think you could add another fifty grams of protein each day?"

"More like fifty grams of enanthate," Dylan muttered under his breath.

It was one of those sentences that, when you don't understand it, just flies under the radar. The pack didn't seem to notice, and went along with their conversations as though it were mere background noise. I glared at Dylan, motionlessly continuing the conversation with Scrawny as unsuspectingly as possible.

He knows, I feared.

Enanthate isn't exactly a common word, and people have a natural way of ignoring things they don't recognize. But that word, at that particular point in time, as whispered and quiet as it was, shook me to my very core. Because regular weight lifters and gym rats don't walk around using words typically reserved for pharmacists, clinical doctors, and—most importantly—steroid users.

Specialist knowledge imbues a certain magnetism to its holder. The rarer the specialty, the stronger the attraction when two people with the same background meet. Sure, meeting someone in another state who went to the same high school as you may feel fun, but it pales in comparison to the exhilaration experienced when you meet someone who takes the same drugs as you. After all, to go to the same high school just means your parents fucked in the same zip code as the other person's parents did. But to know what testosterone enanthate is means one has spent time learning how hormones effect the body. It implies a certain degree of knowledge about the gym, and the social mores existent in such an environment. It means you know to rack your weights and not walk between other lifters and the mirror because its rude. It means you likely know the difference between fast- and slow-acting carbohydrates. Because by the time you're using tools like steroids, you've exhausted all of the easy stuff.

But besides the technical details and educational components, it implies so much more. Steroids are still illegal after all, and you just can't walk up to the pharmacy counter and ask for them. People don't normally take the time to learn about drugs and then never try them. So one has to assume that such deep specialty knowledge comes with a personality which is not only *willing* to bend the rules, but likely *has broken them* at some point before. This wasn't finding someone who went to the same high school as you. This was finding someone who fucked the same girl behind the bleachers you did! Not only is it a smaller crowd, but there is a certain comradery associated with it.

Fear gripped my throat, which I managed to hide through false courage. Countless possibilities flew through my mind with ever-increasing anxiety. Perhaps Dylan had started using. Perhaps he knew someone who used and was just exposing me as a fraud. Maybe he's got a rare medical condition and learned about steroids in some fashion I could not even fathom! It was, in every way imaginable, just like falling in love, but without being able to communicate the emotional turmoil racking one's mind.

I sized Dylan up while continuing the farce of teaching a beginning nutrition class. He wasn't huge, muscularly at least. He was tall, about six foot two, and maybe 150 pounds. He sported wonderfully golden hair and a slightly rugged look. At around the same age as me, I could see his farm boy roots in the practical clothing he wore. I recognized him as a fellow employee, but not someone that I worked with regularly. He had come on board as part of a recent acquisition, but our roles weren't aligned and didn't require talking to one another.

As the timer on the microwave neared its end, I signaled that class was over. I stood up and the hyenas followed suit.

Everyone else needed to get back to work as well. I approached Dylan and looked into the microwave.

"Looks like it's lunchtime for you too, huh? What are you taking to grow?" I asked.

"Not what you're taking, that's for sure."

I smiled. "Well, if tanning products can come in a bottle, I guess muscles can, too. I'm Chris, nice to meet you. I haven't seen a lot of guys your size who even know what enanthate is."

"I'm Dylan," he said, offering a firm handshake. "Yeah, knowing is about all I do. I don't take anything. Someday though."

It was refreshing. I listened intently as he talked about his past, and I asked questions to delve into his psyche more. He told me that he grew up in the country and was used to raising livestock for slaughter. To him, steroids were mostly tools used to put food on the table. He used to be like all the rest I'd dealt with—a weakling nerd who joined the gym to gain size. Somewhere inside him, though, was something different. He had spent six years working on his body, and while he lacked the obsessiveness I had, he made up for it with consistency.

I tried to both listen to *and* understand him.

He shared his aspirations to be big. Really big. But from what I gleaned of his training, he was doing way too much cardio and eating like the wrong kind of athlete. He got the basic ideas while missing some of the key points. He was off just a few degrees from true north, but could be set right easily enough.

"Damn, six years and still only 150 pounds," I commented. "How could someone who is as technically minded as you not take advantage of every available shortcut?"

"More like 170. And, well, not every shortcut is available," he hinted.

"Didn't you say you could get it for the cattle?"

"Eh, not really. It's my parents' farm, for one. And with all the regulations and stuff, if I want 'em, I'm going to have to get 'em some other way."

I paused. I could see want in his eyes. It wasn't the needy lust the hyenas had. They were just hoping to pick off scraps of knowledge—scavenging what they could find—and yet were too picky to eat most of it. But Dylan was willing and consistent with what he wanted and had pictures to show for it, even if his plan was largely wrong.

I had extra bottles of testosterone at home. Parting with a few wouldn't kill me. My stash wasn't gaining me much in terms of immediate gain, and I felt oddly invested in this guy's success. Perhaps I was just in a sentimental mood, or maybe it was the way he presented himself. Either way, selling him a few of those bottles wasn't going to hurt my wallet at all, and since we both had the same employer I knew he wasn't a cop. It was as low of a risk as any, and marking it up twenty percent seemed like a fair return on free stock.

"I've got a guy. Do you need me to draw up a cycle, or do you know what you want?"

He was the last person I gave free advice to. My first drug deal took place at work, next to the coffee machine in the break room. It wouldn't be my last.

Over the course of the next year, I saw Dylan grow as fast as my sales did. Like myself, the larger he got, the more he wanted. I dropped his excessive cardio habit, and taught him the difference between various athletic diets. He worked tirelessly, and the results he earned were all the marketing I needed to flip the next set of bottles that came in. We started training together at the same gym, and eventually a few of the other lifters noticed his gains and approached me about them. It was clear I was calling the shots, telling him when and what to lift. Some of them hinted at either current or former steroid use, and when they had a problem getting chems I managed to fill the gap in their cycle—for a price.

That was when I learned the very essence of becoming a drug dealer. The one formula that gets everyone started.

When you mark it up twenty percent, you only need five customers to eat for free.

So that's what I strived for. Just five, so I wouldn't have to worry about paying for the steroids out of my paycheck. Five guys I could lift with regularly and who had the same goals. Sadly, reality wasn't as kind as the math. The truth was that Dylan and I consumed much more than other buyers, most of whom just wanted beginner-level dosing or the odd bottle on the side. Plus, most of my customers weren't as dedicated or hardcore as we were. So it became transactional, merely financial. Five became six. Six became seven. And my hopes of keeping it a cottage industry were essentially dashed.

So I looked for other ways to make money. I started selling growth hormone and HCG. I resold Viagra and other drugs men bought to perform better in or out of the gym. Occasionally I'd get called because someone who wasn't my customer bought bunk shit or something that wasn't sterile and they were too scared to call their doctor. I began to keep odd drugs on hand—antibiotics and pain killers—usually bought from everyday people I'd known for years—and resold them to the highest bidder.

My suppliers noticed the uptick and unusual requests. Before long it became easier for them to ship the chemicals in raw powder form. I never told anyone that I began to manufacture steroids (not even Dylan), but my penchant for chemistry paid off on the bottom line.

Forget twenty percent. It was closer to *fifteen thousand* percent.

The extra money was nice, but I still kept myself somewhat reserved. The fundamental goal was always the same: try and eat for free. But my decisions were certainly starting to get warped. I bought a new car and started paying for things I never needed in cash. I wasn't what I'd call rich, but I was comfortable. Comfortable enough to buy anything I wanted!

I eventually came to disdain the day job. I became more argumentative with subordinates, but still managed to show respect to my superiors and hide behind my work results while on the clock. I had been in IT long enough that it became boring. Nothing was as fun as training or helping others meet their physical fitness goals. I started doing personal training on the side, though generally avoided coaching coworkers because the nerds were rarely serious. Dylan followed suit, and while he never pushed drugs, he would take the people I wouldn't. Though, in many ways it didn't matter—all his personal training income went to subsidize his habit through me.

Charging kept the riff-raff to a minimum and the hyenas at bay. For some reason, ninety-five percent of individuals won't do shit about something unless they put money down, and even then most of them would drop out after a few months. I trained them hard and demanded results, sometimes when they refused to work for them. Each was a disappointment. Each failed to become another me (or even another Dylan), and it broke my heart every time. I tried to temper my fervor on occasion, but eventually had to give the more sensitive types to Dylan to work with. It was like going on an endless loop of dates but never finding that one true love.

They all expected to have my seventeen-inch arms after one day of lifting. At five seven, it took me years and heavy doses of creatine and trenbolone to get there.

What I'd say: "Keep up the good work champ! Nice job."

What I'd think: *Will this dude even be here next week?*

Still, those that stuck with me for any length of time got the results they worked for, even if they weren't the results I would have gone for myself. My ambition exceeded theirs. Given they were lazy desk jockeys, they were happy with simple things. It wasn't hard to get them down a couple of pant sizes or ready for the beach by summer.

Having Dylan as my protégé was a blessing. A second person meant I could experiment with drugs at twice the rate, and a failed experiment wasn't going to deter someone as eager as him. In no time at all, he was up to 220 pounds and as lean as I was. We eventually found the right combination of anabolics necessary for us to both grow optimally. It was a combination I supplied, and that he grew to love watching swirl inside a syringe.

Our day job offered limited opportunities to work with him, but I took every one I could get. In the gym, I trusted him as my back spot while benching as well. Few could handle that kind of weight should the bar fall. When not talking about bodybuilding, which was rare, our banter was light. The reality was we had little in common outside of our insane passion, and we were polar opposites politically. Regardless, we were the best of friends.

We were training alone in the gym one early morning.

"Hey, snowflake," he greeted me.

"What's up, you fuckin' racist!" I replied.

By this time, I had developed a keen eye for discerning guys who had weak points. I could distinguish the ones who would puss out because lifting actually involved work from those who actually gave it their all and Fortune frowned upon them that day.

"Your guy with the hips has a problem," I said.

"Yeah? His form looks—"

"He's a runt for a reason, Dylan. He's got a medical problem. Low T, I guarantee it. Have his doctor check him out. That's why he's lagging."

He gaped at me with his weird goofy stare that I'm sure got him bullied when he was a puny weakling. He had learned not to doubt me, and that following my suggestions usually yielded positive results.

"How the fuck do you do it, Chris?"

"Do what?"

"Know when someone is hormonally off?"

"I just do. I see enough competitors day in and day out. Either the guy's estrogen is too high or his testosterone too low. Women carry their weight in their asses, men in their abs. Not that you can tell on a whale, but when random white dudes walk around with black booty asses, you know something's up."

"I've read about that, sure. But you don't really just walk around the grocery store pointing out, 'Hey, look at that guy! He must have a hormone imbalance!'"

I stared back in silence.

"Well, knowing you, I guess you would," Dylan chuckled.

"Can you help me re-rack these weights? I've gotta be at work in a bit."

Dylan replied, "Lift them yourself, you need the gains. I've still got twenty pounds on you."

I scoffed. "Yeah, and I'm five seven. What are you, six two?"

"Depends on what convenience store I'm robbing that day."

I started putting the weights away, ignoring the joke. Dylan approached me closely.

"Hey, can you get me some bottles?" he asked quietly.

I looked around. We were relatively alone. Still, I hated doing business in the gym because it seemed the stereotypical place for a dealer like me to get caught. I nodded.

"Yeah, man, whaddya need?"

"Three bottles of tren. Hex if you have it. Four of test—cyp or enanthate, whatever you got."

Dylan's knowledge of chemistry had grown since I first started working with him. The shorthanded speech I first found so attractive in him became the normal way of talking between us. Nonsense to most, but beautiful to the few who understand.

"You know I can't get tren hex. My guy doesn't carry it. No one wants it but you, and that's just because you heard about it on some blog, I'm sure. I can get you trenbolone enanthate and you grow just fine on that. As for the test, I can get any kind you want."

"Well, tren enanthate gives me weird nightmares if I dose it wrong."

I rolled my eyes. "Then don't dose it wrong, dumbass. I have acetate, will that do?"

"Yeah. What'll it run?"

I paused. I knew my price list like the back of my hand. Dylan still didn't know I made it, and God knows I could never tell him. I learned a long time ago that two people can only keep a secret if one of them is dead. It wasn't that I was scared of losing my best and oldest customer; I was scared of getting caught. Still, it was better to feign ignorance than anything. The lie slipped through my teeth as I smiled slightly.

"I'll have to ask my guy when I get off work. I don't know when he can get it."

"That's cool. Let me know and I'll get you for it."

Dylan was always solid on payment. Working for the same company meant we got paid on the same day. It was all money in the bank.

Work was routine as always. Customers came and went (where the word *customers* is synonymous with people who have problems and no idea how to solve them). Service tickets were opened and closed, sometimes on the same phone call or walk-in. When the time came for me to leave, the place looked just as stoically brown and beige as when I arrived.

As I exited the building I was greeted with the kind of hot humid air that transforms cars into furnaces, making their drivers stick to their leather seats and wish they'd bought cloth instead. Mine was one of the better cars in the lot, though not by local standards. Even in Oklahoma, simple luxury was considered wasted. My entry-line BMW coupe was exotic in a field of Camrys and F-150s. After all, I had no need or—more importantly—the desire for the extra seats and towing packages that adorned the more common vehicles surrounding mine.

The drive home from work was equally as boring as my day had been. The Great Plains were visually endless. The horizon faded into the distance without the slightest characteristic skyline—natural or otherwise. Even the downtown area, where a handful of skyscrapers could be seen, seemed to fit entirely in my rearview mirror as I headed back home. Ahead of me was an endless suburban sprawl, with franchised national companies based from far away being the only places to do business.

Once I got home, I went inside to check my inventory for Dylan.

"Out of trenbolone. Fuck."

Saying someone is "on steroids" is about as specific as saying someone's "on cold medicine." Just as there is diversity in over-the-counter meds, there is also diversity among steroids.

There are approximately a dozen primary go-to steroids for performance enhancement purposes. One half are injectables. The other half are orals. A third of the total set have some combination, variation, or alteration that enables them to be either (when prepared correctly). The most well-known anabolic steroid among bodybuilders is testosterone, because it's the only one natural to the human body.

Each of the injectable steroids has its own ester, or salt, form which is used for their construction. Salts, like cypionate or enanthate, are slower to release, meaning fewer injections per week. It's the equivalent of a once-a-day allergy pill. Salts like acetate are generally faster to release, making them more like that aspirin you pop every four hours. Even fewer salts, like hexahydrobenzylcarbonate (hex for short), though uncommon, fall somewhere in the middle. Oral steroids have a few variations, based on how they get processed by the liver and how much havoc they play on your body before the desired effect comes to fruition.

A dozen steroids. Half a dozen esters each. Fuck this is a shit business. Too many products, too many sizes. Too many variations and no one wants the same damned thing!

I grabbed a few beakers from the bottom kitchen cabinet and some latex gloves from the first aid kit. I smiled with enjoyment as I put them on. There was something peaceful about preparing steroids that my normal work day didn't provide. It was calm, and uninterrupted time. There were no phone calls, voicemails, or emails to interrupt my actual work. No one was going to tap me on the shoulder and tell me to get to some other priority or task. But the enjoyment of it really came from the knowledge of how easy it was to prepare.

Meth houses blow up all the time (or so many may think). The reality is, even meth cooks have gotten more sophisticated in their ways. The reason newspapers don't report on this topic like they did in previous decades is methods have changed. Of course, stimulants like meth still involve terrible icky consequences for the ecology when it comes to waste products and the like, but fortunately, steroids are not anything like that.

It is more dangerous baking cookies than it is to bake steroids and, oh my God, so much cheaper than buying them online like I used to. Nothing caustic. Nothing carcinogenic. No dangerous waste products to speak of.

In fact, every component is organic and decomposes safely. And while I wouldn't necessarily pour it in my eyes or take a bath in the ingredients, it's nothing like the crap hard-drug users put in their bodies. That shit's for car batteries and cleaning drains. Steroid-making is done in every compounding pharmacy in your neighborhood (of which, most neighborhoods have two) and there's just simply nothing for the EPA to care about.

The same thought, as always, crossed my mind as I began the process.

"Just keep it sterile, since it goes in the body. If anyone cares about what goes in their bodies, it's bodybuilders."

My cooking method was simple, but effective. I had a few customers that I had built up through various connections, so making a little extra volume than what Dylan and I consumed on any given batch was useful. Bodybuilding is an expensive hobby, after all. High quality protein, eating two-and-a-half pounds of chicken a day, and premium gym memberships were regular expenses. It was a rich man's sport and a rich man's drug.

The smell of rugged pine filled the kitchen air as reruns of *Breaking Bad* played in the background. I liked the show, not only because I could empathize with the main character, but because I thought of him oddly as mentor. Mr. White said to "respect the chemistry," and I always did.

While waiting for my batch to finish cooking, I took a break to look outside the window and admire my car. Meth dealers drive broken ass Hondas. Steroid dealers drive BMWs. I smiled, knowing that I had made not only money today, but helped Dylan and I reach our goals.

After completion, I removed the gloves and discarded them in the trash. My hands, despite the precaution, were always coated in grapeseed oil and smelled richly for it. Once cooled, I labeled the bottles with a marker. I bagged up Dylan's order and set it to the side.

Only got to train once today, but at least I made some good gear.

I pulled up some porn and masturbated to completion. I licked clean any evidence of my deeds, and reveled in the taste of cum mixed with hormone powder.

It was a good day to be a bodybuilder.

THREE

I N THE YEARS I spent bodybuilding, I made a name for myself that I couldn't have without steroids. It doesn't take long for management to notice someone who can execute well at work and look good doing it. So, I got a raise. Then a promotion. Then another raise. I had quickly outpaced my fellow employees on the track toward management and was enjoying the ride for its visibility. I was assigned various projects for customers and executives alike. My plumage shined brightly each day, and I stole the attention and interest of those many years my senior.

"How would you like to go to San Francisco?"

By contrast, Donald, my new boss was a simple guy. Family man. Married. First to the military, and then after retiring from that, to his spouse. His office was decorated as such, with the obligatory pictures of loved ones outlined in red, white, and blue. He rolled back in his chair, showing not only his gold wedding band but also the smugness that comes when a leader gets to give one of his direct reports a reward. He wasn't someone I'd normally go for a drink with after work, but the kind of guy you knew you could entrust with your best friend's kid. Or any random kid. As long as that kid wasn't one of those fags. Which was fine. He never asked, I never told.

"I've never been to San Francisco. For what?" I responded, closing the door to his office.

"Convention. Cybertech is doing a trade show out there, and I know you haven't had any training in a while. It's likely up your alley, and we need some upskilling in the Linux team."

Upskilling. One of those weird words that only make sense in the Beige World of Business. I swear, if you said words like that in a room with a green plant, it'd wilt.

"I don't see why not. Who would turn down the chance to spend company money and listen to nerds talk about technology?"

In gay paradise, nonetheless.

Donald tossed a pen between his fingers. I knew what he was expecting—a song and dance with me gleaming and thanking him for a chance to check out Silicon Valley, endless acknowledgement for investing in me and all. For Christ's sake, it's expected when you've worked in the industry as long as I had. I wasn't just another expendable grunt changing oil in Humvees in some desert war zone. I was one of the few people who understood what the customers wanted. What they needed. I rarely asked for training, if ever, finding even routine meetings boring. I would rather spend my time at my desk eating my forty-fifth serving of chicken and rice, all while producing more output than my peers.

The former master chief seemed content to acknowledge my humor without laughing. He thought of us all as nerds spending too much company money.

"Yes, who wouldn't indeed. It's important that we get this training to the rest of the team. We've got to be ready to meet that demand for some of these upcoming projects. Let's figure out who the players are, get an understanding of how their products work and who's buying what. Then, start water-falling the relevant items to the team so we know what we're supposed to support in the next twelve months."

Detailed marching orders indeed. Apparently, he had his sights set on becoming general at some point.

"Sure. Can you get me the dates? I'm pretty sure I don't have any conflicting appointments, but it's always best to check."

"Of course."

My foot turned as though to leave, while Donald looked at me sternly. Quickly thinking, I froze, while trying to minimize my attempted movement. It wasn't the place of a subordinate like me to call a discussion over, at least not in his office. Perhaps, had my rapport with him been better, I would have been able to casually enter and leave without needing to be dismissed.

"Thanks, Donald. I appreciate the opportunity."

Donald smiled shortly, maintaining the rigidity of his forehead and posture. Giving a shallow wave of his hands, he responded, "Don't mention it."

I closed his office door behind me. The relative calm of his office was replaced with the cacophony of office phones and people typing. It was a busy day at work, and a busy day for me to sell drugs. I made a beeline for my desk to fetch a bottle of creatine I brought from home.

Once in hand, I went over to Dylan's desk. I handed it over to him.

"I think you left this at my house the other night."

Wearing a headset, he glanced up to meet my eyes. He mouthed silently that he was on the phone, but saw I was insistent. When he reached out to take it, I tilted the bottle so he would hear the faint *clink* of glass rattling. Feeling the weight when he took it, Dylan could tell his bottles were inside. He looked me in the eyes and dismissed me away with a wink and a gesture. We were always on good terms. His credit was good with me, and I knew I'd get my $400 from him at some point. Hell, he'd find an extra bottle in there for being so loyal. I habitually gave him extras, partially as a reward, and partially because I never wanted anyone to complain about underfilled bottles.

And no one ever did.

I returned to my desk to delete the obligatory low priority e-mails so I could focus on those that actually warranted a response.

My phone buzzed with a text from my friend Tony. He lived in Kansas now, and I hadn't heard from him in a while. We kept in touch over the years and he was one of those guys who was always interested in bodybuilding, but mostly for the hot men. He was gay as well, and a little bit of a party animal himself.

Hey Bud! I'll be in town for a bit.
Think you could hook me up with some stuff?

I fucking hated doing business through text messages.

Could you call me now?

Yeah.

I stepped into an unoccupied meeting room.

"Hey, how's it going?" I answered Tony's call.

"Not too bad, what about you?"

I paced back and forth like I did whenever I was on a conference call, gesturing with my hands open. "Oh, you know, work as always. You in town?"

"Yeah, I was hoping to stop by for a bit."

"I might could get free. What do you need?" I asked, knowing the answer.

"Viagra, if you got it."

Tony was predictable. That's all he ever wanted. Viagra wasn't one of those drugs most people associate with bodybuilding, but I started dealing it when I heard a few guys had a hard time keeping it up while coming off their cycles. I figured where there's a problem, there's a market. But I could never figure out why he needed so damned much of it. And he needed *a lot*. Tony wasn't a bodybuilder, and I never sold him steroids though he knew I had them. He must have attended more sex parties than I did customer meetings.

"How many?"

"Two hundred?"

"Wow, okay. Let me see what I can do. That's a lot for one day's notice, ya know. Damn, man, if you gave me a month or so that'd be one thing. There's no way these are just for you. What's going on?"

"That's cool, I'll take whatever you can drum up. Some friends are going out west and I need to re-up for them, too. If you saw them, you'd understand."

I heard his shit-eating grin through the phone. I envisioned Tony eating some hot model's ass while they were all hopped up on penis pills.

"Yeah?"

"Yeah, for serious. You should see these guys. Just get me what you can. I know some people out there I can hook them up with, too. I just figured I'd save everyone a trip since I'm passing through anyway."

"Well, maybe you should give this other guy more than twenty-four hours' notice. It doesn't just rain from the sky."

"Maybe not in Oklahoma. Out there it sure does."

My phone beeped. I pulled it away from my ear to look at the screen. A picture message from Tony popped up, showing three very hot, scruffy, shirtless men, none of whom looked like the type I'd take home to Mom and Dad. They looked like they belonged in a prison gang rape porn, tattoos and all.

"Damn."

"Yeah, so if you can help out, that'd be great."

"I'll see what I can do. Hit me up after the gym. Eight o'clock?"

"Thanks, man! You're the best!"

Yes, yes I am.

Work kept me busy and the rest of the day flew by without much of a hitch. I kept the windows up along the ride home. I stopped by just long enough to fetch Tony's pills, which I packed in a baggie, before I was back on the road for the gym. The summer was dry and red clay had started to fill the air along with cottonseed. After getting there, I popped an allergy pill along with my pre-workout.

Another problem, another pill.

It was going to be a good leg day. Well, as much as leg day can be "good." I was doing more with volume than heavy weight. My legs had always been my strong point aesthetically, not that training them was any less of a bitch. I made a point to never train other people on my leg day. I was just never in the mood for their groaning on top of mine.

Dylan, ever the masochist, insisted we do ten sets of ten on the squat rack. We finished the final set then collapsed onto a spare bench. We gasped, the breath we lost twenty minutes prior trying to find its way back into our lungs.

"I think you're trying to kill me," I wheezed.

"I'm trying to get you into another weight class. If only you'd stop being a pussy and add more weight."

"It's not about the weight. It's about the control."

"Sure, Chris."

We sat in a euphoric haze, staring at the ceiling. Beige commercial tiles and bright florescent warehouse lighting glared back on us. It was mostly quiet, despite the sound of other lifters in the distance going from machine to machine. Occasionally, we'd hear plates *clank* or treadmills *whirr*, but in the hot summer months, few braved voluntarily building a sweat in this weather. We were left alone when we trained together, and I enjoyed it that way.

"Read anything interesting?" I asked, hoping to catch my breath while he went into story mode.

"Not really. I've been studying for this new certification at work. What about you?"

Damn. Backfired.

"Kind of," I responded. "I read an article about some Norwegian woman who died."

"Oh yeah? What about her?"

"Well, this chick in Norway, or Sweden, one of those countries, I dunno, she died. Anyway, she made it to like 116 years old. She was something like the fifteenth oldest person in the world and she died, but when she was seventy, she donated her body to science."

"How do you donate your body to science when you're alive?"

"No, stupid, she set it up before she knew she was dying. She just never knew she'd make it that long. So, when she died, her body eventually went to some university to be cut into."

"Well, that's cool."

"That's not the interesting part. The interesting part is she ran out of stem cells."

"What?" he asked.

"No, seriously, she ran out of stem cells. In the autopsy, they found all of her red blood cells came from a single pair of stem cells in her bone marrow. We're born with tens of thousands of them and she had just two left. *She literally lived herself to death*. No cancer. No Alzheimer's. No genetic diseases. She was eccentric, sure, but not in that 'I've lost my mind' kind of way."

"Weird."

Dylan got up. He lumbered toward the treadmill to walk off the last bit of pain in his legs. I guess he wasn't as interested in the story as I thought he would have been. Normally we exchanged information about the body and medical journals with some delight, but since it had little to do with bodybuilding, I suppose it didn't make much sense to him.

Done with the sweat session of the day, I decided to pack my things into my gym bag and head home. I picked up my shaker cup, lifting belt, and other things then started heading for the door. Once I got outside, a familiar truck pulled up.

Tony.

Tony was not the kind of man you'd normally see at a gym. In contrast to my own physique, he was tall and girthy, almost intimidating, with a strength he didn't train for. Though he was naturally well built, his overall demeanor was more playful than overtly powerful. His eyes had collected slight bags under them, which I took to mean he was weary from travel. He was soft around the edges yet had this way about him that convinced you he could pick you up by your elbows and toss you six feet through the air if he wanted.

I can vouch for the legitimacy of that feeling. That was one hot night.

He got out of the truck and we approached each other. We hugged, though feeling the sweat on my body, he quickly pulled back and regretted the decision. Even though we'd sucked each other's dicks before, we kept our touching to a level appropriate for heterosexual comfort.

"Tony the Tiger, how you been?"

"Terrific! How 'bout you, stinky man?"

"Don't you mean . . . YOUUUUUURREEEEE GREAT!" I teased.

"Shut the fuck up, loser."

We walked back toward his truck. When I got inside I was greeted by the musk of cigarette smoke. It was a fairly new vehicle, but had high miles by the look of it. It wasn't equipped with an ashtray but Tony managed to buy one which occupied a cup holder slot. It was full, and then some. The smell of smoke filled every crevice. The upholstery, navy blue with almost chocolate colored stains, was ripped all to fuck. Any reasonable person would assume from the trash bags and tossed change strewn about that the man lived in his vehicle.

"So, what brings you to town?" I started, showing personal interest before it would be appropriate for business to proceed.

"My company keeps cutting sales staff and making territories larger. I never wanted to buy into these larger routes, but, hey, I guess it'll make my numbers look bigger when I apply somewhere else."

"Meh, you'll survive."

"How many did you get?"

I dug into my pocket. The baggie fit easily in my palm.

"Forty-five. Best I could do. But unless you're planning a sex party with the entire Kansas City Chiefs, it should tide you over."

"The San Francisco Giants, actually. And funny you say that! We sometimes do wear jerseys."

"Ha ha," I laughed, knowing he did, indeed, have a sportswear fetish. "That's where I'll be soon enough."

"Then maybe restock soon. That's where all the fun is."

"Meh, it's a work trip. How much craziness do you think I'm going to get into out there if I'm stuck in meetings with dweebs?"

"You'd be surprised," he replied. "What do I owe ya?"

"Call it forty-five. Leaves me dry but I should get more soon."

He pulled out some loose bills from his back pocket.

"Got change?" he asked, showing only twenties and a ten.

"No, but I got a stunning personality."

He tossed fifty bucks onto the center console between us. "Whatever, at least you're cute."

"Awww! Thanks, Papa Bear," I flirted. "I'll throw in some freebies next time."

I leaned over to give him a hug, but, in reality, I was concealing my movement to anyone outside observing us. While reaching over, I dropped the baggie full of pills north of the cemetery for dead smokes and scooped up the cash. He returned my hug and gave me a small kiss.

Though I didn't get to see Tony often, his charm always made me smile. We were very different people, with different goals in life. My time was better spent jumping rope or using the step mill, while his involved filling his lungs with smoke as fast as he could. Though I loved Tony, I left quickly. The smoke was getting to be too much.

FOUR

ORK WAS BUSY, BUT I took the opportunity to book my travel. Having never been to San Francisco, I didn't know if there were any particular points of reference I should use. Other than the obvious convention center, Golden Gate Bridge, and that pyramid thing, I had no preconceived idea of where the action was. Going in late July meant missing Gay Pride by a month.

Refusing to resign myself to the routine touristy museums and humdrum art shows, I downloaded a GPS spoofing app for my phone and then set my location for the area. It let me not only take advantage of all the normal tourism and nightlife apps, but even some of the simpler ones that lacked the ability to look up distant cities.

"Wow," I thought while looking at the squares in Grindr, "there's a fuck ton of people." I had never been to a place where people's distance from me was measured in feet and not miles.

Reassured that population density meant plenty of nightlife options, I started Googling gyms in the area. When I traveled for work, which wasn't often and usually not to large cities, I liked to try local hole-in-the-wall gyms. Juice heads like me don't like the chains for multiple reasons. For one, the equipment is subpar at best. For two, the no-name places were always better and I was likely to find my own kind there.

While deciding which airport I wanted to layover in the least, someone tapped me on the shoulder. I looked up to see

Kevin, one of the technicians I worked with often. I ordinarily would have noticed his cheap Axe body spray announcing his presence before he ever touched me.

"Do you have a moment, Mr. Culver?"

"Sure, Kevin, what can I do for you?"

"I'm working on generating this report for Donald and I was wondering, would you mind taking a look at this script when you get a chance? I'd ask all the guys on my team, but we have a lot of people out on vacation so we're a bit shorthanded."

"Yeah, I'll be right over. Give me five minutes."

Cheerfully, he responded, "Thanks! I'll be at my cubicle!"

Kevin sprung off. He liked me a lot and, in my mind, his look was patterned loosely on mine. Minus the muscle, of course.

I started to follow, but paused. For reasons I can't explain, I thought back to Tony and our conversation in his truck. I wondered what kind of craziness I could *really* get into in San Francisco. Perhaps I was setting the bar too low for this trip. If everyone else was having a vacation, why couldn't I? An idea struck me and I opened a new browser window and searched "Bathhouses San Francisco."

I then minimized the window, locked my desk, and went to find Kevin.

"**K**eep going!" I screamed.

It was seven o'clock and Dylan and I were back in the gym. He was doing a small circuit between battle rope, a miniature obstacle course, and jump rope. I never had a chance to return to my workstation, and had forgotten completely about my quest for hedonism before I left work. Dylan was eager for me to train him hard as he was trying to cut the last bit of fat for beach season. Oklahoma beach season, that is.

I stood with a stopwatch in one hand and, surreptitiously, through the pocket of my shorts, my hard dick in the other.

He was great to watch train. You just don't find his level of dedication in the average guy. But his willingness to do anything to get where he wanted to be was the sexiest attribute I could find in a person. Pure ambition. He wasn't my type physically. Sure, I would have fucked him if he asked, but I generally tended to go for guys who were darker in personality. Yet our shared mindset was a turn-on.

Eat big. Lift big. Dose big.

He collapsed, breathing hard.

"F . . . Fuck you. Fuck car . . . dio. I'm . . . I'm not doing more," he wheezed.

"You're getting fat, tubby tubs. This is how you get on a stage. You like the torture and you know it."

He closed his eyes. He did like it, even if he was spent. And I think he secretly enjoyed having someone as skilled as I was ordering him about the gym.

Masc4masc, am I right?

"Okay, but just . . . let me get . . . my breath," he panted. "There's no reason . . . doing high impact . . . this long," he continued complaining through his gasps.

I was used to being cursed out and criticized by the guys I trained when they were in a totally depleted state. I found it more comical than anything else. I wasn't turned on now as much as amused. I put the stopwatch down and stopped fondling myself.

"Oh, so you're the expert now? Student surpasses the teacher and all?" I teased.

From the floor, Dylan raised his arm and flashed me the middle finger.

"I'm just . . . letting my blood . . . flow to my head," he managed, still exhausted.

We enjoyed using each other. We each got something out of the relationship. He gained satisfaction from being the biggest piece of meat modern training and drugs could make him. I was voyeuristically satisfied that he was doing so on my drugs. It was oddly sexual somehow. I thought in awe about my testosterone flowing through his beautifully engorged veins.

I let him lay in silence for a bit and recuperate.

"You take BCAAs?" I asked.

"Of course," he replied.

"What brand?"

"My favorite: cheap. Why?"

"I was wondering. Mind if I borrow a scoop?"

He pointed to his bag. I walked over and opened it up, being cautious to avoid any needles that might be in there.

He was right. It was the cheap stuff. The nutrition label looked like a superhero comic book cover from the 1970s. From overseas.

"Where the fuck did you order this?" I asked with a chuckle.

"Online. You always do better ordering online."

Dylan's breath returned and along with it, his tren sweat. He was overtly ripe from his workout. Who would have thought giving yourself a hormone imbalance would make your pheromones go nuts? The smell was uniquely pungent. It was a musk that only two types of individuals find attractive—steroid users and gay sex pigs.

I was both.

I opened a spare protein shaker and poured a scoop of comic book BCAAs in with an obligatory round of name-brand chocolate protein from my stash. I shook it until I was satisfied with the consistency, then began to nurse it down.

"Did you buy this because it had a superhero on it? I swear whoever wrote this label doesn't speak English. I doubt you even know what half this stuff even is."

"It's leucine and a few other things. They're chopped up proteins. That's what amino acids are," he said confidently.

"Sure," I replied, somewhat sarcastically. My effort was to purposely leave doubt in his mind that he answered the question correctly enough for me.

"Well, it is. I mean, what would you say, Mr. Wizard?"

"It is. Partially, I guess."

"And . . ." Dylan invited, "what else?"

"BCAAs are the combination of L-leucine, L-isoleucine, and L-valine in specific ratios designated to elucidate the most optimal anabolic response from the body," I said, as if quoting some great scientific text.

"If you had asked me what they are and I had to define them by function alone, that would be the definition. However, that is not what they are anymore so then I'm just an IT guy who works for a big company, or you're a mere redneck asshat who doesn't know how to park his truck. BCAA's identity in the role of bodybuilding is uniquely defined by what they do, in that they trigger an anabolic response at the cellular level called mTOR, or the mammalian target of rapamycin; mTOR is one of the major cellular pathways responsible for both aging and muscular development."

"Fascinating," he said in a monotone, rolling his eyes. He stood up from the floor slowly, signaling that he was not in the mood for a chemistry lesson.

"Quite. mTOR stimulates this process in muscle tissue, and your body has to respond by carrying out the necessary instructions. It has no choice but to do this thing that the chemical is telling it to do. Coming into the nucleus of the cell is a string of amino acids that, through a somewhat complicated process, unwind the very DNA of the cell. It merges with an RNA signal protein and then, boom! Instruction followed! You start growing. Of course, the instructions only make sense for skeletal muscle cells. Well, maybe cardiac muscle, too. But I don't think anyone's ever cut someone's heart out to tell if that grows. But suffice to say, it works!"

"Sometimes I think *you're* the kind of person who would cut someone's heart out just to tell if it grew," Dylan said.

"Maybe. But only if I can use them as guinea pigs or spare parts after I'm done. I mean, if all that superdrol does you in, one day I might come by with a cleaver and a gym bag just to take your liver."

"Not if I get yours first!" he joked.

I was pretty sure Dylan was done listening to my science lesson, but I was on a roll. And while his mind could only focus on one topic at a time, mine worked on overtime. Part of working in IT—as well as bodybuilding and steroid-manufacturing— meant making connections.

"Good luck with that. But then again, BCAAs do mean something completely different if you think of it as what it means philosophically."

"Mmhmm, professor," Dylan said, ignoring most of my words.

"Well, there's a cost associated with this whole cellular DNA unraveling-to-do-your-bidding business. Sometimes when it comes back together, it comes back shorter than it was before. Could cause cancer."

"Cancer—" he exclaimed, suddenly reinterested in the topic. He was visibly alarmed that he may have been poisoning himself at the hands of GNC.

"Now calm down," I interrupted. "No, it's not like that. Well, it won't cause cancer if you weren't going to have it anyway. Amino acids are just chopped-up proteins. To say BCAAs would give you cancer is to say that anything with protein in it would give you cancer. Steak, chicken, quinoa, anything.

"The point that I'm making is that BCAAs burn the candle faster. Your DNA is very redundant and likely to handle a single transcription error without a problem, just like error-correcting memory in a computer. Cells, though, will auto-destruct if they detect too many transcription errors over time. Cells don't last forever, nor would any process let them. We aren't immortal. But the point is, you get to set the terms of this process."

Dylan cocked his head, trying to follow what I was saying as best he could.

"Well, would you want to go out slowly, over a long period of time, easily living life day-by-day like Grandma Norway did?" I asked, trying to simplify it for him. "Or do you want to slam as many BCAAs down your throat as you can and potentially die earlier, but weigh 300 pounds and be on a bodybuilding stage? You could say it's the sand of a chosen life slipping through your fingers."

Dylan gaped at me, while taking the canister. He packed it back into his bag without a thought. My conversation had become merely a soliloquy echoing back into my ears, unheard by any other.

"Yeah, I guess there's that," he offered.

I let silence punctuate the conversation. Enough to ease the mood. It's difficult to transition from an in-depth discussion to something lighthearted when there are two people in a room and only one is on the level. Dylan's attractiveness faded quickly into the ether. Despite his muscularity, we were no longer of the same mindset. Whatever was going through his mind was not present in mine, and my thoughts felt much more real.

"I'll send you the website where I bought it," Dylan broke the silence. "They let you come up with your own protein blends. I'm sure you'll enjoy it since you love all the science."

"Yeah!" I feigned excitement. "I can't wait. Maybe I can get Captain America on mine. He used, didn't he?"

"Sure. I recommend the chocolate. Their vanilla is a bit floury and chalky tasting. But get whatever you want."

"I will. I usually do."

I looked at my phone, which I had ignored for most of the day. Forgetting for a moment that I had faked my GPS location earlier, I opened up some of the hook-up apps.

Between them all, I had 113 unread messages.

Jesus. Fucking. Christ.

Were there that many gay men in all of Oklahoma City? That's what I got in just a day pretending to be a San Fran gay? This was going to be a helluva trip I could tell already.

"See ya, Dylan," I called after I gathered up my things.

Once I was back in my car, I pulled out my phone again and started combing through the profiles of the guys who had messaged me. Faceless and no-name profiles, often worth reading for the laughs, were ignored in the sea of options at my disposal. I looked for ones that enticed my particular proclivities. I viewed the images, sorted them in my head by relative attractiveness, and started reading without responding.

All the fuckers on the apps looked like models. Or porn stars. These were not your local run-of-the-mill queens. These guys looked gruff. And gruff is my type.

Message 114 arrived.

Hey there, I don't recognize you. U looking?

I thought his statement was odd. Did he normally not recognize men he hooked up with? Or perhaps he did, and I was just fresh meat.

Not today. I don't arrive in town for another week. Just checking out the scene.

Are you even worth talking to? I hit the lottery. Like eighty guys hit me up.

Must be your first time. I'm Ryan. Where you staying?

Chris. In a hotel.

There was no way I was going to say which one.

Cool! Well, when you are here, hit me up.

A notification from the app, "Picture album unlocked," followed his last message.

Will do!

I reviewed his album. The boner I'd had earlier while I watched Dylan work out returned. Ryan was twenty-seven (going by his profile at least), dark-haired, and definitely muscular. It was apparent he took care of his body. He was five eleven and had otter-like hair spread across his chest. He wore a full beard with sideburns. There was no doubt from a football field away this guy dripped masculinity. His pictures captured a certain charm about him, and most possessed a mysterious inquisitiveness. In some he was playfully sticking out his tongue. In others, he was sucking someone's dick. In all, though, he looked like he loved the camera as much as it loved him.

Leather and Levi's were his style, but so were the decadent meals he was seen to enjoy. The obligatory landmark photos with Golden Gate and Alcatraz in the background completed the collection. Like most other profiles on the apps, it screamed the things all gay men want to scream: "I'm interesting! I'm fun! Just love me!"

The album contained a fair number of nudes, which are a part of doing business in the world of high-tech hookups. He was not lacking in that department either. The display of a few key back tattoos only titillated me further. His skin had a certain sheen to it, which I presumed was sweat from a rough and rigorous workout. At least that's what I told myself.

I hit the "Favorite" button, put my phone on the passenger seat, and started driving home.

FIVE

COMING IN EARLY TO work and wrapping up existing projects was well worth my trouble. It was a Wednesday, but most of my next week would be out of town. Work had slowed down but I wasn't in the mood to take on complicated tasks.

Plus, I could reallocate my bandwidth normally reserved for new tasks toward playing around on Grindr and Scruff. For the next few days, I was nose deep in my phone.

I used to think I was the only one who fiended over hook-up apps. I eventually started having conversations with random guys I'd hook up with about the topic. It seemed it was a common thing for most gays (maybe straight men, too). For those I talked to, it slowly replaced bars as the primary place for gay men to meet.

The modern apps were convenient, but, in turn, caused their own problems. For one, it was in my damned pocket all the time. So whether I was in a meeting with clients or reviewing a PowerPoint presentation at my desk, there were naked dudes trying to give me their lust. I wasn't unused to it, mind you. But having left my phone locked in a new city gave me so many possibilities for sex.

Before I turn thirty-two, I will have spent more of my life online trying to hook up for sex than not. I was addicted to the predecessors of Grindr before I could even get my driver's permit. And this was a good hit of that rush—the rush of hooking up with new men. The realization hit me hard.

It was 7:00 a.m., earlier than my normal shift. I had noticed Ryan online. A bright green dot glowed next to the profile picture of his beautiful manly abs.

You're up early?

laTe actually.

The capital *T* was hardly a mistake. I shifted in my seat.

I first fell in love with dope back in college, when I was quite the party guy. I started dropping ecstasy every opportunity it was offered, and the transition to meth didn't take long. Meth, while a poor substitute, was available in abundance in Oklahoma and was the drug of choice for those who liked dick. Called Tina or CrysTal, somehow the capital *T* became the signature hallmark of those parTy guys looking to indulge in crazy sex.

I found it was the perfect study aid to getting to class on time and it made sex a thrilling adventure to boot. My cloudy nights (as I called them) were oftentimes filled with personal interviews and confessions, as much as work and sex. I hadn't touched it in a long time. I felt like I outgrew it somehow when the career started calling. Friday nights were always so much fun on it, but by the time Monday came around I just felt like dying. I thought about what kind of fun he must be having without me.

Hahaha . . . is that right?
Well, I'm at work so nothing
stronger than coffee at the moment.

That's a shame. Coffee's not nearly as fun.

Oh, I know.
Got a bunch of guys over?

Nah, it's been quiet.
Though my room is remarkably clean!
Lets me get a lot done and such.
Now it just needs to stop spinning.

I laughed quietly. That was always the shitty part with it. When you wanna get high, it was always great—but when you want to come down, it would take its sweet ass time.

Cute. Yeah, I use pre-workout for that.
Speed just doesn't work well for bodybuilding.

Hahaha . . . that's what you think.
Better than ephedra or anything you can
get over-the-counter if you do it right.

I thought of what a workout all geeked out and anxious from meth would be like. The idea didn't sound that appealing.

LOL, well, I've done my fair share.
It's not the 'T' for me.

Oh? What is?

I smiled. Like he'd understand! He was hot, that was for damned sure, and muscular, but somehow I thought he couldn't handle being in the gym with guys like me.

You prefer tren hex or acetate?

I froze. My mouth dropped open just a bit. His comment caught me by surprise.

Wow . . . familiar with the Dark Arts of bodybuilding? How exactly does a parTy boy get into that game?

I dabble. What about you?

I've talked to plenty of guys on apps, forums, chat rooms, etc., many of whom were knowledgeable to some degree about steroids. Few, if any, talked about cooking them. But one thing I had never seen is a party guy who also liked gear. Meth heads don't go to the gym, and bodybuilders don't typically do hard drugs. I felt my brain tilt back in my head as I recalled how rare it is to find someone in this world who had my background. I remembered the joy of finding Dylan and the relief of being able to sell to Tony, but neither seemed comfortable with the other. They just weren't the same type of people.

And neither of them would touch meth. As far as I knew, I was the only one who had. In the whole world.

How many of us could there be?

I studied Ryan's picture. Dark beard and washboard abs. He clearly understood masculinity and put it on display. Perhaps there was something to him I shouldn't discount so easily. I thought about how much I wanted to tell Dylan I made and how many social encounters I had to pass up because I had to make gear instead. My heart climbed toward my throat. Rational or not, I saw this as an opportunity to connect with a kindred spirit. The kind of connection I couldn't have even with Dylan.

Ryan took the first leap with his capital *T*'s and all. I took a deep breath, closed my eyes, and leapt off the bridge to see if he'd catch me.

Steroids? I make them.

> **That's cool. I need to get back in shape too.**
> **Been trying to gain some muscle back, been**
> **too long.**

I laughed out loud, somewhat insanely, but quietly. Sure, I had the office to myself but I had just told my deepest darkest secret. A secret so sensitive I didn't even trust my best friend with it and had to rely upon this complete stranger to keep it. Finally, I wasn't alone with it.

Well, there's two things I know that help.
Dbol, and not smoking meth.

> **Hahaha... I suppose.**
> **How much is your dbol?**

Well, that depends I guess . . . how much would
you need? I mean, I don't normally give cycle advice
over hookup apps.

> **I didn't ask for advice.**
> **I asked for a price.**

This was new territory. I mean, it's not that I didn't sell it before. But I was used to doing so with people I'd known for quite a while. I knew Dylan worked with me and wasn't a cop. And I'd known Tony forever it seemed. But this man seemed too impossible to be a cop, too knowledgeable to be just a user, and too fascinating for me to not talk to. I knew my prices and I stood by them.

$50 / 50 ct. 10mgs per.

No minimums?

Minimum $300

That's not too bad.
When you gonna be here again?
Bring it when you come to town?

Next week.

I pondered what exactly it'd be like to get arrested by TSA mid-flight from one part of the country to the next. Flying with it would be a bad idea. Given that steroids are so rare of a drug, shipping them made logical sense.

I'm flying, but I'm sure I can
ship ya something if you got the money.

Lemme work on it, brb.

I put my phone down to take a reprieve from the soul-sucking world of gay digital sex. I got up and stared down the hallway from my office, then closed my eyes to make the pixels vanish from view. Purposely avoiding the bright screens, I thought about how much of my life I spent looking at those displays, big and small. *What percentage of my day is subjected to the cruel enslavement of RGB pixels? Whatever percentage it is, I at least found peace at the other end of the phone today.*

And it was a violent peace.

For the first time, I decided to sell drugs to a random stranger I had never met. To someone I'd never seen, except for some pictures online. Sure, I was in the business to make a few extra bills, but I didn't think of myself as a drug dealer until that moment. It was just about getting Tony laid or getting Dylan bigger. *Am I still an IT guy, or have I become something more?*

I thought about how great it could be to not return from California. It would have been nice to escape the shackles of this IT prison and do something more active with my life. We spend a third of our lives at work, and another third asleep. I did everything I could with that remaining third to grow and experience life outside these beige walls.

I wondered what was going on at Ryan's place. Certainly he was just as manic on dope as I used to be, staring at porn and sucking dick, or whatever it was he did when he got high (which, given he was on a gay hook-up app, probably involved rubbing his dick raw).

I felt uneasy. I had to do something to escape my office.

Dylan was too busy for me to annoy, preoccupied with his own projects, so I went to the server room to clear my mind.

I picked up a clipboard and started consulting the inventory, resigning myself to the more administrative tasks of my job.

Still, I couldn't count the servers. In my mind, all I could do was count bottles.

I wondered if I should train or stock up on more anabolics before I left. I was getting low on the good stuff. Dylan bought me out of a lot of my injectables and I never kept that much available on hand anyway. I wasn't normally in the business of actively recruiting new customers, but if this Ryan guy paid up, then I could make some serious money.

Why do I do a job that I hate and that pays less than the one that I love?

Fuck it, I should probably just train. This Ryan fucker won't get me any money anyway, and I got other stuff I want to do before I head out of town.

So after another day of beige work in beige rooms with mostly beige coworkers, I left early, and didn't look back.

SIX

FTER TWO DAYS OF radio silence from Ryan, he finally texted.

Hey, what's your number?

I didn't get right back to him. It had been a particularly arduous day and it wasn't like I'd been pining for him since we last talked. I had been training harder than normal since my routine would be fucked up on this trip. If I brought myself just short of injury, that would be fine. I would have several days of seminars and limited gym access to grow and recover.

Eventually, I told him I'd be available to call later. I was nearly starving from an earlier injection of GHRP-6, a research peptide known to cause a growth hormone response and a hunger so intense you'd eat the family pet if he fit within your macros and was the only thing around.

After satiating myself with more protein and carbs, I retreated to the garage. My mancave afforded me the courage to start up a conversation. I asked for his number, and when I was ready, dialed it. I didn't mind calling guys or even sexting on the phone, but long-distance drug business wasn't something I was used to. I didn't know what to expect. Would this random guy call me every time he got high at potentially all hours of the evening?

The phone rang three times before a deep voice picked up.

"What's up?" he answered. His voice was somewhat groggy, but he sounded happy to talk.

"How's it going?" I asked, pacing around the area I normally reserved for deadlifts. I walked around the space's perimeter, just as I did when I was at work.

"Nothing much. Keeping busy as always. Look, I wanted to apologize for the other night. I don't normally get spun up and then hop on the apps to talk to people."

"Don't mention it. You were actually very well contained for a guy geeked out of his mind. Hopefully you got some sleep in."

"Well, I try not to do too much. You know how that goes. A little dab'll do ya. And yeah, a few hours' sleep here and there. Going to be your first trip out here?"

"Yeah, work trip."

"Bummer. And here I thought you were coming out for Dore Alley."

"Dore Alley?"

A fairly long pause ensued. I could practically sense the guy deflate in his chair. I had committed a faux pas. I just wasn't sure how.

"You've never heard of Dore? Damn! It's a leather event. How could you not have heard of it? Where do you even live?"

It occurred to me I never told him my city of origin. I had turned off the GPS spoofing app a few days ago, and while I guessed he could tell I lived 1,300 miles away, that could have been anywhere.

"Oklahoma."

"Ah, gotcha. I'm from Nebraska originally. I get it. Other than during Pride, your town pretends gay people don't exist, amirite?"

"Pretty much. So all the parade stuff is going to be going on?"

"Well, normal parade stuff for here. Compared to my hometown, it's quite a bit different. I'm sure you'll agree when you see it."

"No doubt."

I wondered if the number of average homosexuals per square mile would be increased temporarily for my stay. The thought fleeted. *Business . . . I should be talking business.*

"So, Dianabol. How much did you say you wanted?"

"Yeah, that's why I wanted to talk. Like, do you have a price list? My last guy had one. What's your shipping cost and minimums and all that stuff?"

I liked that he had ordered shit before, but guessed by his tone that he was just as confused talking to me as I was listening to him. Most people don't refer to drugs generally as *stuff*, after all, especially people who are familiar with variants like tren hex and the like. I had figured he did what I did—order shit online and pray the guy on the other end doesn't run off with your money. That, or he was used to gym buys likely from an overpriced local dealer and was looking to save some money by ordering from me.

I just hoped he wasn't a cop. Sure, the area code on the phone showed 415, which is San Francisco, but where he was located wasn't in doubt. The question was if I was going to be arrested giving him shit. A cop would have already traced the number if that were the case. Oklahoma City's area code is 405, and while we were close in phone numbers, we were miles apart from trusting each other.

"Yeah, I can get you a list. I don't carry everything, mind you. Honestly, I'm kind of a small player in this and typically only make and stock what I use. But if you have a special request I can always see about fulfilling it."

"Well, give me a rough idea."

My mind raced. I had no idea what shit went for out there. There's a big cost of living adjustment between Oklahoma and the West Coast. I had a good idea of some of the Eastern European lab pricing, but I was hardly aware of standard rates. Before cooking, I had always preferred the European stuff, and guessed that he did, too, if he was similarly experienced. I targeted my pricing around there as best I could.

I answered matter-of-factly. "Testosterone cyp is sixty-five dollars for a ten ml bottle. Everything else is more or less from there. Most of the orals I do for about a dollar a pill, $300 minimum. I don't normally do shipping, but you'll make the minimum, so I'll cover that for you."

"Sixty-five bucks for a bottle?" he asked, raising his voice toward the end.

I paused. I didn't know how to interpret the intonation of his question. Was he curious? Angry? Was I overpriced? Sure, there were plenty of cheaper guys out there. Bargain basement was twenty-five dollars but was sometimes fake or underdosed. Even with drugs, price correlated with quality. Of course, in countries where it was legal, that twenty-five dollars was likely close to fair market price straight from a veterinarian. I charged Dylan sixty-five dollars and since he didn't argue too much I figured it couldn't be that bad.

It's not like it's soda pop. You can't just walk into your competitor's shop and price compare.

"Y- yeah. Something wrong with that?" I stuttered.

"No. I mean, no, of course not! That's fine, actually."

"I could probably give you a discount if you order in bulk—"

He interrupted. "Well, let's start small, man. How about three bottles of dbol and five of test."

"That should be fine. I can get a total to ya, one second."

Quickly thinking, I tried to calculate what that would run. Ninety pills in a bottle. That was the minimum order right there. *Fuck, this will buy me a good time for my trip at the least, and at most, enough extra cash so I can replace some of the equipment in this damned garage.*

I scribbled numbers on the whiteboard normally reserved for tracking gym lifts. Retail cost as well as my margin.

I circled my answer, which I shared with him. "If my math's right, your total comes to $595. That seem fair?"

"And this all ships from within the US? You aren't re-ordering this stuff from overseas?"

Ryan was proving his experience. By insuring that all of the components were already stateside, he knew I took all of the risk of importing it.

"Yup, from the great state of Oklahoma. Just text me your mailing address and all of that."

"If you want, I can pay you once you're here," he offered kindly.

"Oh, it'll be in advance. Nothing ships without cash. You can mail me a check or Venmo it to me."

Venmo charged a three percent fee. On a fifteen thousand percent markup, they could wipe their ass with three percent.

"Oh man, this is way too convenient," he said.

I thought back to his pictures on the app. I pictured him in a tank top, ready to hit the gym and work on his body just for me. The idea turned me on and I wondered if he was on a cycle when he sent those pictures or if that was him before he ever ran any gear.

"So, do you normally buy drugs from a guy you just met?"

"I dunno, if he's hot, I guess. Plus, with your body, I can at least tell they work."

Oh boy. This guy is a player.

"Ha! Yeah, I have blood work, too, if you'd be interested in numbers behind the bottles. I'm only running 400 mgs of testosterone per week right now and routinely peg out the charts when I order my blood work pulled. Definitely superhuman stuff."

"All I need are those abs. That's what sells out here."

What sells?

It suddenly occurred to me that he might not use my drugs for personal consumption but could flip them on his end. *Fuck, I should have marked them up more and pillaged his customer list.*

"My gear and some cardio, it'll be all you need."

"What's your e-mail? I'll Venmo the cash to ya right now."

I told him. A few moments later my phone vibrated. Good to his word—pennies from heaven, followed by a shipping address.

"Awesome. I'll get it shipped as early as tomorrow."

"Right on. What do you do for a living?" he asked, somewhat curious.

"It's kinda boring. IT work, basically . . ." I trailed off.

I didn't mind talking about work, but so few people could keep up with me it didn't usually make sense to go into too much detail. "It's kind of technical. I work with an operating system called Linux."

"I used to do that, too. Gave up the grind for more fulfilling endeavors. That, and recompiling kernels just wasn't for me."

"Oh, wow. You actually know a thing or two about everything, don't you?" I asked, surprised.

"Well, Silicon Valley is literally in my backyard. I can see half of the dot-com startups just walking down the street. If you're a sysadmin here, then you're basically as common as a grocery store clerk out where you are."

"Funny, I used to be a grocery store clerk, but yeah, it's managed services work actually. So all the firms that can't afford an expensive West Coast company get stuck with me. Where I end up doing twice the work for half the pay."

"Yeah, but at least you have a house, I'm sure. Here, you have to marry into money if you want to live without a landlord. Or just be homeless."

I sat down and started listening to his voice more closely. It was great to hear. Both foreign yet familiar. And I was enjoying the conversation as well. It's customary when doing drug deals to book-end the meeting with polite pleasantries unrelated to the actual business at hand, but this was different. It was natural. As natural as talking to Tony or Dylan, and I had known them for years. His voice was deep and confident, and most of all friendly. Underneath was a certain calming tone to it.

"I can only imagine, based on what I've heard. Maybe you can show me around when I get into town? I've been out east a few times, but I've never been on the other side of Vegas. Perhaps we can get a bite to eat or something?"

"I promise you, I can do better than that."

"I look forward to it! And since you got me the cash so fast, I'll overnight everything to you so it should beat me there—"

He interrupted again, "And you can pump me full of your steroids and get me nice and strong?"

Fuck.

The way he said it. Quietly aggressive. Strong, yet submissive. A hypersexualized guinea pig in the making. The verbal equivalent of taking my hand and placing it on his throat as an invitation to fuck him harder.

"Uh, sure. I can show you how to inject them," I stammered, surprising myself by being a bit flustered.

"Oh, I know how to inject them. You just need to be the one who does it."

My pants became tight, filled with a raging boner. This guy was hungry and I was happy being his full seven-course meal.

"Absolutely. I'll pump you full of whatever I want."

"Great! It's a date. See you then!"

He hung up.

He seriously gets a rise out of me and then hangs up? Goddamned cocktease!

"Fuck!" I exclaimed.

I contemplated calling him back, though I couldn't come up with a good enough reason why. *The bastard!*

I had a hard time putting the thought of sex aside when I stepped back into the house. I fetched the requested bottles from my stash and then retreated to my study to start packing them up. I nestled them gently in a box with some soft bubble wrap I had on hand. I found it relaxing, packing his order, and also attractive. While I addressed the package, I fantasized about how wonderful it would be to have my steroids fill his muscles. I took a certain pride in knowing my work was not only appreciated, but desired.

It occurred to me that I should label the bottles in a more distinct way. At some point he'd want to order more than one injectable, and I had to be able to distinguish between the two. Dylan was happy with the steroid name hastily written in permanent marker on the outside. It was always extra sloppy because I did my damndest to obfuscate my handwriting. But that seemed too plain compared to the sexual imagery I found flooding my mind from this most recent phone call. I wanted to make a good impression with Ryan—one that left him wanting even more and showed that I knew what I was doing.

I didn't care to brand my gear one way or another until then. After all, testosterone is testosterone, just as aspirin is aspirin, and Dylan didn't really care as long it was in his price range. Yet Ryan was ready at a moment's notice to throw money to me, and I was sure better deals would follow if I executed this one well. I had to ensure my package wasn't just another undifferentiated commodity, but rather something that expressed the unique quality of masculinity that I was delivering.

"What does one name a steroid brand?" I muttered to myself. What is the point of a brand, after all, if not to imbue a cold product with warm feelings, like sexiness or excitement? An electric car is just an electric car, but a Tesla is a wholly different beast. No Coca-Cola ad I'd ever seen actually featured soda. They featured people laughing at parades and ball games, and joyful fathers teaching their kids how to ride a bike for the first time. Emotion is what they advertised, not sugar water. I had seen plenty of bottles of prescription testosterone from the gents at the gym who took the Lighter Path of getting it prescribed. Most of them were from the same bland pharmaceutical companies that make things like contact lens solution and other crap. All more beige things in this world.

Then there were the bottles I had seen traveling on the Darker Path—the illegal as hell ones. I remembered a few from the days before I started brewing them myself, back when I was lucky to scrape by a bottle here and there in the gym. Names like Scorpion or Snake Venom. The names went way over the top in the other direction, with logos that screamed, "I'm cool! No, really! Pick me because I'll make you deadlift a thousand pounds and will go great with that American Fighter T-shirt and Monster energy drink you always carry around."

I did not want to be that predictable.

I looked up steroid lab names online. I felt a closer kinship to these goofball names than anything in a Walgreens. Many of the posts I found were old or discussed labs that had been busted by the DEA years before I even thought of touching a barbell. I got ensnared in these old posts and loved reading how fondly some brands were talked about, and how certain individuals "repped" for them well. Some of the older forum posts from decades beyond talked about an often-forged yet decommissioned brand in Europe known for its amazing quality. It went by the name British Dragon, which seemed to be consistently regarded as a top player.

When these older lifters wrote about it, it was with a beautiful nostalgia. As if their first love was found in the bottom of those bottles. It must have been damned good to capture the essence of youth and virility so well.

"Why not American Dragon?" I answered myself. "Give it the old red, white, and blue treatment."

I pulled out some address labels, found some stock photo images of a dragon, and spent fifteen minutes making a simple but descriptive print of my new logo, the compound, and its concentration. The result looked good, but not great. I stared at the computer screen for what seemed like forever. This logo could never encapsulate the full-product experience that steroids gave me, even if a picture is worth a thousand words. But I decided it would do for now.

File. Print. And I waited.

My printer whirred to life as my labels were cast into existence, and with them, my new future. I sat back silently and listened.

It was the sound of power.

SEVEN

MY RAPPORT WITH RYAN grew quickly over the days before I left. By the time I touched down in San Francisco, my drugs had arrived ahead of me. He had expressed complete satisfaction from himself "and others" and had complimented me on how everything was so delicately wrapped and discretely shipped. He even liked the labels, saying they were "a hit with the guys." Apparently, he had a small group who wanted to buy some bottles and were all excited about their new supplier.

He had promised me a VIP tour of the city when I arrived. I had no idea what that would entail, and he was light on the details when I asked. I liked the idea of having a tour guide for such a large place and got excited when I thought about it. He volunteered to pick me up from the airport, though I made plans to hail a taxi (or try out Uber for the first time) since one can never be sure when they're arriving or how reliable a newfound friend can be.

I sat in the airport waiting for my luggage. I had to admire the sheer volume of people coming into the city. Silicon Valley has multiple large airports; the Oklahoma City Will Roger's World Airport has only a single terminal. This one had more visible TSA officials than my airport had total employees.

"Part and parcel of being a huge destination hub," I thought. I took a few minutes to people watch and silently guess about ethnicities and languages.

I was as close to Japan and Hawaii as possible while still being in the continental United States. Oklahoma City has a pair of Chinese restaurants and an Asian grocer, but the number of Asians in the airport would have easily filled both of those places. There were families, other business travelers like myself, and a lot more security than I had anticipated.

On my way to baggage claim, I eavesdropped on the numerous conversations going on around me. Apparently, the Customs and Immigration Office was an actual thing. I overheard a few tourists complaining that it was running behind that day. A currency exchange sat quietly by the wayside, unattended. I reminded myself that there are other forms of payment than US dollars.

The luggage carousel was tightly surrounded by people, and I made no attempt to throw myself into the herd. My bulk would have empowered me to push my way to the front, but I was in no hurry to wait around. I enjoyed watching from afar. Few by few, people left with their bags and made openings where I could see past them. Most left with smiles on their faces, eager to be reunited with loved ones. Some, though, looked more somber, and went to find ground transportation or perhaps their next business meeting.

Mine was one of the last bags to get loaded. I typically travel light, and my small bag seemed almost comical next to me. My precious few earthly belongings were limited to clothes and some protein, my smart phone being the most complex tool I needed for my job. Nearby, a solo male traveler was being questioned by airport security. I didn't catch the conversation, but it appeared they were prepared to randomly search him. Random searches were basically unheard-of back home. When I got closer, I heard security ask the man if he was travelling for business or pleasure. I didn't know how I would answer if the question was posed to me.

I made my way for the terminal exit.

It was hard to rationalize the differences between my home state and this place. California is older than dynamite. Oklahoma is younger than plastic. California was proving itself not only much older than Oklahoma, but wiser. Multicultural and bright, the sun blessed my eyes and warmed my muscles as I departed the sliding doors of the terminal. I was greeted by warm radiant air which escorted me to the departure road.

Though I had texted Ryan as I was landing, I hadn't heard back from him. Thus, I wrote off visiting him first thing. I was expecting to have to fight for a taxi, much like the television shows of my childhood had portrayed on the busy streets of New York City. But there were no checkered cabs to be seen, nor were people vying for space on a crowded curb, hands in the air and waving dramatically while whistling through two fingers. Instead, polite signage greeted me in unexpected friendly ways. They indicated that Uber and Lyft pickup points were available every so many feet.

I downloaded the Uber app and followed the instructions while pondering the similarity of it all. Uber, like Grindr and Scruff, represented a dark underbelly of a city, an ad hoc network of people connecting and disconnecting in short and transient ways. One was for sex, the other for a ride, but both more or less were based on the same idea— putting two people together who needed something from each other. And while I wasn't planning on bumping uglies with my Uber driver, the idea of flirting with him like it was Grindr was appealing.

Hell, maybe I should try and sell him a cycle, too?

After a few minutes, I saw Miguel in his recent year BMW 3 Series wind his way down the track. He popped the trunk and assisted me with my luggage. As he loaded it, I noticed how remarkably similar his car was to mine. The luxury I prided myself on through my paycheck was a mere taxicab out here.

As I got into the passenger seat, I took the time to look at him. He wasn't quite my type. He had dark short hair and was mostly unkempt, but flirting was still on the table. Sometimes the goal is just information and not sex, and I figured he may have what I needed. My energy level was high since I'd been freed from my airplane seat. Gaining two extra hours on the time change just helped my mood even more.

"First time to San Francisco?"

"Yes!" I said, almost too eagerly. "It's always been on my list of places to go."

"Good! Good!" he said, showing his broken English.

Realizing the language barrier made flirting for information difficult, I remained glued to the window of the car as we left the airport. After a few minutes and some distance, I could see the giant words *South San Francisco* written on the side of a hill. They were white and large enough to be read from nearby planes. The ground near them was beautifully iconic and quite a departure from the red clay I was used to seeing.

My phone vibrated. It was Ryan. My heart perked up a bit as I was eager to see him. I told him I was in an Uber, and he responded by telling me to stop by whenever I could. I thought of how awkward it would be to show up with luggage, and asked for an hour or so to check into the hotel.

Miguel and I eventually found ourselves in the heart of the city. Giant, enveloping structures of granite surrounded us as I stared at sidewalks teeming with people. I had been to New York before, but only briefly, and not long in the heart of Manhattan. This wasn't something I'd call unusual, but there was a certain youthful energy that was present here which the East Coast just didn't have. I lowered the window in an attempt to take in the view. The cacophony of people reverberated off the walls of every structure. San Francisco had an allure that New York and other large cities I had visited never possessed.

Even the homeless people smiled more.

At the end of Fifth Street, my hotel was a behemoth of security. A fortress of glass and concrete appeared to offer rooms high enough up to transcend the scuffle the city afforded down below. It had a dominating appearance and was a good choice for someone like myself who liked a view.

My driver assisted by unloading my things while I navigated the decision of having to tip him or not. The new ride-hailing tradition of Uber was as foreign to me as the social mores of San Paolo. Even still, I decided generosity was universally appreciated so I palmed a five note to him upon saying my goodbyes. Miguel may have been a foreigner, but he was hardly stupid. He thanked me, accepted the cash, and disappeared back into the ocean of traffic, in my mind, already moving on to the next encounter with a naive visitor.

Checking into the hotel was much more familiar to me. The normal exchange of a driver's license and corporate credit card for a room key and Wi-Fi password took place with nary a problem. Security cameras abounded both inside and outside the facility, keeping a watchful eye on the transients. After checking in, I escaped to the most unusual elevators. A complicated numeric keypad replaced the more traditional buttons I was familiar with.

"Is there something wrong with how elevators are designed? What start-up company thinks elevators are a disruptive technology?" I mumbled to myself.

Soon, I arrived at my room.

Simple. Quiet. Secluded. The beautiful sterility that I had expected from a room where I would sleep for a while but not live in. It was plainly designed but still had an artistic modern flair to it not afforded by my normal beige work conditions. I dropped my bags onto the bed, took a breather to admire the view and then washed up, as if I could remove my native land's red clay from my face.

I logged my phone into the Wi-Fi and felt safe having ready access to any necessary work e-mails. I shot off a text to my boss letting him know I was ready for assignments as necessary. Then I texted Ryan telling him I was on my way. Using the address he gave me from the previous steroid shipment as a reference, I marked my destination in the Uber app.

"Come on over, Chris!" he responded.

Ryan's place was in a part of the city called the Mission, which, from what I could decipher from Google Maps, was an older part of the city. Work placed me firmly downtown near the Moscone Center, a good twenty minutes of city driving away. I was comforted to know that I could escape either to the silent solitude that only a business-class hotel can afford, or to whatever debauchery Ryan had in store for me, at a moment's notice.

My second Uber driver was decisively less interesting. He was a white gay man in his early thirties who gave off a vibe of pure narcissism and elitism. He told me he lived in Berkeley but drove to the city where the work was. I espoused how great it must be to live in the Gay Capital of the World, and he poured out his feelings about how nothing new or worthwhile had occurred in the city since Harvey Milk died. He felt that San Francisco was nothing more than a tourist trap and a place where dreams went to die.

I offered him a room back in Oklahoma. He declined, as I had expected.

When I finally managed to escape the bleak reality of my chauffeur, I found myself in the middle of a street deep in the Mission. The car door shut behind me and the sidewalk offered a small littering of pedestrians on each side. The towering might of skyscrapers was replaced with beautiful Spanish-style homes and I had hardly noticed. A calm breeze filled the air and fog capped the mountains in the distance. A rainbow palette of color filled the streets as far as I could see.

The homes were plentiful and much older than those in The Red State's 'burbs. Siding is almost never seen in Oklahoma. Residents opt instead for brick construction over anything wooden. In my world, all I ever saw were McMansions. Homes were manufactured and put together, not architected and designed. Oftentimes they looked identical, with only the orientation of the home being slightly adjusted to give the appearance of individuality. The charm and uniqueness of each one here was exhilarating. They were all special, each commanding a presence on the street.

Some had dark roof tiles, others light. Almost all were three stories high. Some invited you in warmly with deeply sloped sidewalks while others sat more imposingly at the top of a flight of stairs. Plant life was hard to find, being replaced with paved sidewalk as far as the horizon would allow, which was not far given the steep hills I surmounted along the way. Even without flora, the area was rich with life.

The distinctly urban sounds of neighbors talking and cars driving by surrounded me. No one conversation was distinct enough to be heard, though each had substance of sorts. The noise felt more pink than white. I stood outside what I took to be Ryan's place. An upper floor window was open. I pulled out my phone and called him. He answered on the second ring.

"I'm here," I said.

"Great, be down in a second," he said excitedly.

A few moments later the garage door opened into a deep tandem bay. A shirtless barefoot male came out.

He was remarkably beautiful.

He was muscled, lean, and possessed the air of someone who took care of himself. At nearly six feet he was taller than I was, though he weighed about the same. His shoulders were broad and capped with round balls of muscle. He was dark haired with minor acne on his chest (normal for steroid users). His bootcut jeans hung from his hips, and deep Adonis lines carved out his abdominal frame.

A well-kept, dark, scruffy beard covered his face, though his chest was much more thinly covered. His fine hair invited a warm touch and was likely the product of years of high-end conditioning and care. An oversized phone was in his front pocket, as if I needed an additional invitation to stare at his designer jeans. The dirty garage gave way to darkness, with no car in sight.

As he approached, I noticed his gait was strong and steady. He walked as if he had places to be and things to do. He didn't wear cologne or deodorant from what I could tell. Instead, he had a natural scent that was pleasant and warm—a warmth I enjoyed as it got nearer.

"I'm Ryan," he said, standing too close to shake hands with. If he were anyone less attractive, it would have felt uncomfortable.

"Hey, I'm Chris."

"I figured," he said, giving me a gentle hug. "Come on, let me show you how to get into the house. It's easier to come in through the garage than the front door. The roomie prefers it."

I stood there, mystified. Not at his words, but by the sheer elegance of this creature in front of me. I was a thick bodybuilder type—rarely did I get invited into the home of a man as gorgeous as Ryan.

Or, better yet, be given the keys to his kingdom.

"The code is nine-six-six-three. Just remember *WOOF* and you'll get in."

Indeed, the keypad was lettered like a landline phone. I followed him just inside the entrance.

"I have my own hotel and I don't need to stay with you," I said, somewhat reluctant to proceed. "It's awfully nice of you to give me the code to your house, but I don't normally enter the home of a man who I know deals without calling first."

Ryan smirked and leaned over to me, placing his hand on my back gently to pull me in.

"Why not?" he whispered. *"They're your drugs."*

He typed the code onto the keypad and the garage door started to close behind us. I looked deep inside. Where pure darkness was expected, a strip of light was found instead. A semi-opened door gave way to more sunlight. Ryan led the way, and as he opened it, revealed an outside wooden staircase. We began climbing to the upper floors of the house. I watched his immaculate ass with every step, shifting my eyes away only to admire his strong back muscles. His acne was slightly worse there, but the blemishes were well worth the beauty of this beast.

Each muscle was defined and thick, rippling as he grabbed the wooden handrail during our ascent. He took the steps two at a time while I did my best to keep pace tackling them as singles.

We approached a door. As Ryan turned the knob, he glanced toward me and paused before opening.

He whispered, "My roommate doesn't like it too much when I bring company over. If he's around, try and be quiet if you can. I just had a group leave, so it's just us three for now."

"I'll contain my disappointment," I whispered back.

We headed inside.

"They'll be back later, for better or worse."

Through the door was a kitchen. Ryan quickly turned around and brought his finger to his mouth to hush me as I followed him into the main part of the house.

He opened another door and led me into a small bedroom.

The space was small, no bigger than eleven by fifteen feet. A bed on a black box frame took up the middle. A simple metal desk with a computer on it was up against the wall blocking the window I had seen from outside, which allowed the window to vent in sound and air, though only minimal light. Three separate computer monitors were attached to the machine, with two televisions mounted on the other walls of the bedroom. The place was disheveled and messy. A standing mirror, some protein powder in a glass jar, and a mountain of USB cables and hubs were draped over nightstands and dressers.

Little was available in terms of walking room, and the easiest path to the other side was by climbing over the bed. Especially given that both of us were large.

The shipping wrapper that had contained the steroids I sent him was in the waste bin. The bottles baring my new logo were on the desk. Nearby was a large box of syringes of various sizes and types. On the shelving behind the headboard was a small plastic baggie containing a crystalline substance I took to be meth along with a glass pipe.

Thin white drapes danced with the wind in the open window, or at least attempted to as much as the computer monitors would allow. The sound of the occasional pedestrian walking down the street came through easily. Had we not been at least a story up, I was certain we could reach out and touch any stranger passing by.

It felt more like a dorm than a full-sized living space. It seemed the man's whole life was in front of me, with everything he had in the world compressed into one tiny room. He took a seat in front of the computer desk while I sat on his bed, for lack of any other option.

"You got my stuff?" I asked, in an effort to get the conversation moving.

"Yup, looks good. I like the logo. So, you're American Dragon, huh?"

"I guess you could say that."

"Just you? No one else?"

I paused before answering.

"Is . . . Is this real? I mean, I don't normally get asked right off if I'm conspiring to run a steroid lab."

Ryan clarified. "Well, I mean, you look amazing, but I wouldn't expect it to be a one-man-shop kind of deal. Not that

I ever thought about how hard it is to make them. It was kind of happenstance that I found you when I needed to re-up on some stuff. I know plenty of drug cooks but I wouldn't know how to make steroids. I honestly wouldn't even think it would be the drug I'd want to make. I've just always bought them in the gym."

"How do I know you're not a cop or something?" I knew he could sense the unease in my voice and my posture even while sitting. I was unusually rigid and unmoving, almost at attention.

Ryan looked at me, kindness and understanding in his eyes. I felt he realized how crazy this must be on my end, given my background, and sympathized.

Ryan got up from the computer chair and moved to the bed. He sat close to me—much closer than the relative strangers we were should. He placed his rough, masculine hands on my thighs and brought his lips near mine.

"Would a cop do this?" he whispered.

Then he kissed me. Not just as a single finite discrete event, but with his whole being for what seemed an eternity. I couldn't fight him, and instead my stiffness melted into spontaneous pleasure. His open hands traveled flat and hard against my torso down to the button fly of my pants, which he had no trouble undoing. My raging hard cock protruded from the opening.

His hands, having freed my cock from its enslavement, began pulling my tight T-shirt up my chest, with his teeth making the slightest bites against my nipples. I felt the urge to help and removed my shirt, tossing it against the wall in front of his computer. His mouth traveled south, the top of his head pushing hard against my chest, as his kisses migrated across my skin. Then he pushed me flat against the bed and went full throttle sucking my dick.

He didn't waste any time with shallow attempts, and instead pressed ever onward in an attempt to swallow my whole member. Slight gagging noises punctuated the moment intermittently, and his beard occasionally brushed against my thighs. My hands scrabbled the air, clutching at nothing, and eventually found a home on his muscular, acne-ridden back. I ruffled my hands through his scalp to communicate pace and tempo. Within a few moments, ample amounts of precum started flowing into his mouth.

"You taste great. Did I prove my point?" he asked after removing my penis from his mouth.

"You don't have to stop there, you know," I muttered.

"I'll stop when I want," he said firmly yet seductively.

Getting to his feet, he grabbed the pipe and the torch lighter from the headboard and put them on the bed next to me. It had been a long time since I'd smoked with anyone. I couldn't have told you the name of the first person I ever kissed, or the first time I muttered the words "I love you" (with meaning or without), but I remembered vividly the first time I rocked a meth pipe. And I remembered loving every moment of it.

Meth does something for sex that nothing else does. Medically, they say it delays the male orgasm, but I always thought that was bullshit. My first time, I was orgasming non-stop for hours. All without the need of physical release. Meth had become such a phenomenon in the gay community that mixing it with sex was called "party and play".

It was hard to not take the mantle of drug cook and turn down Ryan's offer. The invitation was too good to pass up.

He leaned over the bed and resumed sucking me. I struck the lighter to life. Before I could start my first puff, a knock came to the door. Ryan leapt from the bed and I instinctively hid the pipe under a pillow before covering my half-hard cock with the sheet.

Ryan glanced over toward me. After giving him a go-ahead signal, he opened the door narrowly to peek out. Relief allowed his shoulders to drop.

"Hey, Tom."

Ryan let our interloper in and motioned for him to close the door behind him. Tom entered and closed the door. He looked at me briefly, seeming not the least bit surprised to see a shirtless stranger with a hard-on in a precarious situation.

"Oh man, if I knew you had such delicious company I woulda shown up before the party started."

"No party right now, not that he would mind. This is Chris, my friend from Oklahoma."

Tom devoured me with his eyes. "I need to get to Oklahoma some time. How do you do?"

Tom was redheaded, six foot two, and fair-skinned. He possessed a certain gentility and sophistication that neither Ryan nor I had. You could tell he was the kind of gay who went to opening night of a new ballet because he loved the arts and was raised around them, but he wasn't the kind to dance in his mom's ballet shoes, because only faggots do that.

I nodded in greeting.

"Well, I'm glad he doesn't mind because I need a fuckin' light."

Ryan edged around Tom and quickly began putting some foam padding up along the door that he retrieved from behind the mirror.

"What's that for?" I asked.

"Sound insulation."

"Ah," I said. I wanted to ask more questions, yet was too afraid.

Tom sat down. He reached into the satchel he'd brought in and pulled out the most unusual-looking meth pipe I'd ever seen. Most pipes I'd seen were simple: round glass bowls on the end of a six-inch-long pipe, ending with a single breathing hole at the top for oxygen to enter as the dope liquifies. Tom's had the addition of a water reservoir. He pulled out some money and handed it to Ryan, who gave him the little baggie by the headboard in exchange.

"Does he bottom?" Tom asked Ryan as though I wasn't in the room.

"No, I'm all top," I responded.

"Damn. Well, it's all good. I don't need to be fucking right now, anyway. I'm rubbed so fucking raw and I need to wait a few days for the rest of the hotties to arrive. I just need a pick-me-up before I get back to the rest of my day. God, I hate this fucking shit."

Tom loaded his pipe and burned off a token amount. Though it had been years since I'd done speed, I never forgot the terrible taste of the first hit. I learned to always blow that hit away, as the impurities that came with it weren't worth any buzz it could give you.

"Tom DJs for some of the Dore parties," Ryan explained.

"No shit, that's pretty cool!" I said excitedly. "Dope with great company as well."

"Pfft. Yeah, it sounds that way," he scoffed. "Except you have to be up at all fucking hours of the night, smoking shit just to keep up with everyone else who's smoking shit, and the bastards won't even pay me until I finish the week. Like the bartenders have to wait that long for tips! I swear, this is the last year I do this shit. From now on, I'll just do fucking weddings for basic white bitches," he spat bitterly.

I saw the fatigue in his face. Bags had started to form under his eyes.

"Can't be all that bad, is it?" I asked.

Tom lit the pipe. A long slow inhale took place followed by a quick exhale. I was enamored by the bubbles he formed in the pipe in between the two breaths.

"No," he exhaled, "of course not. It's more exciting than the alternative, I suppose."

He motioned the pipe toward me.

"I've never used one of these before."

"Oh yeah, Ryan said you're from Oklahoma. Probably don't get all the good stuff out there. Use it like a normal pizzo. Just the water cleans out the shit so it doesn't taste nearly as bad. I left my regular one here last night if you want to use it instead."

"It's under the pillow," Ryan volunteered.

I suddenly realized I was going to use this man's dope and pipe in his absence, and I felt like an asshole for it. I grabbed his water pipe, handed back the regular one for him to replace in the bag, and gave it my first go. The dope crackled and tasted more sterile than I remembered, but went down without even a hiccup.

"Wow, it definitely tastes cleaner. Though it's been so long since I've done any I'm probably not the best critic."

"So you're the steroid guy. What kind of advice do you have for getting me big?" Tom asked.

"Stop smoking meth?" I suggested as I took a second hit to clear the pipe.

"Well, I'd love to. But I wouldn't mind being the jacked hot DJ at some of these parties! I mean, it's about image as much as the music. I started my first cycle this February."

I handed the pipe off to Ryan who looked down almost in quiet sadness before he handed it to Tom without taking a hit.

"February? That's kind of recent. No offense, but I wouldn't have pegged you as someone who juices."

"Yeah, I barely get to the gym in enough time."

"He's one of the ones I'm going to switch over to using your stuff," Ryan offered. "It's too early to tell, and he does have challenges getting enough calories and gym time in. I suspect that if we were to put him on a more standard schedule he'd be fine as far as growth goes."

Tom swatted flamboyantly at Ryan. His feminine streak, however minor to others, seemed to be exaggerated around our masculinity.

"My last party started at ten in the morning. The one before that, eleven at night. Plus the day job . . . I'll just do what I can with what I've got. May the grace of God be ever in my favor! But tell me about *you*! What on earth brings a well-hung, muscled-up country boy out west. How does one get into the steroid business?"

Tom sat on the bed with me and seemed keenly interested in my answer. Maybe it was just me craving attention, but I fell in love with him. His personality seemed not unlike mine. He valued relationships and friendships, and drugs were merely a means to enhance those however he could.

"Well, I got into it to subsidize my own habit, I suppose. Bodybuilding is such an expensive hobby. Between the gym memberships, chicken, shakes, and steroids, you have to do something to give yourself an edge. I was quite the engineer in college and chemistry was fascinating to me—"

"Engineer! Oh, no wonder you fell in with Ryan! He was an IT guy before he went all freelance."

"Yeah, I'm an IT guy as well. You do consulting, Ryan?"

Ryan looked at me. Tom and I were bubbling along high as hell, and had left Ryan behind completely sober. Tom and I were on a different plane than he was. Relatively speaking, the meth didn't speed us up as much as slow him down and leave him in the dust. A shadow of regret and a feigned practiced smile overcame him.

He stared through me.

"Not in IT, not anymore. I consult for drug users and chemists."

EIGHT

FEELING THE MILD EUPHORIA, I did my best to listen without jittering or interrupting Ryan as he spoke. He was articulate and impassioned. He was confident with his words and easily managed to bring Tom and me into the conversation.

"It's the same as what you do for bodybuilders, only I do it for everyone else. Think about it this way. When a bodybuilder comes up to you, you ask questions about goals. Does the person want to get shredded and down to six percent body fat? Do they want to bulk up and gain twenty pounds of muscle? The exact stack that you recommend and sell to them varies based on where they are in relation to their goals. I do the same thing.

"I got fed up with information technology. The meaningless prattle of it all. Who cares if e-mail goes through? Who cares if a server has uptime or not? The whole point of IT was to save time by introducing automation into people's lives, but it has only made us slaves to the machines we created. It's like living only to feed the washer and dryer at home, not because they are better alternatives to handwashing your clothes, but because if you aren't actively feeding them, then your home is broken. And you're a broken person for not using them. Everyone in this damned city is an IT guy, and we've all become cogs in this machine that exists for someone else's pleasure.

"So I decided it wasn't for me. I was always good at chemistry, and dope is certainly an easy thing to come by any time there are gay men around. It affords certain pleasures that we all know, but also corrupts the body in serious and dangerous ways.

"I take my knowledge of the biological sciences and apply that toward helping people maximize their pleasure while minimizing the fixed costs and variable risks of chemical dependency. I can't stop someone from using drugs, but I like to think that I can stop them from using them in a stupid way. They can always take my advice or they can do the opposite and ignore it, but the service I provide leads to a better, safer party experience.

"Plus, I provide a few other great services to my clients," he continued. "Besides product deliveries, I do party planning— making sure guests are all of the same mind and type, as well as providing the idyllic mix of out-of-town visitors with in-town regulars. I'm the guy you call if someone's overdosing, and I'm also the guy you call because you're out of lube at your sex party and everyone is too tweaked out of their mind to go get more. I understand the issues and the problems, and I take my problem-solving experience to you."

I couldn't tell how much Ryan had practiced that speech, but he gave it without pause or stammer. It was something he clearly thought long and hard about, and made me reflect partially on why I decided to deal. I almost seemed too greedy in comparison. I was so focused on my own revenue and supply, yet he seemed almost altruistic in his approach. I decided not to press too hard into the thought right then. How much of it really made sense I wasn't sure.

I felt detached from what was going on around me. On the journey to better understand my host, I had enough of Tom's crystal in my body that Ryan's meaning was somewhat lost in translation. The meth had calmed me down from a day full of airport woes, but the conversation was getting heady.

"He's actually quite good," Tom chimed in. His weary look had faded and his pick-me-up was in full effect. "Ryan has saved more than one party of mine from going bust, and he does a good job of regulating my usage to my particular needs. He makes sure it enhances my job performance without having me be such a geeked out bastard that I'm like every other homeless homo in this city."

Ryan looked over to Tom. "Yeah, which is why I think you've probably had enough, my friend. And I should probably give Chris a tour of the city like I promised."

Tom abided and put his pipe away.

"Of course, darling! My God! First time in the city, he tells me! San Francisco is a terrific place and I'm sure you'll enjoy every moment of being here. It's the City of Impossible Things, you know. And Impossible Things happen in pairs! God! You two are just fantastic together! A real power couple!" His voice seemed incredibly energetic for someone who had just pulled an all-nighter.

Tom joyfully hugged our host and me before making his way toward the door.

"Be sure to close the garage door on your way out," Ryan said as a final goodbye.

"Of course, babe. Let me know if you want any extra tickets to the events this week."

Tom left. I was somewhat giddy, both from my chemical high as well as the sudden realization that there were likely eight million people just like Tom I could run into. A whole world of adventure was waiting for me outside.

"I like him. He's fun!"

Ryan rolled his eyes while explaining. "Eh, Tom can be a handful at times. He has some depression issues and the dope hits a certain pique point with him. You saw him in one of his good moods, and we were right to be done with him before he started turning all mopey."

Ryan got up and handed me my shirt. He grabbed some keys from the desk before turning to me.

"So, yeah, I have to go to the hardware store for some new shelving. You're more than welcome to come with me if you'd like. I can give you a walking tour of the city at the same time. Not sure if you're hungry or not—"

"That'd be fantastic!" I interrupted. "And no, the shit kills my appetite."

"Oh, of course. That makes sense, especially if you haven't used in a while. Well, *mi casa es su casa*, as they say." Ryan handed me a key.

"This is for if I'm not around and you need a place to stay. Feel free to grab a protein shake if you need to keep up with your macros. There's a gym down the street, Fitness SF, where all the gay musclebears like to train. You also have a host of restaurants within stumbling distance. I only ask that you text me before you come so I can make sure my roomie doesn't have anything going on and I don't have any business transactions to take care of."

I smiled while pocketing the key and getting dressed. "Like I said, Ryan, I don't normally go to a dealer's house unannounced. I mean, we can compare business practices whenever you want, but steroids are different than what you deal in. I mean, people get shot over meth deals and I'm hardly interested in something like that."

He looked at me with some confusion. "Don't be stupid. No one is going to shoot anyone around here. For one, the city is about as bleeding heart as it comes. Everyone's on meth and no one owns a gun. Look at Tom for example! What you think of as a drug deal in your state—or in Nebraska, where I'm from—is infinitely more violent than anything you would ever see here."

"Okay, but I'll text anyway," I finished.

As we were leaving, he put his hand on the small of my back.

"And don't call me a dealer. It just sounds *so awful.* Dealers buy and sell things. I offer professional party planning services."

Ryan showed me the rest of his house, starting with the kitchen. I learned that it was not uncommon for individuals to rent out a single room at a time instead of the more traditional apartment where I'm from. That single room was all Ryan had of the house, and everything else was shared space for anyone living there. There was no living room or den. Those had been carved out to create other units and had since become disconnected from the house. Just two bedrooms, each with its own resident, neither of whom seemed to want to speak to the other.

"Considering how much I hate my neighbors at home, this isn't a bad setup when you think about it. Seems more human somehow."

"I agree. I like keeping a certain distance from my neighbors, too."

Shit, did I say that out loud?

That entire train of thought occurred in my head without any sort of transition. The words *this, setup,* and *human* likely had no meaning in the current conversation to Ryan. Somehow, though, he understood what was going through my mind.

I guess he was used to random tweaker speak. I was pleased; it oftentimes got lonely in there. "There" being my head.

We left the house through the front door. Ryan locked up behind me. The afternoon sun was beaming down on us when we emerged and started walking. It was bright and comfortable to be in.

"The hardware store is about a fifteen-minute walk away."

"You can't walk anywhere in fifteen minutes in Oklahoma. You have to drive everywhere."

"Pfft, you had it lucky. In Nebraska, exits on the interstate are sometimes sixteen or thirty-two miles apart. If you missed your exit, you occasionally had to drive an entire township over."

Ryan jumped to the lead, since he knew the way.

"How did you make it here?" I asked.

"Same as anyone, I guess. Tired of living in a conservative people-less hellhole. I was too good at understanding people and computers to live in a state that had neither."

We walked along the street for a few minutes while Ryan told the history of the city. To be honest, my ears were mostly closed because my eyes were feasting on all they could devour. Our fifteen-minute walk easily grew to half an hour, though I didn't mind at all.

The houses all hugged each other perfectly, with no two adjacent ones sharing the same color. Only the rare exception had any sort of separation or alley between them. Signs littered the way showing the dates and times that sidewalks were closed for street sweeping. The shops were all mixed-use buildings, with tenants living above where they worked, and every shop seemed to bustle with some activity. I looked for the dirt. The grime. The seedy underbelly of the city.

"I was expecting more boarded-up buildings and graffiti for a city this size."

"Well, you'll see plenty of that, I promise. I'm not sure what kind of food you like, but there's plenty of fusion restaurants here. Melting pot of cultures means you get unusual cuisine, but all of it is good."

"I'm open to trying something new. I'm on an expense account, so money isn't a big concern."

We paused in front of an Italian restaurant. The doors were wide open and inviting. The fresh smells from the kitchen filled the street and the sound of silverware and plates clinking could be heard spilling out.

"Then, whenever you're hungry, just walk around. Don't bother looking online, that's a fool's mistake. Look at the lines in the restaurants and decide from that. I also look at what everyone else is ordering, too. After all, who wants to eat the second-best dish at the third-best restaurant? Especially if work is picking up your meal tab. This place is good if you want to give it a go later."

Meth be damned. He was starting to make me hungry.

"I need to work on this shelving before everyone gets back so I won't have time to take you to the Castro and show you the Gayborhood proper. But, if you're interested, it's literally stumbling distance from here. Just follow the setting sun."

"The weather is perfect, too."

"Yeah, you think that now. It'll get cool tonight. It always does. And fog every morning. We named it even."

"You named the fog?" I asked.

"Karl. Karl the Fog. He has a Twitter account and everything. But then again, we have the whole Twitter company, so of course we would have an account for something like fog."

"That's cute."

Ahead of us, a walking path etched the outline of a large open field where several hundred people were present, most of them basking in the sun. A sign read "Mission Dolores Park." The natural slope of the terrain made it easy to view downtown as well as the picturesque homes of the Mission. Unlike in most of the city, a few trees dotted the landscape. We didn't enter, but continued alongside the edge while Ryan pointed the way.

"The dog park is a good place to go if you want to people watch. It's a favorite of mine when I want to get out of the house. Or just enjoy some sun. You can do all the same on the nude beach, too, and, if you're lucky, get a blow job at the same time."

"I thought nude beaches were only in small getaway towns away from everyone."

"San Francisco is a nude beach. We had public nudity legalized until a few small bad apples fucked it up for everyone. Now you can get by with it on fair days only, like Dore. Honestly, you picked the perfect time to come down."

I continued in silence, enjoying the view. I wondered how many of these people Ryan knew personally. In a city this large, certainly they all were strangers to him. But he was so charming and so comfortable with people, I pondered how he couldn't know them all. Their bad habits and good.

"I keep hearing you mention Dore. What the fuck is that?"

He pointed to a street sign. "If you follow Harrison up, you'll find Dore Avenue. It's the location of the largest gay leather and BDSM sex fair in the world. It happens once a year, and you're here during it."

"Whoa, you're kidding me, right?"

"Nope, not at all. Folsom Street Events puts it on. Folsom is a fairly mainstream event now. The *Fifty Shades of Grey* bitches took over that whole event. Most of them are fucking soccer moms that wouldn't even let you put a finger up their ass. Since that movie and book made it big, the real sex pigs like you and me ended up having our event taken from us. So now we have our own. It's almost exclusively male-focused too, and while the lesbians get a tiny part of the fair, most of it's for the kind of porn you like. Hell, you probably got off to porn made during the event at some point in your life and don't even know it."

I was confused. "What makes you think I'm a sex pig?"

"Well, you smoke ice for one, and love it. Everyone who smokes is a sex pig. What starts as vanilla sex turns rough. Then what starts as rough turns violent. Plus, I read your Scruff profile, remember? You did your homework on me, what makes you think I didn't do mine on you?"

I had no idea what my Scruff profile said. It wasn't something that I updated regularly.

Ryan stopped, got close to my face, grabbed me firmly by the shirt, and said in a gruff, direct tone, "I'll rip your clothes off right now and make you fuck me like the faggot I am."

My eyes widened. I was startled and tried to take half a step back. It took me a moment of looking into his eyes to figure out what he was getting at.

"Aggressive sex? Yeah, that was part of my profile, wasn't it?"

He broke character, smiled cheerfully, and said, "Oh, yeah. And I like it, too."

My heart slowly fell from my throat back to its normal place in my chest. He released me from his grip, put some distance between us, then twirled around lightly on his feet, almost like a dancer.

He pointed to a small building. "That coffee shop also has great ice cream."

"I bet it does. I used to always buy my dope at ice cream stores."

Ryan paused, then looked at me as though I was insane. All I could return to him was a guilty look.

"Really?" he asked curiously.

"Yeah, it always seemed fitting. And as an alternative to what? Buying it at a school or church where the penalties for getting caught would be so much worse? No way. Always the ice cream shop. Besides being ironic, I would buy milk for the calories before I went tweaking too hard."

"That's oddly clever. I wish I had thought of that."

"What you call clever, I call convenient."

We walked into a hole-in-the-wall store. It was a worn-down ACE Hardware, a chain well-known to populate strip malls and the like.

"I had no idea you had ACE Hardware in San Fran."

Ryan paused for a moment.

"Land's too expensive for a Lowe's or a Home Depot, and while we don't have strip malls we do have small retail spaces. So ACE kinda fits in. Though, now that you're a local, I have to tell you something. You keep making a really big mistake. Please stop calling it San Fran. No one calls it that but touristy jackasses. You can call it SF. Or San Francisco. Or even the city. But don't ever call it San Fran!"

"Noted, but I'm hardly a local," I replied somewhat questioningly.

"Nonsense. You're an SF Gay now. Don't let anyone tell you otherwise. You just need to learn the rules is all. There's also some good pieces of advice I should give you. I know not every town has every app. Grindr works in most places, and if you're just looking to get off it's a start, I suppose. Obviously, we met on Scruff so you're on that one, but there's plenty more apps that are popular here which may not have a big user base where you're from."

Ryan was feverishly hunting the aisles for shelving products and mounting hardware while he spoke. Occasionally he'd pick an item up and look at it, only to replace it when he decided it wouldn't suit his needs. He seemed somewhat distracted, occasionally looking in the distance to find some new thing to investigate.

"I'm on all the apps," I confessed.

"Pfft, I somehow doubt that," he retorted.

"Seriously, I am."

"Really?" he said incredulously. "BBRT? Grommer? Growlr? Jacked? Adam?"

"Yup. And Recon even. Tried 'em all. I don't get on all of them unless I'm traveling, but I've been hooking up online since gay dot-com was still relevant."

"Wow. You impress me, Chris." He glanced back at me with an element of surprise on his face.

"Because I was a horny teenager with a computer?" I asked.

"No, because I can see the pig inside you. Because you were hooking up before it was cool. We would've run into each other sooner if we weren't a couple states away. It seems like you genuinely love meeting people, even if they aren't into everything you are. That, or you're literally into anything with a pulse."

"Depends on the year and if I was smoking at the time."

"Makes sense. But now that you're an SF Gay, you're going to have to raise the bar. Especially with a body like yours."

He pulled what appeared to be a washboard off the wall and put it in front of his abs. He edged out a seductive single bicep, kissed his own arm, and then replaced the object on the shelf. If I had taken a picture it could have been on the front page of a porn magazine. He was mischievous and dark, but playful and lighthearted at the same time.

I chuckled. "For sure. I certainly am a lot pickier than I used to be. Mostly because, well, I can afford to be. I wasn't always in shape. I used to be a fat asshole."

"Me too, actually."

"Really!? I can't picture you fat at all."

We had made our way to the back of the store and were surrounded by conduit and baseboards. Ryan pulled out his cell phone. He handed it to me, unlocked, something IT people never do with their electronics, and continued his search.

"Holy fuck, you were a whale!" I exclaimed. I took a moment to admire the goofy smile in the image.

He seemed unphased by the comment. "Yup. Moving to a city where I walked everywhere helped. So did the dope. Plus, there's too many gay guys around to look ugly, my friend. I had to do something to get noticed and stay relevant."

I handed him back his phone. I pulled out mine, found some old pictures, and angled it so he could see the sins of my past as well.

His mouth gaped. He looked up at me, then back at the phone.

"Wow! That's impressive."

He resumed his search along the peg boards and hardware parts. We were bouncing from aisle to aisle and I was beginning to think we were walking in circles.

"I thought so, too. About four years of work."

"Well, in that case, no leaving the peninsula for you. Rule number one: they come to you," he instructed. "You can have your pick of the litter. In Oklahoma, twelve miles away may be an option. Here, three miles is too far."

"Three miles?"

"Way too far. Maybe two. I mean, look at you. I can get you into any club you want. You definitely aren't going to have a hard time finding a good lay, plus you have your own hotel room and my place. Yeah, you're going to be a busy, busy guy."

"There's that many guys three miles from here?" I asked, puzzled.

"God, shut up and hold these. I'll show you in a minute."

He tossed some brackets and precut plywood slabs into my arms while he stretched to reach for something on the top shelf. I stood there, frustrated by his dismissive response, when I noticed a bearish yet brawny guy gazing at me from down the aisle. He licked his lips in a seductive way that would practically be considered a felony in Oklahoma.

"Wow. I guess you're right."

"Good. Jesus, you country boys are slow on the uptake," he commented.

"And here I thought I was more spun up than you."

"Very funny. Now, try not to get raped in the store before I get my shit paid for."

"Yes, sir!" I said.

It took me a moment to notice that Ryan didn't actually fetch anything from the shelf he reached for. He had just been showing off his physique to our mutual admirer. Ryan slapped me on the ass as we headed toward the checkout. The bear down the aisle took that as a cue to leave, my ass being property tagged by Ryan, who posed enough of a threat that I was deemed not worth pursuing.

"In this part of San Francisco, you're in the minority if you're straight," Ryan whispered as he walked past me.

Ryan paid for things with cash and we departed back toward his place. The street was still bustling with Tuesday traffic, and the sun was beginning to wane into evening.

"What time do you have to be at work tomorrow?"

"The convention starts at nine o'clock, but that feels like eleven to me. I'm not used to jet lag working in my favor."

"Well, don't get too excited. I want you to show up in good shape, especially since you're clearly a lightweight. If you stay up all night, you're going to look like shit tomorrow and I don't want to be blamed."

"Well, business comes first."

"Speaking of which," he responded. "I need more stuff from you."

"How much are you thinking?"

"Well, I was wondering what type of pricing tiers you might offer?"

"Pricing tiers?" I asked, confused.

"Yeah. You mentioned bulk earlier. How much would I have to order to get bulk rates?"

The question caught me off guard. Dylan and I used more than anyone I sold to. "Bulk" for me was anything heavier than that.

"I suppose I never thought of it before. I mean, I already give a bit of a discount for buying twenty-five mls at a time instead of ten. But I guess at $1,000 I could offer a flat rate discount. How about fifteen percent off?"

He sized me up with a glare, our hands both full of tools and parts. It was the type of hard-nosed negotiation where you both want each other to be happy. His eyes were serious and kind at the same time. I thought of all the great businessmen of the past and how they negotiated. Andrew Carnegie and John Rockefeller. Barings and Rothchild. Hell, for all I knew, Bill Gates and Steve Jobs both bought tools here when they were in Silicon Valley together.

"Sounds good. I don't suppose you'd be willing to do half cash now and half credit?"

I contemplated for a moment. Dollar signs lit up in my brain like a neon sign. I don't think I've ever been that greedy before in my life.

"I don't see why not. My interest rates are *very* reasonable."

"Awesome, because I need about twenty bottles of test and some other things as well."

"Twenty?!" I repeated. The number was a bit higher than I anticipated.

"Yeah, is that a problem?"

"No! I mean, God no! That's well over a grand there. It sounds like you're closer to $2,000 more than anything."

"Well, your stuff is very popular, I'm not gonna lie. The entire time we've been walking Tom has been texting me. He and all his friends would kill to look like you. What can I say, kid? You're a walking billboard."

I was in awe. My head hurt from the possibilities. Tom was right that impossible things happen in this city. I thought about all the times I undersold chemistry to the guys back home and questioned those decisions. I thought about how much I wanted to be big and loved for bodybuilding. Here,

Ryan managed to give me both the adoration I needed and the social status I craved. As an added bonus, he threw in fat stacks of cash, free dope, and sex on the side. And he made it seem so easy. All of this was done while giving me a tour of the city, and the most difficult decision he had to make was picking which shelving he thought would look best in his home.

My heart swelled with excitement—the excitement you get when you realize you've won the lottery or beaten an opponent in a game of skill before they themselves knew it. My life in the last twenty minutes had changed more than it had in the last twenty years.

I looked at all the stores. The people. The houses. Every single one of them was colored with the full spectrum of the rainbow. Then it dawned on me.

Rainbows don't have beige.

"What's in it for you?" I asked, wondering where the missing color went.

"For me? Professional kindness to a peer in the same industry. Well, and I mark it up, of course. You don't have to deal with distribution for anything on this coast. I deal with your stuff exclusively and you deal with me exclusively. Minimizes risk, maximizes profit. For both of us."

"Exclusive is fine. But you can't possibly be marking it up that much."

He stopped for a moment. He smirked deeply. He almost couldn't contain himself.

"Have you noticed how everything costs more in the city?" he asked.

"I guess so. I mean, the tools and stuff were a little high, but not enough I was going to say anything about it."

"Well, what you're used to paying for food in an airport, we're used to in the grocery store."

"Really!"

"Yeah," he said. "And it gets so much worse."

He paused. My mind was still spinning on dope so I missed the point he was going for. Finally, the idea cracked through. The conclusion he was trying to walk me toward was so obvious.

"Holy shit! Exactly how much does a bottle of testosterone go for out here?"

"About twice what you charged me, retail. Before the discounts you just threw in," he grinned uncontrollably.

"Son of a bitch. You're making two hundred percent."

"More actually, if I repackage your twenty-five ml bottles as ten mls. Like we agreed, it's an exclusive deal here. No Lowe's. No Home Depot. Just me playing the part of Mr. ACE Hardware. I'm the only shop on the corner in a crowded city. Tripling up on money is pretty good for a distributor agreement, I think at least. I figured you'd find out sooner or later. After all, that's what they call you guys, right? Sooners?"

I was floored. "Yeah, that's the football team. Motherfucker! How much turnaround are you looking at from this?"

"I already have the next twenty bottles sold at $130 each. You promised me sixty-five dollars per in your price list. That's about $1,500 this weekend alone, profit to me, and that's just the testosterone. I haven't even bothered to do the math for the other steroids. It's a win-win for both of us."

Maybe Dylan and I weren't the big consumers I'd thought we were.

"Damn, I guess it is. And that's only in a weekend? How many users, er, customers do you have? I mean, I have a very small discreet clientele at home, and I don't think any of them would snap their fingers and just instantly want twenty bottles to appear."

"About a dozen. Most of them are guys wanting to look good. Not bodybuilders, mind you, but that just gives me extra income opportunities around cycle planning and the like. They'll pay me for diet advice. Fuck, I have abs too, you know. But even better, your price list indicated you have TNE available."

Freebase. Testosterone No Ester. It was my favorite way to jumpstart a cycle, and unlike enanthate or cypionate, TNE was known to hit hard and fast. Enanthate usually took weeks before strength and libido gains could be felt, while TNE took about thirty minutes.

"Twenty bottles of TNE? That's going to be a bit harder to get ahold of. I was thinking you meant enanthate."

"No, twenty bottles of enanthate. I'll want *another twenty* of TNE after that."

Gears. Cogs. Turning. Why? Why would he want TNE? It was great for advanced bodybuilders like me, but why on earth would he care for it? It was fairly exotic to some degree. This was weirder than Tony's Viagra orders. My mind raced ahead of itself, extrapolating possibilities of who these clients could possibly be.

"Wait a minute. If they're not bodybuilders, then the only benefit I can think of is what it does for sex drive. Holy hell. It's because of the shit, isn't it? The dope. You got a bunch of guys using it to fight crystal dick so they can fuck all night?"

He went from leading the way to dancing ahead of me. Literally, the guy was dancing on the sidewalk.

"Bingo!"

"That's . . . that's . . . brilliant!" I stuttered in awe.

"Not only is it brilliant, it's genius. When tops take too much ice they all go soft, and there's nothing worse than a room full of spun-up party bottoms. Everyone wants dick but no one can get hard. TNE helps give them a nudge in the right direction. Instant chem tops ready to fuck on a moment's notice."

I thought about Dylan and all of the time I spent teaching him proper steroid usage. I always emphasized that it was to be by the book, and that there was a difference between being stupid and reckless. As a willing acolyte, it took years for him to be able to keep up with me and to slowly chip away at any ignorance he may have had. Ryan was way ahead of most, perhaps even me, but he seemed to lack any sort of fear about the forces he meddled with.

"But, wait, that's dangerous isn't it? Every drug has its fixed cost and potential risk. Isn't introducing a hormonal substance without the patience and practice of a bodybuilder harmful? I mean, how do you get them off of it? I'm not even sure what 'recreational steroid use' looks like in this capacity."

"Do you really think meth users are worried about cardiovascular health? Not that it matters, because it's lower risk than what you do," he argued. "Giving someone a single shot for a night of fun, sure it'll throw them out of whack for a while, but compared to the months or years of use that you're doing? Please. As long as I make those few days worthwhile, it'll be worth any cost you could imagine. And they're happy to pay it. Besides, in two days they'll be back to normal, and these guys are happy with that."

He was right. Any claim that my way of doing things was healthier than his was just ego. His science was impeccable in that it was accurate, and his assessment that gay drug users didn't care about health was spot on, too. Fuck, most of them had HIV or were worried about where their next meal was coming from. Many more were homeless. They had other priorities in life. I had read every medical endocrinology textbook I could get my hands on, and while I considered his approach to medicine akin to playing with fire, I could not for the life of me consider it more dangerous than what I was doing with Dylan back home.

In all reality, I had already paid the ultimate penalty as a steroid user—I couldn't come off them. My body needed synthetic testosterone to function properly at that point. I didn't mind it for myself, but it was certainly a price not every person should pay. Diehards like Dylan and I loved the fact that we controlled our physiology. We'd rather be gods bound to the chains of injection drugs than mortals free of chemical shackles.

But was someone like Tom capable of making that kind of decision for himself? Or even Ryan? Certainly, he shared my Machiavellian tastes for chemistry and was familiar with the Dark Arts. Few gym bros and juicers I knew were even familiar with the hypo-testicular axis, which is the male body's mechanism for regulating hormone release. And even those who were aware of it oftentimes lacked the finesse to play God with it in a safe and repeatable way. I had dedicated years of my life to understanding it, and returned my clients safely back without even a scratch. Was this Ryan guy so altruistic? Was he as capable a deity as I?

He certainly had his own set of results. The picture he showed me in the hardware store was a testament to the fact that he understood his own body, at least. But could he be responsible for someone else's?

And Jesus . . . Meth? Forget playing with fire, Ryan was consumed by it. If his primary customer was using my drugs to counteract the side effects of meth, would that not make me complicit to some degree in its use? Sure, it was one thing for me to offer steroids to Dylan, who was going to be a user whether or not he got them from me. But leveraging them as a true lifestyle drug for a self-induced problem was something else entirely.

The idea mesmerized me. Controlling my physiology had long been a turn-on. But the trust needed to give someone else that control, for no other reason than sheer enjoyment, was a level of perversion unlike I had ever imagined.

"I suppose that's a risk that the user has to take into account," I hedged. My libertarian streak showed its colors in the San Franciscan sun.

"Exactly. Just as they have to take into account any other side effect of a drug or lifestyle choice."

"I guess."

We walked the rest of the way back to his house in silence. Ryan took the things out of my arms and plopped them on the bed when we got back to his room.

"Awesome. Thanks for helping carry things."

"No problem. Makes me wonder how you do grocery shopping on your own."

"When every day's a sunny day, why not make a market trip part of your standard routine?"

Fucking great logic, Ryan. Again, I get it: Oklahoma's a shit hole and you live in paradise.

"Makes sense."

"I'm going to put these shelves together. I also have a few deliveries to make later today. Why don't you explore the city a little on your own? Try and get a good bite to eat. If you want to come over and chill later, you certainly can. The roomie will be back probably around ten o'clock, but that doesn't mean we can't have a small get together here. Or we can all head to your place."

The idea of using meth in a hotel room paid for by my work sounded like a bad one. It was the kind of idea that would leave me homeless in a gutter.

"I think a bite sounds great. I'm sure there's something worth seeing that isn't all touristy and shit. I'll let you know afterward, that work?"

"Sure! Well, call or text me and we'll figure it out.

We kissed gently, but briefly.

I went to step away, but before I could, I had to kiss him again. This time, more romantically.

Was this how we were always going to say goodbye? Or hello? Was there actual passion between us, or were we just two drug dealers caught in the moment? We were both using each other, and we were each complicit in doing so. We enjoyed our respective God complexes because deep down, we believed the real God either didn't care or didn't exist. There was a certain cold, hard, calculated logic inside us.

And there we were. The materials we purchased from the hardware store soon found themselves on the floor, our clothes ripped from our bodies. Sweat dripped down and filled the sheets. The same wind that made the drapes dance in the window caressed us. Any sound of passersby was muted by our passionate moans of ecstasy.

Ryan got up briefly and looked around.

"What are you looking for?" I asked.

"The pipe."

"Tom took it. But not now," I pleaded. "It's not something I want."

He reached for a syringe and a bottle of TNE. I looked at him, took it, and began drawing up a shot. He started sucking my cock while jacking off his own. He quickly got hard. Once the barrel was full, I handed him the syringe then laid down on my side on the bed, pressing my face into the blind comfort of a pillow. I had never trusted anyone to give me a shot before.

I couldn't see anything, but the sound of liquid being sloshed around filled the room. I presumed it was rubbing alcohol as, moments later, a small area of my ass was met with the cold wet touch of cotton. The piercing pain when he broke my outermost skin layers with the needle lasted only a moment, before it penetrated deep into the glute muscle.

"Are you ready?" he whispered sweetly.

"Yeah."

He began to push the syringe plunger steadily. I felt the oil begin to fill my body. Oil-based steroid injections generally don't hurt. This wasn't about pain or pressure. This was sheer ecstasy. The ecstasy of losing control. The incredible feeling of getting exactly what I wanted was more than I could stand.

I was rock hard when he withdrew the syringe. I looked up and saw him gently place the cap back on the needle before discarding it in the waste bin. A single droplet of blood formed on my skin. Ryan licked it up eagerly, smiling fiendishly.

I got up and we switched positions. After having him ass up, I began eating him out hungrily. I savored every drop of his sweat. Though I had not seen him smoke from a pipe, I detected the unmistakable smell of meth from his body. I pushed his face down into the pillow like mine was and slid my hard cock inside him. I fucked him deeply and passionately. My balls ached, both from the testosterone and from the powerful release of shooting my semen deep inside him.

"Thank you," I whispered. I got up, got dressed, and left the only way I knew how.

NINE

THE CITY WAS SO very much alive. While the convention afforded me a free lunch, I decided to bail midday and try one of the places that Ryan had pointed out on the tour the previous night. I settled on an Italian restaurant near his house which seemed homey and inviting.

I thought back to my favorite restaurants growing up, the kind where the hostess places fresh butcher paper on the table while seating you and where the waiters write their names in crayon upside down in an effort to wow the patrons. It worked back then, but not now. I remembered as a kid enjoying the ability to write on the table while waiting for the meal to arrive.

This was not that kind of place.

The restaurant was classy without being overtly elegant. I had expected disposable napkins or even the more familiar paper towels found in barbecue joints back home, but instead discovered thick cloth napkins and tablecloths with a high thread count, all in a rich red. San Francisco, like most of the West Coast, had limited amounts of landfill space afforded it. Anything that could be cleaned and reused was, even in a simple café like this.

Glass salt and pepper shakers were on each table, along with parmesan cheese and crushed red pepper. They were all in the familiar, cylindrical shapes found back home and added a fresh fragrance to the table. I inhaled a small whiff of the pepper, a habit I've always enjoyed at Italian restaurants, and surveyed the rest of the dining room. Each table was laid out similarly and many were occupied by fellow diners. The only thing that was served in original containers were the sweeteners; the white, blue, pink, and yellow packets were corralled in tiny glass boxes. Each a miniature rainbow.

I enjoyed the sound of voices exchanging ideas, not about technology, but about life. I overheard a couple near my table on a first date. The man was eager to get into her pants, as evidenced by his constant handsyness more commonly seen at a bar at night than in a café midday. She wasn't having it. Instead, she was giving the waiter hell, asking if every ingredient was organic, gluten free, and dolphin friendly. The poor guy followed suit, asking similar questions of the waiter in an effort to seem just as concerned about the cuisine. Given the clumsiness of how he asked them, he didn't seem to care how much dolphin existed in the tuna, or if the chicken was free range or not. He only cared about getting laid afterward. The waiter wore the same smirk I did while listening to him try to pronounce the items on the menu.

My waiter was cheery, though clearly harried. He occasionally smiled knowingly to his peer with the high-maintenance couple, but he had plenty of people to entertain on his own. I was one of the few solo diners and thus at the bottom of the queue any time I needed something. I didn't care. I was more in love with the moment than the food, and I didn't mind savoring both slowly. I made a point not to touch my phone since I had already done my research on what was available on the Grindr meat market.

Okay, well, of course, a quick snap of the entree and a log of my macros was fair. The double serving of chicken spilled over the bed of spaghetti it was placed on, but such was the norm for me. I guessed at the protein content, took a picture of the receipt for expense report purposes, and returned to the splendor of the day.

I stumbled my way aimlessly about the street for a while. The sound of the occasional gull was foreign but pleasant. I contemplated attending some of the evening seminars at the convention, but decided against it. Instead, I committed to enjoying the extra time afforded me by waking up early. I was aloof and carefree, in no rush to do anything other than see the city.

But then I got a text from Ryan.

Got a present for ya.

O rly?

Ya, you going to be back by?

I can be. Should I head over?

Sure

What the hell is this about?

I caught an Uber, confident that I'd arrive at his place before the surprise would be lost or spoiled on some other trick. After sending him a quick, "I'm here" message, he peeked out from the window above and waved me in.

It caught me partially by surprise. I recalled that window being blocked by his desk.

W-O-O-F. Garage. Stairs. Kitchen. His room.

Ryan was alone, sitting on the floor under his partially dis-assembled desk. Some mail and Amazon packages were on the bed, and the packing material was sprawled around him. The computer monitors and cables were carefully stacked in the far corner of the room. He was in full-blown tweaker project mode, a wrench in one hand, socket in the other. The shelving we'd purchased the day before was mounted, and looked good.

"Whoa," I said, eyeing the spectacle. I closed the door behind me.

"Got the shelves put together and I need to rearrange the desk over to the side. I don't like the way the light is all backlit and I'm staring at the sun all the damned time when I'm at the computer."

"Looks like a lot of work."

"It is, but I got something in the mail that you're going to need. I wanted to give it to you now so you'll have the full ben-efit of it."

"Oh?"

He tossed me a bottle containing two different-sized pills. One was a larger blue oval, the other a small circular grayish/green. The label was written in an Asian language. I was not fluent in Mandarin.

There was only one thing I could tell with perfect authority—whatever they were, they weren't steroids.

"What are these?" I asked, pouring them into my hand.

"The blue one is Truvada. Well, the generic of it, tenofovir. The actual brand name Truvada I couldn't get from overseas. The smaller one is doxycycline."

"You bought HIV meds from overseas? Why?"

"Absolutely," he said while intermittently popping his head out from under the desk. "So much cheaper than anything you can get here, even with their discount program and government subsidies."

"What am I going to do with HIV meds?" I asked, puzzled.

"The point is for you to go on PrEP. At least while you're here. I know you weren't expecting a large sex festival, but it's going to happen. I figured you might appreciate it to minimize any sort of risk to yourself."

I was dumbfounded. I had heard of PrEP before but hadn't ever considered doing it. It was a drug regimen where HIV-negative individuals were given retrovirals in an effort to prevent them from getting infected. It wasn't a cure for HIV, but the statistics on reducing its spread were incredible at nearly a hundred percent. A chemical condom that was better than a physical one. Those who were on PrEP and engaged in bareback sex with HIV-positive individuals were considered virtually not at risk.

"Well, that's considerate. Will it even be effective if I take it now? Don't you have to be on it for a while?"

"You should be fine as long as you start it now," he said. "One in three gay males in San Francisco is HIV-positive, and while I'm undetectable, I can't say that for everyone you're likely to run into while you're here."

One in three. Could it really be that high?

Ryan finished assembling the desk and looked proudly at his work. He stood up, slid the drawers in and out a few times to test them, and then started the precarious task of unloading and sorting items on his shelves. I laid down on the bed, nestled between the various packages. I ran my hand over the impression our bodies left on the sheets the night before, and relaxed on my side.

"And the antibiotic? Is this free?"

"The antibiotic is a nice little hack. Truvada will keep you from getting HIV, but doesn't do anything against a bacterial infection. Of course, you can cure that after the fact with a select number of antibiotics, or you can start a course now. As long as you continue it for a couple of weeks after you get back, you won't even get a symptom. Call it insurance against gonorrhea. Just don't get crabs, and you'll be fine."

"Gee, thanks. I never would have thought of such a thing."

"Absolutely. It's just $250 for the Truvada. The doxy I'll toss in. They really weren't that much anyway."

I felt slighted somehow, though not entirely surprised. Had this gift been a deception? Bait and switch after he sold me on the bill of goods? If so, it worked and it worked well. Given how much money I was already up for the weekend, giving ten percent back felt more like tithing than thievery.

I decided I still needed to put up a fight over it, even if just a small one. It wouldn't have been good business practice to let a negotiation be so one-sided.

"Helluva gift. I thought you said you got this for me," I said with some disappointment.

The door opened.

My muscles tensed. Instinctively, I stashed the bottles under the thin bedsheet to cover my chemical dependency and sluttish pride.

In walked a masterpiece of a man. He was nearly Ryan's size in build, though slightly thinner. His chest development was the product of years of training. Where Ryan and I got our muscles out of a bottle, this beast (no older than thirty-one) was much more naturally proportioned. I guessed he did it the hard way. He had fairly dark hair like Ryan, but lacked his machismo, beard, and sheer confidence. He made up for it with an obvious athletic ability, moving gracefully with fine motor control that most chemical bodybuilders—and all tweakers—lack.

"H- hey . . ." the stranger stuttered, more scared than anyone I would have imagined barging in to a random drug dealer's room unannounced would be.

Completely unphased, Ryan said to me, "I didn't. I got you him."

"I think the $250 is worth it," I said with a smile.

"Did I come at a bad time?" the stranger asked.

"No, not at all!" Ryan said, as if noticing the intruder for the first time. "Come in."

"Uh . . . Hmm . . . What do you want me to do about the car? I'm double-parked and I can't park in your garage unless you give me the code?" the stranger asked.

"Shit, okay, excuse me a moment, Chris."

They retreated downstairs. Puzzled, I wondered how our interloper got in the house. Was he not privileged to the secret W-O-O-F code? Was he more welcome through the front door than I, for various reasons? Or was he not aware of Ryan's job as a professional party planner?

So many questions. But I did take a tiny leap in assuming that the man loved cock. It appeared everyone Ryan knew was gay. Fortunately for me, gay men have a terrible habit of leaving their phones running at all times with a collection of hook-up apps installed. If I wanted to learn more about this new individual, chances are all I had to do was pull out my phone and run a quick search.

Voila. His name was Ehren.

Based on his profile, he was a lifelong resident of SF and a fan of dogs. He was frequently outdoors in his profile pictures, running with Ruffles, his retriever. I assumed his athleticism was forged during his former rugby days and he appeared to keep it up during his free time, which he spent playing ultimate frisbee outdoors. He was the masc4masc type that I enjoyed so much. Gym selfies revealed what many would refer to as toxic masculinity, but what I referred to as sex appeal.

And he was versatile. That was a turn-on.

They came back in, cutting short my online stalking.

"Cool! We got it parked! Ehren, this is Chris. Chris, Ehren."

"Hey," I said.

"How's it going," Ehren replied.

I moved over to the farthest side of the bed that I could, with things still occupying it. Ehren sat down, keeping to himself and maintaining some distance from me while Ryan gathered his packages. He was clearing the bed to make more room for both of us.

"So," Ryan started, "I need to do some errands." His speech pattern was slightly altered, almost brief in wording.

"Yeah? Do you need us to go?" I asked.

"No!" he exclaimed. His labored breathing showed that catching his breath was still a good several hours away. "Not at all. Please stay. It's convenient. For all of us, I think. I need to borrow Ehren's car for this. Do anything you like. Turn on a porn. Talk. Keep to yourselves. Whatever." Long pauses seemed to fill each sentence fragment he formed.

He had the bed mostly cleared, though the floor had quite a few things on it now. I was at a loss. He was super high and detached. He needed the car but also didn't want us to come with him. I presumed he didn't have the desire to leave either of us alone in the house. I surmised he opted to put the two of us together in an effort to minimize risk over leaving either of us alone in his room.

"That's fine, I'm a pretty friendly guy." I replied.

Ehren's eyes perked up.

"You two will get along great."

Ryan grabbed a drawstring bag. It had some things in it, but I couldn't determine the contents. He made his way for the exit.

"Don't forget to take those pills," he said, finally closing the door behind him.

Two very confused and nervous men were left, our only companion was the awkwardness of finding each other attractive. The afternoon sun was still high in the sky.

"Wow. Well, he's a mess. How long have you known Ryan?" I asked to break the silence.

"Far too long, it seems," Ehren replied.

The conversation wasn't going to be of any particular use as long as it was focused on the absent person. How was I supposed to describe Ryan? My sex and drug dealer? A guy who buys my steroids? Perhaps this unfortunate soul had a similarly regrettable first-time story, having met him in a seedy bathhouse or the like.

"Here, let me clear off some of this shit so you have a place to sit," I offered, favoring helpfulness over exchanging small talk. I moved an extra pillow and box out of the way.

"Ryan told me a lot about you. He was right, damn! You do work out."

"I get it all from a bottle, man," I hinted.

"I don't mind where you get it from, I can certainly use more of that myself."

Did Ryan give me a piece of ass or a potentially paying customer? Does he expect me to sell my wares, or just bust a nut?

"Well, steroids have their benefits," I said, since he was comfortable with the subject.

"I heard they make your dick huge."

I replied with a laugh. He was cute, though naive. "No. Not hardly. The actual reality is it makes your nuts smaller. But, I guess by comparison, you could say your dick gets bigger."

"Mind if I find out how much?" The sentence was forced through every ounce of courage he could possibly have.

He was so nervous I could almost feel the bed quake with his apprehension. I remembered the pictures of when Ruffles was a tiny pup, and when his rugby career was only a high school hobby. I felt I already knew so much about him. More importantly, though, I knew Ehren's buttons and how to push them. He had listed his fetishes, his turn-ons, and his desires in men—and I wanted to exploit each of them.

I edged closer to him on the bed.

"That depends on if you're capable of taking what I give you, bro."

I could feel attraction fill his veins. It was exactly what he wanted to hear. To feel like he was used by one of his team-mates on the field. To feel a sense of camaraderie and physical attraction, and to have someone who was better at sport than him give him recognition and desire. He wanted to feel used as much as wanted.

"Oh, I can take a lot."

He was so noncommittal. He couldn't look me in the eyes for too long and seemed so unsure of himself. I thought it apparent I was going to fuck him, yet he still questioned his worth in my eyes. This truly was going to be easy. And easy it was. He just needed a more experienced hand to show him the way.

He was not unattractive. God, I've seen unattractive men. Men who have resigned their bodies to the computer gods. Those who consider games things to be played while eating snacks in their mom's basement, not battles won on a grassy field. He wasn't one of them.

Ehren was a man who, with the right confidence, could move mountains and achieve great things. The fact that he was older than me and lacked it made me think one of two things: either he came out of the closet at a later age, or had no experience with drugs whatsoever. Typically, both made the best closet cases. Either way, it was my job to make sure that he got what he needed in small controlled doses.

Fuck it. If someone's going to make the first move, it might as well be me.

I reached over and tugged lightly at his shirt. He grabbed it to assist. It came off with all the caution of a frat boy preparing for his hazing. I tugged the band on his black gym shorts, then lowered it enough for his cock to fall out. It was small and retreated, not from cold but from fear.

It was plump, with a certain heft to it that I enjoyed watching. His hands hovered in stasis above my head and it wasn't until I started to blow him deeply that I could feel them try to find a home and relax. The tension in his fingers broke in waves as his hands eventually settled to rest on my upper back. It took a few minutes of this for me to feel the pulse beat in his throbbing cock.

Ehren seemed sober, going by the firmness of his cock, but nervous given how rarely his eyes were open when I looked up at them. While I was tempted to try and find Ryan's pipe and get this guy spun up, it occurred to me that I neither knew where he kept it, nor was certain if it would have scared the poor boy away. Ryan may have been a tweaker, but he was brilliant at keeping his stash safe via the forced detente he invoked by his absence.

"Do you bottom?" I asked quietly.

His eyes drifted open and he nodded. A gentle nudge on his hips was all the cue he needed to start rolling over. Stepping off the bed, he slid his shorts off completely while I stood on the bed and stripped myself bare. I was the more cumbersome of the two, having to avoid hitting my head on the ceiling, but he didn't seem to notice or care. I was mostly hard before but seeing Ehren's nearly perfect skin and rugged musculature naked before me got me the rest of the way.

Ryan had been sport enough to leave an extra bottle of lube on the headboard for us to enjoy. I reached over to pick it up. It was a clear Swiss Navy bottle, which I took to be his favorite brand once I spotted a few empty ones tossed behind it.

How many others does he invite up here to fuck in his absence? I forced myself to think the answer was many, and got turned on even more.

When I looked back, I caught Ehren's mouth watering as his eyes focused on my cock. Given our recent and brief introductions, I wasn't sure if he had seen dick pictures of me before, so I couldn't tell how much was lust or just surprise. I was hardly the longest guy ever (seven inches of pure cut All-American white cock) but girthy as a motherfucker. Still standing on the bed, I relished watching his mouth close around me. Ehren visibly struggled deepthroating me, though he was certainly trying heartily.

Sensing his struggle and thirst, I motioned for him to get back on the bed. Placing a pillow under his thighs, he laid there ass up, his face buried deep in the pillow.

It didn't take much to penetrate him with the mix of pre-cum and lube coating me. Still, it took for goddamn ever before I could even get close to cumming.

My partner wasn't complaining. He released bellowed grunts with every thrust while I pounded away at him. There was no talking, no cries of "Yes" or "Oh God." Just raw grunting. Nonetheless, we were having a helluva time even though I couldn't bring myself to cum.

And I wanted to cum in him, badly. But I felt I could keep this up for hours and had no idea when to expect Ryan back. It was delicious torture, and I needed to put him out of his misery. I unmounted him, hooked my arm under his leg and flipped him to his side. I quickly forced my mouth around his cock while thrusting two fingers into his hole. Soon, his whole body seized up, and I saw his eyes open for what appeared to be the first time during our whole encounter. He came in waves, which I took as a cue to keep pressing my fingers deeper and deeper toward his prostate. His cum was partially in my mouth, but mostly on my beard and chin. It took only a moment in real time, but given his final releasing grunt, I can only presume it felt like much longer to him.

His cum was sweet as hell.

When I finally edged away and produced some distance between us, I was greeted by a wild, geeked out face in front of me. Nothing but pure pleasure looked back.

"Wow. You're amazing," Ehren finally said.

"You should see me when I want to get mine."

"Oh, Jesus! Don't tell me that. I'm surprised I could keep up with you as it was."

I gave him a pat on his bare leg. "You did just fine, bro. You're fun."

"How long are you in town for?" he asked.

Ah, the deception was revealed. A crack in the armor exposed.

"Oh, you know I'm from out of town?"

"Yeah, Ryan told me. Said you were his steroid guy. Damn, I knew you were muscled from the pictures he showed me, but I wasn't expecting this!"

"I'll take that as a compliment. I'm just here until the end of Dore. I'm American Dragon."

"What's that?"

"That's my lab name."

"Interesting. I thought about doing it once," he responded weakly. Going from the lack of confidence in his voice and the topic, I guessed he'd never seen a bottle of steroids in his life.

"Well, don't start unless you're comfortable being on them forever."

"So I hear. Listen, some friends of mine are going to the bathhouse later tonight. You're more than welcome to come with us. I'd love to see what the finale of that show is like before you ditch town and head back to wherever you're from."

"Bathhouse? Wow, never been. It's a fucking Wednesday though. Is there even anything going on there?"

"I actually . . . I wouldn't know. I've never been," he confessed.

I couldn't believe my ears. "Wait, what? Aren't you from here?"

"I am. Whole life. But, yeah, believe it or not, I wasn't out until recently, and San Francisco doesn't have any bathhouses."

"Come on, San Francisco is gay sex Disneyland! I've heard about the sex parties out here since I was but a wee little gay. What are you talking about?"

"Sure, there's sex parties. If you're into that kind of thing. I mean, I don't go to those, usually. But you have to get to Berkeley on the mainland to find the nearest bathhouse."

"*Usually*, huh?" I poked at him. "And how far is that?"

"About a forty-five-minute drive, assuming no traffic. Two or three hours at the worst."

"Fair enough. Well, I'm flattered you'd choose me as your, um, partner for your first time going to one."

I hoped *partner* was the right word.

"Nah, it'll be fun. Ryan's finally getting me out of my shell. Here. Put your number in my phone and hit me up if you are free for the night."

I saved his number. He saved mine. It was truly a genuine, friendly experience. Sure, he was a closet case, but going by his online profile before, and geeked out face afterward, he had just had his wildest dream come true. And who doesn't like watching people at their finest moment?

We took a few minutes to regain our composure before putting our underwear back on. Shortly thereafter, Ryan returned to find us both nearly naked on the bed. He was calmer in his appearance and speech. He was coming down from his high, and it showed.

"Oh, hello. Glad you two had fun."

"Thanks," we eked out together. Nervous Ehren finished getting dressed, and I followed suit.

"So, you have me for the rest of the night it seems!" Ryan announced to me. "I managed to get a lot of my stuff done and cleared my calendar. I can't promise I'm going to be around a lot this week since this is my peak time of the year, but I can definitely show you around town if you're up for it."

"That sounds awesome," I answered.

"I have a few things I need to catch up on. Do you still need my car?" Ehren asked.

"No. And thank you. It was super helpful. I got everything I needed done. I managed to borrow the roomie's for a few hours. He doesn't want me making deliveries in his. He's parked on the street across from the house. You got me out of a bind, thank you."

"Not a problem. See you tonight, Chris?" Ehren asked hopefully.

Oh gosh! New possibilities! New adventures! I didn't want to fully commit to Ehren's invite, especially now that Ryan was back and had some time to spare for me. I didn't want to choose the second-best option or the third-best entrée. To be honest, I didn't want to miss out on any of them. So I hedged my bets, answering Ehren as best I could.

"Maybe? But you'll see me before I leave town for sure."

"Cool. See ya guys."

"See ya, Ehren."

He departed, leaving me to Ryan and whatever adventures the city truly had to offer.

TEN

FOLLOWED RYAN ACROSS THE street. An older white Buick with a cranberry interior was parked in the alley. It was the kind that my grandmother used to have. Hell, it was the kind that all grandmothers had.

I got inside and closed the heavy door with a thud. A high-pitched chime rang until Ryan did the same. We got situated and he started the car.

"The roomie lets me drive it. To be honest, I'm glad to have it when I need it. He's very understanding, just not understanding enough for me to make deliveries with it."

"I get it. I'm honestly surprised anyone here has a car. It's so easy to walk everywhere."

He smiled. "I got it for you."

I wasn't in need of transportation so I didn't quite understand what he meant. Lyft and Uber were very viable options, especially since I was on an expense account. I wouldn't have thought of borrowing a car if he came to visit me, though I would have driven him around to see "the sights." Except I couldn't think of any I would show him.

"Very cool. Where are we headed?"

"Well, what do you like?" he asked excitedly.

I laughed. "I think we're well beyond what I'm into, aren't we? Why don't you show me what you're into?"

He pursed his lips and drummed his fingers on the dashboard. He seemed to fidget when he was thinking. He glanced at the clock and down the alley to check traffic before suggesting an option. It was six o'clock.

"Well, I guess we can start with the simple stuff. Ever hear of Clarion Alley?"

"Nope."

He engaged the car. The cab shifted back against the heavily graded steep of the San Francisco hill. In a moment, we were off and driving along the city.

"It's an easy choice because it's so close. And free. Clarion Alley is known throughout the world for its graffiti art. It's routinely redone, and no piece stays for too long."

He was right. It was no more than a few blocks away. And, oh God, was it an alley! It was almost too narrow for the land boat of a Buick we were in, with no possibility of a second car passing alongside. Artistic admirers on foot were appreciating the murals as well, finding our presence in a car to be irritating. Still, they moved out of our way. We idled through with only minimal time to examine any one particular piece.

"They look beautiful," I said, not really paying much notice to them. I was more afraid of Ryan hitting a pedestrian than artistic qualities.

"They're all right. Sometimes they're better than others. I know a few of the artists, or did. When I moved here from Nebraska it was easy to find people who did art."

"How did you possibly find yourself with all of these artists?"

"Everyone knows a starving artist," he replied.

"I don't. Unless you used to be one."

He laughed.

"Not at all. I had it made. I was just like you, you know. Closer to two hundred grand a year than one, and the whole world at my feet. Just … It's kind of depressing when you think about it."

"What makes you say that?"

He stopped the car almost midway through the alley, placed it in park, rolled down the windows, and pointed. "Look. No, seriously, look at them."

I did. Each of the pieces was on separate panels reserved for individual artists. To call it graffiti art would be appropriate. It lacked the nebulousness of the post-modern abstract shit you see in museums. Lettering was limited, but always in stylistic blocks iconic of graffiti. Images were clear and conveyed meaning through every imaginable shade and pigment. People were drawn with all colors—black, brown, red, white, and yellow. The emotions on their faces were simple enough for children to understand, including happiness, aggression, sadness, and joy. Pastoral depictions of nature overcoming the wrath of technology (and the technology companies that resided in the city) were also common.

Looking down the alley at the other pieces, I noticed that they all seemed to convey related themes. It wasn't as I had expected—a bunch of people with spray paint cans defacing the side of a building or bathroom stall like at work. Instead, this was a collection of modern cave drawings, each depicting moral tales of good conquering evil. Nature over the machine. Humanity over governments.

They were all messages I could agree with, and when the gravity of their meaning hit me I looked back to Ryan. I could see the idealism reflected in his eyes. Each creation made as huge an imprint on him as the most moving church gospel could. Messages about how love knew no bounds, that the wealthy don't own humanity, and that people of color are just as human (perhaps even more) than their white oppressors.

Each painting was a message of hope. Each devoid of beige.

When Ryan started to speak, his voice cracked with emotion.

"It'll all be gone soon. It won't mean anything. It'll be replaced with another message or picture. That was all I was doing, you know, with programming and software development. Nothing but PowerPoint presentations and staff meetings. It took two years after I left for every line of code and every system I stood up to become deprecated or destroyed. No one was left to enjoy the art that went into making it work, the science of why it worked, or the engineering that kept it together. I went into it to make art but ended up just making concrete. And you can't even see the concrete for the pictures, can you? Now I have meaning."

Ryan put the car back in drive, rolled the windows back up, and rolled forward. The canvas wasn't on my mind, even though we were pushing people into it as we nudged through just for my own gratification.

"I can see that. It's certainly not my favorite part of the job. I get a lot more out of the steroid thing and personal training than I do the regular career. It's nice being able to talk to individuals about their goals and their dreams." I paused while I thought for a moment, then added, "And the story behind the dreams. I've listened to a lot of people say they were going to the gym to get their girl back, and every time I laughed at them. I laughed because they never were the ones to stick with it. They always washed out, and either she would fully spurn them, or they'd stop training when a new one showed up."

"Who did stick it through?" Ryan asked.

"With training? Or with steroids?" I responded, unsure of what he wanted.

Ryan readjusted himself in his seat. A half beat passed as he thought of another way to ask the question. "Who got what they wanted?"

I was a bit puzzled about how best to answer him. Open-ended questions are always difficult, but this was as important a question as any.

"I don't know. I guess it was the people who understood what they wanted, and what they needed to get there. The ones with a plan and a clue. I always saw training as a way to express myself as I was meant to be. To make the shadows on the cave wall match the actual thing."

"Ah, Plato. I'm not a fan," he said rolling his eyes.

"How could you not be? As a computer guy—"

"I'm too practical for that," he interrupted. "Aristotle makes a lot more sense. Who cares about perfect circles when there isn't one, or about shadows on a cave wall when the shadows aren't what get you?"

I have always enjoyed deep conversation, and this was the first time I felt uninhibited to experience it in a long time. We hadn't even gone a mile from the house and were neck deep in it. It seemed no topic was off the table. We just passed through every conceivable element of politics and the humanities, all conveyed in art, and moved on to talking philosophy. At home, I felt my topics were limited to work. I basically lied whenever bodybuilding came up, either through omission or direct intent. I was filled with a sense of happiness and had to punctuate it with a drop of humor.

"I suppose shadows do get you if you tweak too hard," I joked.

We exited the alley and returned to the flow of normal traffic, leaving the art and subject of politics behind us.

Ryan smiled. "I try not to be on a first-name basis with the shadow people, but it's been known to happen. I'm usually the one talking people off the bridge, so to speak. I'm used to it by now, and I don't think it's anyone's favorite side effect."

"I can imagine. Meth and psychosis are dangerous things. Certainly, you've seen more than your fair share."

"Absolutely," he said. "As common as cows where you're from."

I tried to think of my own experiences with meth, but I had never personally been chased by shadowy demons or figures that disappeared into walls. I had simply heard they were the most frightening things one could experience this side of Hell, and one of the reasons meth users die so young.

They're frightened of things that never were.

I paused for a moment to add gravity to my words.

"There was an underground blog I read once. Very underground. I'm not sure if it's still online, but if you look for it you'll find it. It was from a porn star that I used to love. I forget his name. In it, you could tell his mind was slowly losing itself to meth. He recalled seeing the shadow people out to get him and it always intimidated me. I liked his blog because he was a heavy steroid user as well, and he talked about the intensity of his training and what he was sacrificing to get the results most people would kill for. Have you ever read it?"

"Pfft," Ryan replied. "I probably met the guy or sold to him. You may never have seen a porn star at home, but I've met dozens. Dozens in my house! After a while you just get used to it, like everything in the city. And hey, steroids and meth go together wonderfully. Stay lean and keep the muscle."

I stared at him. Could it be that Ryan knew this individual? The idea took me aback, but so far Ryan hadn't let me down. Moreover, the idea of things going together "wonderfully" that can make you die before you're forty seemed counter-intuitive.

Ryan turned on the blinker, and we turned right. "This is the Bi-Rite. They have amazing ice cream. The lines will go on for a mile some days. The weather isn't hot like what you're used to at home, but people love the flavors they offer."

We slowly rolled past the shop, and a line did, indeed, stretch around the block. I couldn't imagine waiting forty-five minutes for ice cream.

Not able to think of what to say, I ended up repeating myself. "I used to do all my deals at ice cream stores."

"So you were telling me."

"Do you think of what you do as selling ice cream?" I asked meaningfully. "After all, guys call it ice, or ice cream, or use emojis for it. Do you think of it as selling a treat, even though you've seen the down side that it can bring?"

"I think about that a lot," Ryan answered, keeping his eyes on the road.

"So do I," I admitted, also looking forward. "Being with you, as someone in such a similar line of work as me, has made me really question my own motivations."

"What you sell is a lot different than what I do," he said glancing to me.

"Sure. I don't think of it as selling drugs. It's even easier to think that since steroids don't get you high. No 3:00 a.m. deliveries or people fiending for bags or bottles. And there's no such thing as 'roid rage. It's been scientifically proven to not exist."

"What do you think of it as?" he asked.

"Selling confidence."

"Con- fi- dence," he muttered, drumming out each syllable on the dashboard with his fingers as he contemplated the idea. "Is that what you put in the bottle to make it so good?"

I thought about it and smiled. It was kitschy to think I could sprinkle in confidence like a little seasoning added to grilled chicken. But it was really an answer to his earlier question. Who got what they wanted? Who were the winners in the steroid game, and what separated them from the losers or those who refused to juice? Guys like Dylan and I had leapfrogged in our careers and had become better able to command a presence in a room full of strangers. We were used to testing our strength in the gym. When issues outside of training set us back, we remained resolved to find solutions. We became better problem solvers, better thinkers, and, I think, overall better men.

"Without a doubt," I said. "I've always been a cerebral juice head. The prescription should cure the disease, and it shouldn't just be like all these fucking YouTube guys competing on who can handle the highest dosage. More drugs aren't always the answer, and the guy selling them is too often trying to make a quick buck. I found it made more sense to understand what exactly the individual wanted, what they already had, and then formulate a plan to connect the two. If that isn't confidence building, I don't know what is."

Ryan smiled heartily, as if what I said was funny. "Seems like a very altruistic way of looking at yourself."

"More like what I wish someone would have done for me."

I looked at my reflection in the passenger window. I was so jealous of Dylan. When it came to finding a mentor, he had one in me. Who did I have to look up to? It was lonely paving my own way, and I felt it so heavily.

Ryan must have sensed my mood going south. His hand touched my leg, then he pointed out the window.

There were no colorful turn-of-the-century houses or sky-scrapers. The buildings appeared to be a mix of industrial and commercial use. Some were unnamed, others had bright sig-nage. We were in a part of the city that was more worn down and tired than old.

Ryan parked the car illegally in a no-parking area then con-tinued showing me the sights.

"This is SOMA, or South of Market Street. It's where you'll find approximately half the gay clubs. This is going to be packed as fuck when the fair starts, and most of the night life you'll want will be right in this area. Half of the buildings may look deserted, but they are the ones with the best par-ties. It's not dark yet so I wouldn't expect too much going on right now. The closet cases are finding hookups on Grindr before they make it home to the wife, and the go-go dancers and party guys won't be up for the next few hours. I'd expect out-of-towners like yourself to have good hook-up options about now."

He couldn't describe places without describing people. The two seemed inextricably linked in his mind. He saw the entire ebb and flow of the city, knew where every gay man was at the drop of a hat, and where the nightlife was to be had even with the sun still up.

"Happiness," Ryan said, looking into my eyes. "I think of it as happiness."

It took me a second to realize he was back to my initial question.

"Is it real happiness though?"

"Is your confidence real?"

It took me a strong heartbeat to answer.

"No," I admitted.

"Neither is mine. But that doesn't mean it's not useful in its own way."

His words fell slowly off his lips. Sadness replaced the idealism I'd seen earlier in his eyes. He smiled weakly, then put the car back in drive and merged into traffic.

We rode in silence as the older worn-down warehouses were replaced with more modern and beautiful skyscrapers. We were back in the heart of downtown. A large building loomed in the distance, nearly half a dozen stories high, dwarfing a beautiful dark church.

"This is the MOMA," Ryan said, breaking the quiet. "The Museum of Modern Art. It has so many exhibits that I never got to see them all. It's seven stories but honestly feels like so much more. If you had extra time and a full day to spare, you could easily get lost in there and never find your way back."

"I was more in love with the church, actually."

"Saint Patrick. It's old. But yes, very beautiful."

The church was almost out of place. It looked nearly black compared to the rest of the shimmery glass buildings surrounding it, all of which looked down upon its steeple. Still, it seemed to be an active social location even on a weekday. Its design was meant to be imposing, and it probably had been when it was built 150 years ago or so. Now, it was merely a pawn lost between the mighty towers of commerce and capitalism. The last remaining vestige of virtue in a world full of vice.

He spoke. "I'd like to ask you a hypothetical question. If you could condense all the happiness in your life into a brief small amount of time, without losing any of it, would you do it?"

I thought about it for a moment. Seemed like a fairly open-and-shut question.

"Well, I presume by the offer that there is a cost associated with it. The cost being that you'd never feel happiness again afterward, am I right?"

"Exactly," he said.

"Seems like an interesting offer you have there. And kind of a fatalistic one. To live without any happiness would make you want to kill yourself."

"It wouldn't be robbing you of happiness. Just shifting it around a little. You get the same amount of net happiness by the end of your life, regardless."

I thought back to the conversation Dylan and I had in the gym about Grandma Norway. Did I already make my decision when I started to use? Did I already make the decision for Dylan when I empowered him with drugs? Did Ryan already spend all his happiness?

I answered as best I could.

"That sounds more like ecstasy to me."

He looked over at me and smiled, glancing back and forth between me and the road a few times to keep control of the car and still focus on me. I'm not sure if he thought I was referring to the drug MDMA, or that it sounded like a fantastic way to die. He seemed enamored with it, and drummed his fingers on the dashboard in silent thought. It was a clever diversion.

"I suppose so. I forgot I'm talking with a chemist."

I smiled. We were in each other's minds and we both knew it. They were places of dark thoughts, but they were shared nonetheless.

A car pulling out of a parking garage cut out in front of us. Ryan slammed on the brakes and reached his hand across my chest as if to keep me in my seat. The cars didn't touch, but Ryan and I did.

"Watch it, motherfucker!" Ryan screamed, flipping him off.

The other driver returned the gesture, but traffic had already resumed moving forward. My nerves and emotions slowly settled back down.

"I hate driving in this city. You're staying downtown, in the Tenderloin, so I'll skip that. I figure you'll want to stumble around that area more than anything and find adventure on your own. You said you're staying at the Parc 55 Hotel, right? If so, you'll have plenty of good hook-up opportunities there."

The idea of hooking up with anyone else bored me all of a sudden. I wanted to spend my time with Ryan.

"The wharf, however, you'll enjoy. We'll drive by there and you'll see where all the shopping is."

A giant cable bridge shone off in the distance. The sun was beginning to set and the lights on the bridge were just starting to come to life.

"Is that the Golden Gate Bridge? The color looks off to me," I asked dumbly.

"No, that's the Bay Bridge. Golden Gate's on the other side. Personally, I've always liked this one better. I find the lighting on it to be so much more beautiful. Golden isn't lit up at night."

Though I had never seen the Golden Gate Bridge, I instantly decided that this was the more beautiful of the two. It seemed so much more stoic than its iconic counterpart. Large signs labeled "Pier XX," each with two-digit numbers, identified one building from the next. Massive rope anchors were scattered throughout. I could not tell if they were there for function, aesthetic, or some deprecated facet of the region's previous primary use.

Long rectangular buildings lined the street as far as the eye could see. People were carrying shopping bags and trinkets as they went in and out of them. The shoppers were much more touristy than I remembered them being near Ryan's house. Regardless, it was amazing watching people teem the sidewalks like I imagined fish teemed in the sea.

"It's the end of the world isn't it?" I asked.

"It is?" Ryan sounded confused. "No one told me!"

"Edge. I meant edge."

"Yeah. The analogy gets brought up on occasion."

I spoke, "Have you ever sat down and thought about it? We'd both be burned at the stake for witchcraft for what we do, if it were a hundred years earlier."

He gave a short dismissive laugh.

"Ha! You know, now that you mention it, I never thought of it that way."

"Were you ever religious growing up?"

"No," he said.

"Me neither. Though I have learned in my many travels that the Bible, depending upon the translation you use, refers to the burning and killing of sorcerers for various reasons. But the older alternative definition of *sorcerer* is something I'm reminded of from time to time."

"Which is?"

"*Pharmakeia.* Drugs."

"Interesting," he replied, trying to keep the tone light. "I'll keep that in mind if I ever become a priest."

I noticed a Ben and Jerry's stand near the shoreline, surrounded by happy teenagers getting ice cream sandwiches.

I was reminded of Ryan's earlier question. My one sentence answer was a clever diversion, but I felt the need to give a more honest one.

"I know I glossed over the answer earlier but, to be honest, I am not sure I could condense all my happiness into a single period of time. I mean, meth does speed you up. Rather, it makes me feel like the world is slowing down when I'm on it. It is relaxing, though I know to everyone else I must feel like I'm spun up in a million different directions.

"There's a certain irony there. I know that by going faster, I can get more things done. I first started using in college, and it enabled me to do many great and wondrous things. I managed to complete my senior year without a hitch, graduate with nearly a four-point GPA, help my parents with their business, and deal with a friend of mine who committed suicide.

"I burned the candle at both ends because I needed more light in my life. I know I needed it, and if I wasn't burning brightly enough at that point it was for a damned good reason.

"But what you're proposing is something stronger. When I think of that drug-empowered light, and the things I did, or could do, I don't think of it as happiness. I think of it as a list of accomplishments.

"Does burning the candle faster help me get things done faster? Absolutely! But exploding the candle wouldn't let me get anything done. It just melts me away into slag."

We had nearly completed the trip around the shoreline. Ryan was driving steadily onward and remained silent. He kept his eyes focused on the road. I could tell I had hurt him in some way, but I wasn't sure how. Perhaps I hit too close to home regarding his own reasons for use. Or maybe I undermined the reason he sold this poison to his friends. Perhaps he hated me for saying that, or perhaps he was thankful that he didn't have to.

Either way, the car made a sharp turn back inland, deeper into the city.

"Is life just a big to-do list to you?" he asked almost bitterly.

I considered my words carefully.

"No. Absolutely not. There are things that I feel I need in my life in order to have a happy one. It's important to feel the value of a moment. To feel the sands of time slip through your fingers. To cherish what little time or happiness or whatever you have on this earth, is crucial. You should respect it because it's finite as much as short. *But it's not always your sand to lose.*"

"Are you sure about that?"

"Of course I am! Confidence is what I sell. And I have an overabundance."

He left the comment alone. We sat in the car in silence, each with our own thoughts as the ocean faded away in the rear-view mirror. Ahead of us was the largest rainbow flag I had ever seen. People, many obviously gay by their dress and mannerisms, filled the sidewalks completely. Buses and cable cars became objects Ryan needed to navigate and avoid through the traffic, which slowed to a crawl. The occasional queen would leave an Uber or Lyft, and kind exchanges ranging from unusually long kisses to very personal touches were shared all across the avenue.

"This is the Castro. Gay headquarters you could say. The flag's a staple and flies year-round. Like I said, I don't have time to give you a full walking tour, but I'm sure you'll stumble down here eventually."

"It's amazing," I said. "I recognize the theater from pictures."

"The theater's just a theater. It's nothing special," Ryan said while gesturing dismissively at it. "Half the movies suck in my opinion, but I never cared for that faggy shit. The real action is at Orphan Andy's."

"What is that?" I asked.

"Late night diner, around the corner. If you catch yourself awake at random hours, chances are you can go there for some socializing and meet interesting people. It might shock you who you'd meet there."

"Try me."

"Porn stars. Celebrities. Drug dealers. Politicians. Everyone goes there," he said.

"Cool."

"There's also all the other things you'd expect nearby. Shops, bars, you name it. There's not a lot of chain places around here. San Francisco doesn't like chain places too much. It was a big deal when Starbucks moved in. The last thing we want is for everything to become a suburban wasteland like any regular interstate drive back home."

I thought back to my daily commute in Oklahoma and the endless sea of McDonald's and Shell gas stations.

"It's the last thing I'd want for this place, too," I answered.

"I don't know how you're doing on time," he said, drumming his fingers very briefly, "but there's one last place I'd like to show you before we head back to the house. It's not on the list of places I normally show people. That is, if you have time."

"I don't have to be anywhere until tomorrow morning."

"Good."

As we left the cable cars and homosexual neighborhood behind, Ryan's sadness was visibly swelling beyond his control.

A drug dealer's charm is powerful, and his masked a lot of emotion. But it couldn't mask the tears that were forming in his eyes yet refusing to fall upon his cheeks. He placed his hand on the center console and I felt compelled to rest mine upon his. Emotion permeated the car and I couldn't help but feel the importance of whatever lay ahead of us.

Looking forward, I saw one of the largest wooded mountains I had ever seen in my life.

I was reminded of the murals and the depictions of nature overcoming the evils of the city. I felt us drive into those ideals with every passing building. Lights and street signs became dimmer and less frequent. Giant pine trees lined the serpentine road every inch of the way while the sound of the old Buick engine raged as it fought the force of gravity against us. There were no restaurants or ice cream shops. No neon signs or gay bars. Skyscrapers and capitalism all faded as we drove back in time to when even that old church seemed new.

"The Presidio," he muttered.

We parked at the top of the mountain, in one of only a few dozen spots. The only signs of industrialization were a few nearby radio towers which took advantage of the area's relative altitude. A few people were out, but not many. All of them were tourists, I could tell, mostly with families. Coin-operated binoculars were along the edge, which overlooked a remarkable view of the city. Ryan and I got out. The wind was violently brutal, even by Oklahoma standards, and made opening my car door nearly impossible. We braved the air which had become deceptively chilly.

We stood there, looking over the distance, for what could have been an eternity. We looked down on the city. Our city. We were at the edge of the world, as night was starting to claim its prize of the places Ryan had showed me.

He sighed and relaxed a little.

"They call using meth 'chasing the white dragon,'" he said, refusing to look at me. "It's a much tougher dragon than you're used to."

He took my hand and we huddled close to one another. Any high that Ryan or I experienced earlier in the day was replaced with solemn emotion. We weren't drowning in happiness or confidence, but connected by love, sadness, and despair. We also felt the joy of getting exactly what we wanted and the pride that comes with living the life you want to live. Even as he looked over the view, and I looked at him, I had never seen so much emotion in a loved one's eyes. It was the emotion that swirls in the gut-wrenching void after all happiness in the world is gone. I had no idea when he'd last used, and I suspected he didn't remember. I hadn't even seen him use the whole time I had been there.

I looked forward to match his gaze, becoming lost in the depths of the city below us. The individual houses were each worth more than all the dreams I could imagine. Each room with a renter, and each renter with a light. The souls of the city, countless beyond comprehension.

"I slam," he whispered.

No other words were said. I knew what that meant. From what I could guess from the IV drug users I'd known in the past, he had five years, maybe seven, tops. He knew the math better than I did. I held him tightly. I held him tighter than I had ever held anyone in my life.

And I hoped it was enough.

ELEVEN

NIGHT HAD FALLEN OVER the city. In San Francisco, night comes without darkness. There was so much light pollution that no single star was visible. Where one would expect a million candles to dot the sky, nothing but a semi-dark veil could be seen.

I wasn't sure if it was appropriate to say anything or ask where we were going once we got back in the car. Fortunately, Ryan volunteered the information.

"I was hoping to take you to Mr. S Leather before all the crowds got stupid. But I think they'll be closed by the time we get there. I don't suppose by chance you have any leather, do you?"

"Nothing that I brought with me," I hedged.

"Well, let's make sure you get the tour of them tomorrow. Until then, how about we check out The Eagle? There's always something going on there, and it'll likely be a good opportunity to see if that's where you want to spend your downtime."

"There's an Eagle in Dallas. Is it run by the same people?" I asked.

"No. Virtually every major city in the country has a gay leather bar called The Eagle. But they're not related to each other at all."

"Well, then why—"

"Look, don't even bother asking," he interrupted. "Everyone asks why they're all named the same thing. It's just one of those things. A universal mating ritual of the horny gay man."

"I guess today I learned something new about traveling. If I'm ever lost and want a good drink, all I have to do is ask 'Where's The Eagle?' and I'll fit right in."

He pointed to his head, as if to express that I had, indeed, discovered some universal truth. I was eager to give this new place a shot.

"Dallas was fun, so I'm sure I'll enjoy this. But I can't stay out too late. I don't want to show up wasted tomorrow for work."

"I'm actually glad you said that," Ryan replied with a sigh of relief, "because honestly, I hate going there now. Watching a bunch of people drink just isn't a fun night to me anymore."

I wanted to think his willingness to abstain from booze was rooted in some holy purpose. Or that he generally preferred nightclubs over bars. But the odds were that he, like I, did not see sobriety as a cardinal virtue. I suspected he made the same value proposition that I did a long time ago. A $200 bar tab isn't shit compared to ten bucks of speed. Alcohol is a shitty drug, and people who enjoyed it were simply inefficient. Watching a bunch of people get drunk on a shitty substance while you're the only one sober makes for a depressing night.

"Well," I said, "I'm sure a cameo appearance won't be too bad. Plus, I'm two hours later than you when it comes to time zones. I'll get tired soon anyway."

"Only if you want to be," he offered.

The thought rattled around in my head for a moment but fleeted soon. In my right back pocket, my phone vibrated. I fetched it and saw the screen flash a picture of Dylan licking his bicep with an exaggerated sexual glare. The picture always made me chuckle, in the way that only straight men trying to turn on a gay man could.

"I may have to be up late," I said with some intrigue. "Duty calls."

Ryan glanced over at the phone to see the picture.

"Oh. Wow, you've got good taste! Need any help with that?"

"All the damn time," I replied to him before speaking into the phone. "Hey, sexy! How's it going?"

Dylan's voice seemed tired, but enthusiastic about something.

"Hey motherfucker, where were you tonight? Weren't we going to train today?"

I looked at the clock in the car. It was late enough now that I would have been finishing my gym session with Dylan.

"Huh? Oh, did I not tell you? I'm sorry. Work sent me to San Francisco for this trade show."

"What?!" he exclaimed. "Bitch, I can't get them to send me to shit. How long you there for?"

"Just a few more days. Don't get your panties in a wad, I'll be back before you know it."

Dylan didn't usually mind me skipping a training session or two. And the same went the other way around. But we'd grown so close that going to the gym by ourselves just wasn't the same.

"You better! If you stay out there for too long you'll end up a Democrat or some shit. I just wanted to say, you missed a helluva deadlift day. I pulled 550 sumo with just wraps. I was going to belt up and go for six but I ran out of gas. You shoulda seen it go up, man. It just shot up!"

"I believe you. You sound like *you* just shot up."

Ryan glanced at me oddly while maintaining his calm driving. His expression was one of confusion, with a single eyebrow raised and his forehead cocked slightly to the side. I presumed he could only hear my end of the conversation, which likely left him wondering what drug I was talking about and exactly who I was talking with.

Dylan continued, "Ha, I wish. That's the best I've ever done coming off a cycle! And I'm not on shit! Except for some Clomid."

"Well, that 600 will come your way soon then."

"Fuck yeah it will!" he said, unrelenting in his excitement. "I was going to bench big this Sunday, but I guess I can find someone else to back spot me while you're out. I'm sure between all these guys, I can find one of them man enough to handle it."

I smiled knowing we were the two biggest guys to train there at that time. Halfway joking, I replied, "If not, find two who will half-ass it."

"True. I'll see you Monday after you're back?"

"Absolutely."

"Cool. If you make it down to Venice Beach though, take pictures!"

I almost couldn't keep from laughing into the phone. Dylan had obviously never been to California. Venice Beach was nowhere near San Francisco.

"I will," I chuckled.

Dylan hung up. My smile remained as I thought back to the gym in Oklahoma and training with him. I pictured him all wide-eyed from pre-workout, covered in lifting chalk and baby powder, thrilled to make a new personal best at a difficult lift. Even for those who "cheat" at sport, it's always a big moment to make a new milestone. While I couldn't be there in person, in some ways I felt like his call was a thank you for helping him get there.

I was honored and somewhat speechless that he took the time to call me.

Ryan finally had to break the silence.

"Six hundred bucks? Shot up?" he asked, scared of my response.

"Oh, no, dude. Nothing like that. That was my buddy, Dylan. We lift together. He made a new personal best on deadlift."

A wave of relief came over Ryan when he realized it wasn't an overdose call. His confusion remained, muted substantially. He put his eyes back to the road.

"How do you do it?" he asked. I was sincerely unsure of what he wanted to know.

"Do what?"

"You have a career, you fly around the country for your day job, and you manufacture and sell steroids on the side. Plus, you have time to train yourself and others, and that's when you're not competing in bodybuilding!"

"Ha, I'm a little type A, I guess. But, come on, I'm not the interesting one here. How do *you* do it?"

He glared at me, as if to ask if we really needed to revisit the topic.

I got the hint.

I pondered for a moment how much easier life would be if I never had to sleep. What would it be worth to gain a third of my life back from the Sandman and apply that to training? Or to work. Or to producing testosterone for sale. Of course, that wasn't an option. Bodybuilding can't be fueled by meth binges. My body grew when I rested, but Ryan had no such luxury. His clients were creatures of the night and he had to hustle during their hours. The things that enabled Ryan to keep his lifestyle, and be this incredible guy, couldn't enable mine.

There was a subtext of desperation. It wasn't just that he was curious or wanted to pay me a compliment. He was looking for hope. And a way out.

"I've naturally always been an overachiever. Driven. I can't just do steroids; I have to make them. I can't just work on computers; I have to be the head analyst for my company. Every time I'm idle, hell, even when I'm busy, all I can think about is how much more I could be doing. It's like ADHD but I don't have a hard time focusing. If anything, I focus too much. I develop tunnel vision with everything I do and throw myself into it fully. It's just not enough to do something, I have to be the best I can be. No half measures," I said.

"Must be nice," he faltered, followed by a couple of drum beats on the dashboard.

"I don't know. It has its downsides, too. I have what I call my curse."

Ryan laughed. "You? Cursed? Oh, I'd love to hear this. Tell me *your* problems!"

"Absolutely!" I replied, "Ninety-eight percent of people live their entire lives cradle-to-grave, and never once learn what they're good at. It's a depressing existence to be a human being when you think about it. Most of us are born in the wrong time, or under unfavorable economic or geographic conditions. And that's presuming we even make it past adolescence into adulthood. There's a serious chance that you'll never actually reach any sort of meaningful potential because you won't be given enough resources to find what you're good at.

"That's where my curse comes in. Only a small number of people will ever manage to figure out what they're good at. Me, I'm one of those people. I know what I'm good at."

Ryan looked over to me and raised both his eyebrows. He rested his wrists on the steering wheel and lifted his fingertips in his confusion.

"That doesn't sound like a curse."

"It is when you hate it."

His confusion seemed to wash away and was replaced with sympathy. His fingers resumed their normal position managing the wheel and his eyebrows fell to their regular resting place. His lips quietly mouthed "oh" as my words sank in. I felt we shared a bond; both of us were disillusioned by the high-paid world of technology and entranced by the idealistic color of liberalism and drug dealing. He activated the turn signal and piloted us into the driveway of an abandoned warehouse.

At least, I thought it was abandoned. The clock in the Buick showed just after 10:00 p.m. It was dark, with relatively little street lighting available. There were no windows on the building's first floor, making it impossible to see inside. No other cars were in the small secluded parking lot, but I saw plenty of signs warning that trespassers would be towed.

We got out of the car and Ryan popped the trunk. He pulled out a leather vest and a bulldog-style harness. He put on his harness and tossed me the vest.

"The Eagle doesn't have much parking. We can park here, but not for long. Take this. It's a loaner, you're not keeping it."

"Sure, I appreciate it."

We started walking across the street toward a small dive bar located near a highway overpass. A line had formed outside, and a bouncer could be seen in the distance checking IDs. The place looked like most gay bars—fairly divish and dark—but it was larger than most of the clubs Ryan had shown me in SOMA. Dance music with a heavy beat pulsated throughout the area. Based on the line length at this time of night, a good time was promised therein.

While we waited in line, I removed my shirt to make the vest pop more. Ryan began fitting his harness tighter around his chest. The couple ahead of us were a cliché in the gay community. They were attractive and hung closely to each other. One whispered to the other while looking at us. The second gave Ryan "elevator eyes," examining him from top to bottom. I imagined that if given the opportunity to drag a third back to their lair, they would have taken it.

As we approached the bouncer, I overheard him asking for the night's cover charge. I reached for my wallet.

"You don't need that," Ryan said.

"That's sweet of you, but you really don't need to get me."

He whispered to me, "I didn't say I was paying."

I was confused. The moment we ended up at the front of the line, the bouncer looked at Ryan with a devilish smile and he waved us in. Ryan leaned into his ear, gave him a kiss, and then led me inside.

"Oh, I didn't know you knew him," I said.

"I don't know his name," Ryan replied, speaking loudly enough for me to hear him above the music. "But I know what he likes. That's more important anyway."

Ryan had the whole city wrapped around his finger.

Inside was a large bar, hundreds of shirtless men I would have taken home on any given day, and a plethora of dance lights. It surprised me. It was clean and amazingly well attended.

"It's not normally like this, and thank God it's only Wednesday. By Friday night this place is going to be so packed it'll be standing room only."

He took my hand and led me toward the music. Being insulated by the body heat of the crowd, I didn't feel the cool San Francisco air when we stepped out onto the patio. I found myself only able to look up and see the sky, but not ahead or behind me in any particular direction. My bulk usually let me push myself any way I wanted, but I was unable to navigate in the sea of men over six feet tall. Taking advantage of Ryan's relative height and familiarity with the venue, I followed him as he eked a path directly to the bar.

"Do you want anything to drink?" he yelled.

"Sure, Red Bull and vodka. Sugar free if they have it."

"Cool," he gestured with a thumbs-up.

He repeated the order to the bartender who immediately started making it. Ryan pulled out a few bills from his jeans pocket to pay before handing me my drink. He ordered nothing for himself.

The familiar taste of alcohol on my lips was sweet. I enjoyed the flavor of vodka mixed with various stimulants, but not as much as I enjoyed Ryan holding my hand.

That was especially wonderful.

Even with Ryan and the alcohol soothing me, I felt a bit uncomfortable. My guard was fairly high, not because I was scared of people but because I was surrounded by strangers. The music was loud enough to prevent most socializing, and it seemed many here were already very familiar with each other. My natural instinct was to retreat, but Ryan squeezed my hand and pulled me ever deeper into the dance area. I was afraid of becoming lost at sea without him. I kept one hand on my drink, the other, in his.

I like to think I swam much more than sank.

It didn't take long for people to notice us. Eyes quickly darted toward the two muscle-bound gods of the dance floor. Not that we were dancing. We were mostly swaying to and fro without any real rhythm. Still, the occasional feel was copped, and more than one individual brushed up against us with a kind "excuse me," as though that made the sexual advances acceptable in the moment.

An attractive go-go dancer performed on a box near us. He was a tall otter, with a thin happy trail of dark hair running down to his Nasty Pig jockstrap. It was a popular brand of gay men's underwear out of New York City. He wore nothing else but a smile. I looked around at the rest of the bar. Most of the men were equally as gorgeous. Many had well-manicured beards and mustaches, deep tans, and slabs of muscle. My eyes floated with just the sheer number of options available to me.

I knew Ryan wouldn't want to stay long, so this was my chance to enjoy a brief moment together. The sands of time were slipping through my fingers, and I wanted to enjoy every granule. I tried to burn every detail of each moment into my brain. I reveled in the go-go dancers making their way up and down the bar, and the DJ throwing himself and the crowd into the music. They were all intoxicated, every one. On what, I wasn't sure, but it wasn't as rich as the experience I had that morning. And I didn't care.

The dancers floated from patron to patron, preferring to flow through the crowd instead of lingering with any one person for too long. Some of the older gentlemen enjoyed their cigars, which surprised me because I thought the whole state was non-smoking. Rules, it seemed, were for those who needed them. Younger guys wearing pup hoods played with each other's bodies and attire and caught up on whatever gossip was going on that day.

Closer to us, a long line was forming outside the bathroom. I noticed guys seemed almost excited to wait in it.

Ryan explained. "The bathroom situation is very unique. They occasionally open up the trough urinal. Three guesses what you'll find in there."

"Let me guess, it's a *who* not a *what*."

"Hahahaha," he laughed. "Well, I didn't say it. But you thought it and we're talking about it."

"That's so funny," I said, admiring some of the guys in yellow piped pants. "Water sports wasn't my thing too much."

"Meh, if they aren't sober it's like a free hit."

I contemplated his response briefly. "True, I guess."

Ryan started dancing, though I wasn't sure why. Perhaps he was trying to bridge the distance I was putting between myself and everyone else. It seemed so spontaneous. He was sober, as was I, more or less. Still, his movements didn't seem to match the music. He was a lot more elegant and practiced than normal dancers in a standard nightclub. His feet were almost motivated by purposeful precision rather than the hypnotic teetering of an alcoholic sway. I felt it was either to get me to loosen up more or to divert or capture someone else's attention. Being unsure of the situation and unable to follow his choreography, I wriggled my body side to side.

"Where did you learn to dance?" I asked with a laugh.

He was taken aback. Apparently, he thought I should be impressed by his dance skills. To be honest, I was. A lot. His moves just didn't fit this music.

"I used to do ballroom with an ex."

"You!?" I exclaimed incredulously. "You used to do ballroom dancing?!"

"Yeah," he said matter-of-factly. "Juilliard was a decent school."

"Really? I thought you went to school for computers like me."

"No, I'm good at computers. I prefer dancing," he explained, commanding attention of some nearby spectators. "But who can make money with that? What, you think you're the only one with that curse you mentioned?"

He paused for a moment, then approached me. He took my empty cup, put it on the bar, then placed my hands on his sides. The nearby drunkards and leather daddies cleared a small circle for us to dance in, for fear of being stepped on by Ryan's aggressive dance moves. He led, I followed. Between the two of us, there were three left feet and I had all of them.

We ended up shifting closer and closer to the music. With each step he injected me with rhythm and meter where I had none. He filled me with a confidence I had never sold—I had built an amazing body but had no idea how to use it. Ryan was an understanding teacher. And while the room we had to dance became smaller and smaller, I somehow didn't mind as we got closer and closer together. We eventually ended up so close together that any semblance of form or function faded into the crowd.

Happiness doesn't always come in crystalline form.

My lesson was interrupted when a hand grabbed my ass. Hard. It wasn't the subtle passing on a dance floor, but direct purposeful intent to get my attention. It was not Ryan.

I swung around to see who it was. Speechless, Ehren was there, a wild look in his eyes and a hungry look on his lips.

"Motherfuck— Oh! Fancy finding you here!"

"Indeed," he replied.

"I thought you went to the bathhouse," I said, somewhat confused.

"I was going to go after this, but now that I found you here, I want to steal you away for the night."

I looked back at Ryan. He looked inquisitively up toward the sky, shrugging as he kept with the rhythm. I couldn't tell if he was indifferent about which option I would choose or if he had orchestrated the whole thing.

"Well, I'm kind of taken for the night," I said sweetly and jokingly. "You'll have to ask *my boyfriend* if I'm free."

Ehren looked at Ryan. Ryan's eyes closed to get in tune with the music.

"I think I'll have him," Ehren said.

Ryan opened his eyes, stopped dancing, and looked at Ehren. "You're welcome to him. I'm just here for a bit myself."

The idea of finishing what I had started with Ehren was incredibly tempting, but how could I leave Ryan? Perhaps in the San Franciscan world of high sex, low-meaning drug deals, and party guys this was the norm. But it somehow felt wrong to me. Not only was it rude by any sort of social standard I was raised with, I was feeling a great connection with Ryan.

I wanted them both but knew Ryan's time was more precious.

"I don't want to leave you alone," I said to Ryan. "How long were we planning on staying? Didn't you say we needed to leave soon?"

"Not much longer really. I have to return the car anyway. I just figured you'd like a drink out, and a dance party to cap the night with."

"I can bring him back to his hotel," Ehren suggested.

Ryan looked at me and saw the confusion in my eyes. I was lost in thought, begging for someone to push the needle one way or the other in their favor.

Ryan leaned into me.

"Go with him," he whispered in my ear. "It'll be fine. You have till Sunday with me, but you may only get tonight with him. You've got unfinished business with him I hear, and I have some myself with our bouncer friend. See you tomorrow?"

"Wait!" I said, pulling back and looking into his eyes. "I'll go, but only if you promise me something."

His eyes looked back into mine and softened. "Sure."

"I get to keep you when I'm done with him."

He smiled. "Of course. I'm always easy to find."

With that, he faded away into the crowd. In my mind, he went off to square up with the bouncer for whatever number of crystals our entrance to the party costed. I wondered what the going rate was, but more than that, I missed his touch.

Thinking of Ryan's hand but feeling Ehren's, I turned my attention to him. My mind was thinking about the whole evening with Ryan and what it all could mean. The trip to The Eagle felt so non-accidental, so purposely set up. I resigned myself to do what Ryan would have done, which was not only fuck the hell out of Ehren, but also try and win some business along the way.

"So, you're going to drop me back at my hotel, huh? What, are you going to kick me out of your place when I'm done with you?"

Ehren looked at me intently. He was hungry for cock and was going to have it, whether it was mine or not was not really a concern. Ehren grabbed my hand and started leading me out of the crowd. As we exited the club, the bouncer that let us in was gone, replaced by another. Ryan was nowhere to be seen.

Ehren led me behind The Eagle to his car in the parking lot. "Hop in."

Ehren's expensive Audi was much classier than Ryan's white Buick grandma-mobile. I got in and was greeted with warm ambient lighting and a top-of-the-line sound system. He took his seat behind the wheel and soon we were on the highway.

"So, your place, huh?"

"If that's all right with you. I think you'll like it. Better view than your hotel I'm sure."

"I don't know, it's a pretty nice hotel actually."

He grinned devilishly. "Oh, I'm sure you'll like this better."

The booze and the time were starting to wear on me. Fatigue was making my eyes heavy, and while I was having a thrilling time, I was almost ready for the night to be over. While I normally do a decent job of keeping my bearings in a new city, the number of times we had zig-zagged down unfamiliar streets had me at a complete loss. I knew we were downtown because of the building density and the height of the skyscrapers, though exactly where, I was unsure.

Ehren spoke as I was nodding off. "So, Ryan tells me you're the steroid guy."

"Well, I mean, I use them."

"Of course you do. But Ryan tells me you make them, too."

I commanded myself to be more awake. "Yeah, I thought I told you that. American Dragon being my lab and all."

"I thought you just meant that was your favorite brand," he explained. "Ryan was going to hook me up with some and he said it was legit. I was like, 'oh man, we're going to be using the same brand. Must be a good one.'"

I laughed somewhat quietly. "Well, I'm kinda partial to it myself."

"No doubt."

Ehren drove the car into what appeared to be an underground garage. After badging in, we descended a couple of levels where a mechanical gate closed off a section reserved for his car. It was as though his car was incarcerated. One gate for the prison, another for the cell. It was an incredible amount of overkill for someone who I had taken to be middle income.

I was mistaken. Ehren had money.

We walked over to the elevator. Artisan wood oak paneling lined the inside and recessed lighting ensured it was brightly lit. It was a stark contrast to the drab, industrial look of the parking garage. The ride upstairs made me woozy. The buttons and the numbers seemed to whir past me. I kept my head down, trying to focus on the floor of the elevator, which I insisted to myself was stationary in space.

All I could tell was were headed to one of the upper floors.

"You know," Ehren admitted, looking forward at the elevator doors the whole time, "I thought about getting into the manufacturing business."

"Is that so?" I said. "Well, it can be good."

"But not for steroids."

I looked over at him. I felt like a fucking dumbass when I met his eyes. They never blinked. The aggression and confidence were unmistakably abnormal for Ehren.

He was more spun up more than a thirteen-hour clock.

I smiled. "Let me guess."

He put his finger to his lips to shush me from saying anything else.

The elevator chimed and the door opened. In front of us was a lush hallway, clean and manicured down to the slightest detail. By the time we got through the main entrance to his apartment, I realized that we were indeed no fewer than twenty floors up in what had to be something that cost ten times what my house did. A beautiful chandelier graced the entryway, and a long breakfast counter with three hanging lights greeted us. Simple artistic drawings adorned the walls. A sound system which cost more than my car was in the living room and the kitchen was equipped with the finest appliances available on the market.

It was a vast departure from anything I could have afforded, even with my clandestine side business.

"There's certain risks involved with going your route over mine," I warned. "You live in a very nice place, and it certainly wouldn't be ideal for it."

"I'm sure. But there's ways of managing that risk. Bathroom's over there in the corner if you need it. I'll be in the bedroom, but you can come in whenever you're ready."

"I'm good," I said as I followed him into the bedroom.

The bedroom was similarly highly fashioned, though small like Ryan's room. A nice bed, already made, with high thread count sheets was in the corner. Traditional light switches were replaced with a fanciful home automation package. The room lit up upon our entrance.

On the nightstand was a bubble pipe and a lighter.

"Do you mind if I . . ." he trailed off, but I waved him on. Obviously happy with the answer, he lit up and took a giant hit. The room filled with a deep bellowing cloud that I did not expect given the amount of time the drug spent under the flame.

I gestured for him to hand it over. He did and then started to remove his shirt.

I took a hit and noted a strong and overbearing chemical taste from the meth.

"Jesus!" I said, exhaling as quickly as I could. "What is up with this?"

"I do an acetone wash. It helps keep it extra pure. It actually makes it safer, believe it or not. If you're not used to it, though, the taste can be a bit overpowering."

"I'll say. Damn, you guys in California do dope a lot differently than we do in Oklahoma."

My host was naked and jacking himself off. He was already three steps ahead of me, and I felt it appropriate to follow suit and begin my own striptease.

A drunken one at that.

"Is that so?" he asked. "Tell me how you do your drugs."

"You guys just overcomplicate the shit out of things. Bubble pipes, acetone washes. It's supposed to be about getting high, not like collecting decorative art."

I hit the pipe plenty and before long my body was covered in an oily sweat. My sweat mixed well with Ehren's. The sheer amount of bodily fluids covering us made every motion slick and intense. My eyes began to focus a bit better with the bump of energy from the pipe.

Ehren ripped open the curtains. Where I was expecting a gorgeous panoramic of the city, I was instead surprised with a solid brick wall. Nothing to see but the skyscraper next door. What the apartment had in interior beauty it lacked in anything external worth seeing. At least the wall was mostly devoid of windows, providing us safety from any prying eyes that could have been floating twenty stories up in the air.

The advantage did however come when the lights were adjusted just right. Our heaving sweaty bodies were reflected back to us. I watched as they fucked in perfect rhythm. We fucked for five straight hours. Angrily. Violently. And the more we watched me penetrate him in the reflection of that win-dowed glass, the more we both wanted.

The drugs were good or, I should say, effective. I had no idea if the whole acetone wash thing made them safer or not. I couldn't tell if Ehren made it all from scratch or if this acetone wash thing was a process he went through after he bought it retail. Maybe he was already cooking meth in the apartment.

Maybe his earlier comment was to get a rise out of me. Maybe this dope was the same shit I smoked earlier and he got it from Ryan. Or, perhaps Ehren was Ryan's source and Ryan sent me to evaluate him and report back. Maybe the point was to discover his secret to making the best stuff, and exfiltrate the recipe back to him so he could promote up the supply chain.

Or maybe this entire thing was nothing but a coincidence and I was just somewhere in a skyscraper fucking the shit out of some fag who loved muscle and drugs as much as I did.

I decided I was putting too much thought into it. Ehren took dick like a champ. He took everything I gave him and he wanted it as hard as I could give it, even harder.

But it wasn't about him. I wasn't even looking at him in the reflection while we fucked.

I was looking at me.

TWELVE

THE NEXT MORNING STARTED early. I felt like I hadn't slept at all and for the most part, I hadn't. Any sleep I had was shallow at best. My eyes shook and vibrated in my skull. It didn't hurt, but I was cognizant of every minute that passed in my darkened hotel room. I barely remembered Ehren driving me home the previous night or plopping down in bed. Still, the little time I had to rest was needed.

Once my phone alarm rang, I got up without fighting for an extra snooze interval and brushed my teeth. I opted to skip breakfast, applied an extra layer of deodorant to mask the lack of a proper shower, and ventured outward.

The hallway and ride down the elevator were quiet, thankfully. I could still hear EDM pounding in my ears even though soft classical music was all that was being played. It wasn't until the doors opened at the lobby that I saw the flock of IT nerds, many wearing conference badges, bustling through the area on their way to the convention hall a few streets over.

Once outside, I zig-zagged through them while trying to be as inconspicuous as possible, which was quite a feat considering I was so much beefier than most of them. They weren't all the same tubs of lard that I was used to seeing at home, but they were still obviously sedentary and used their bodies solely to get their heads to meetings. Staying downtown afforded me the convenience of a few shopping locations. When I found the local pharmacy, I ducked inside to pick up a pair of sunglasses to hide my hungover eyes and enough energy drinks to kill a cow.

My pace quickened as I left the store. The sun, golden and resplendent, was starting to shine in all its glory. I felt protected behind my shades, able to think of the baser things I had done the other night. I thought of Ehren and wondered what his daily commute would be like, and if his coworkers would mind him showing up obviously fucked up from an evening out.

I pushed the thought out of my head as I opened the doors to the convention center. Immediately inside was a check-in counter. The density of conference badges and laptops increased exponentially as I approached. Pulling out my driver's license and removing the relative protection of my shades, I, too, became adorned with a giant conference badge which indicated that I belonged.

Not hardly.

I silently followed the herd to an escalator downward. I tried to focus on the drumming sound of its motor, but that became difficult as the number of people had increased. Conversations about various aspects of technology and industry issues were starting to invade my mind. As I reached the lower pavilion, booths of household IT names—Intel, HP, Dell, Cisco—seemed to stretch on as far as the eye could see. Interspersed between them were a few new up-and-comers, each hoping to play with the "big dogs." They displayed their aspirations through expensive suits or high-gloss posters. Each booth was headed by a sleek and hip representative, too polished to be technical, too unrefined to be management. Instead, they were relegated to the dungeon of sales and marketing, complete with colorful brochures and cubical toys.

"Oh, fuck this," I muttered to myself, not feeling like interacting through a hundred handshakes.

I power walked through the booths, stopping at the most-populated ones to edge my way through and grab business cards without interacting with the sales trolls. Evidence, I figured, was important. Proof that I was here and had conversations, however meaningful or meaningless, was what Donald would want back at home.

Occasionally I found tables packed with an assortment of food provided as free snacks to attendees. One exhibition hall was converted into a dining area, and even offered a free luxurious breakfast. No expense was spared by these companies as this was one of the largest hallmark events of the year. Unable to resist my hunger any further, I stepped in, grabbed a plate, filled it to the brim with scrambled eggs and bagels, and sat down to enjoy it at the quietest table around.

Nearby, I listened to a pair of employees from a bank talking about recent gossip.

"I heard Tetracom isn't going to be here this year," one whispered over to the other.

"Oh, why's that?" the second chewed out, in between strips of bacon.

"They caught their CEO selling coke at an underground casino-brothel. Guess they're not going to be around much longer."

"Jesus! Yeah, probably not!" the second one said in surprise.

I couldn't help but smile to myself. "What a lucky guy," I thought.

The room filled with the sound of buzzing phones, mine being one of them. The keynote speech was about to start, and people got up to leave their breakfasts behind so that they could listen to the industry news. I followed them into a huge auditorium, enjoying the peace that came with being part of the herd, and sat as close to the back as I could get away with.

This was one of the larger conferences, nearly 20,000 people registered according to the scrolling marquee displayed behind the presenter. Not all made the keynote speech, though most did. The auditorium space could have filled that and was nearly standing room only. I guessed the remaining balance was giving small group presentations, break-out sessions in a more traditional classroom environment, or demoing new products to teams. Secretly, though, I hoped there were others like Ryan and me who were capitalizing on the event in more creative ways. After all, this wasn't just a place to exchange vendor business cards; it was a celebration of the year's harvest of tech.

"How should I celebrate?" I asked myself. The program assured that a few Top 40 bands were going to play a free outdoor concert for attendees later, but such exuberant displays of Silicon Valley's wealth weren't really for me. I could've gotten on Grindr to find other cocksuckers in the crowd, but I had the feeling they were going to be fat guys who just weren't up to my standards. Still, I pulled out my phone to check anyway.

Finding my expectations matched reality, I texted Ryan.

SAVE ME!

I glanced back up at the presenter. He was a CEO, and a highly paid one at that. He displayed all the confident speaking behaviors and well-articulated gestures commensurate with the same. The crowd hung on his ability to not only describe what he was seeing in the world of technology from his ivory tower, but also seemed to wait, with baited breath, for the man to name his successor. Still, to me it felt preachy, a trumped-up version of the classic corporate discussion of "customer values" without actually naming anything a human being needs.

Finally, Ryan responded to my mayday call. I looked down at my phone with relief.

How's it going?

Good... class is boring.

"Class?" I thought it was a convention???

Is there really a difference?

Point taken.

I was so glad that he understood. He had been there before when he was a professional slob and knew my pain. Not the pain of sitting in a classroom, but the pain of having your head crammed with deep knowledge that may never come in handy. It made more sense to go out and explore the world to find meaning I could impart by exchanging ideas with people.

To try happiness.

To sell confidence.

Maybe to fall in love.

I looked at my phone and tried to derive meaning from Ryan's words. I envisioned him preparing a shot, and that the phrase "Point taken" meant he was starting the ritual that would have him high on life for hours. Chasing the white dragon.

Come over if you get bored.

That was all the invitation I needed. I'd had enough. It didn't make sense to pretend anymore. There was nothing for me here. I didn't even acknowledge the presenter as I headed out.

My energy level was high as I bounded up the escalator and exited the convention center. I felt I had permission to enjoy my time. Not that it was Ryan's to give, per se. I could have enjoyed a random walk about town without him, but he made it feel more like I belonged there. A sense of ownership of the city swelled within me as I stormed the streets, removed my conference badge, and entered my hotel.

By the time I made it to my room, my work dress shirt was already half unbuttoned. I used my keycard to enter, quickly changed into my more comfortable gym clothes, and hailed a Lyft to Ryan's.

A few minutes later found me downstairs, entering the car of an older Indian woman. I assumed she was as new to the city as I was, as her eyes rarely left the GPS and nearly no words were exchanged. I don't even know if she really spoke English. It took a good half hour for her to manage her way through traffic and deposit me outside Ryan's house in the Mission.

W-O-O-F. Garage. Stairs. Kitchen.

As I opened the door to Ryan's room, he greeted me warmly. "How's it goin', babe?" he asked.

He was seated in his computer chair, cleaning. Familiar progressive house music played softly in the background. My cares and worries about the day were already melting off my face.

I hugged him. "Not bad, how about yourself?" I noticed what could have been forty-two million browser windows open on his desktop, including instructional YouTube videos playing on the two television monitors.

"Good, trying to keep busy."

"Looks like you're succeeding," I said, amazed at his ability to process and handle work.

"Oh! Yeah, I guess you haven't seen any of the work I got done last night."

"Last night? Did you even sleep?"

"Some," he said dismissively. "I had a few friends come by and help me with things so I could focus on my new organizational system. It's quite handy."

"New organizational system, huh?"

He was excited to show me his work. "Yeah, I've got quite a few projects that I'm keeping up with that aren't related to drugs and I need to be able to keep things clean and separated. Plus, it's just been too long since I've rearranged my life."

I laughed. "You don't need to explain the need to organize your room. It's your room, after all."

Ryan began opening drawers and showing the method behind his madness. The contents of each were meticulously organized.

"Yeah, well, I didn't want you thinking I was in tweaker project mode. Still, you'll enjoy this. On the chemical side, I keep my anabolics in this drawer. The other one contains my post-cycle and ancillary support drugs. The third one is all the nootropic drugs, which I'm almost out of. They're great as non-hormonal pre-workout options or for recovering from a night of partying."

"Nice!" I replied, happy for his sense of accomplishment. "A drawer just for the anabolics I make. Wow, I feel special. But, why would I possibly think you're just in tweaker project mode?"

He looked down. A small baggie sat on the keyboard in front of the computer. I wouldn't have noticed it if he hadn't pointed it out.

"No reason." He picked up the baggie and put it in a fourth, yet undescribed, drawer. When he opened it I peeked inside and saw what appeared to be a plastic silverware separator, each compartment holding various drugs in different baggies.

"Seems like you had a good system already," I said suggestively.

"Ha! Not hardly."

"Well, do you need any help?"

"Not at the moment. I do have a couple of people coming by later, so I hope you'll excuse me if I need to make an escape. You're welcome to stay here upstairs. I can meet them in the garage and all of that."

My excitement rose a little. "Anyone like Ehren?" I asked hopefully.

Part of the warmth from Ryan's face disappeared. "Oh no! No, these guys prefer to be quite confidential and private. It's nothing personal, but I don't think they'd take kindly to having extra people around, if you know what I mean."

"Of course," I said, not wanting to press the issue. "My customers like discretion, too. It's your house, your business. I'm glad to be here as a guest. If I need to step out and do anything, I certainly can."

"No, that shouldn't be necessary," he said, trying to return to a more cheerful tone. "I know it takes a bit of cash to Uber and Lyft around everywhere, and I'm sure you'd appreciate some time with me. Sadly, I don't have a lot to spare today."

I faked a dramatic faint as I sprawled out on his bed. "What? You can't drop your entire life while I'm in town to entertain me at my every whim?"

He mimicked my overacting, raising the back of his palm to his forehead. "I know, life is pain!"

Ryan went back to cleaning around his new newly installed shelves. I removed one of the bottles of testosterone from his anabolics drawer and he didn't seem to care. I played with it in my hands. Both the bottle and I had taken different paths, yet ended up in the same place. There was a certain magic to it when I thought about it that way. I focused on every aspect of it I could, from the hardness of the glass to the puncture marks on the rubber seal.

"I really need to clean up this label job. It's kinda shit," I remarked.

"Yeah, I was thinking about that actually," he said, glancing at me between scrubbing surfaces. "I spent some time looking to see if I could find cheaper alternatives to yours out there and some of the labels are actually pretty cool looking. Not that most guys care too much. They're not buying it because it looks cool, but I guess in the world of competing products you're going to have to figure something out."

I didn't know if I should feel insulted because he had considered purchasing from other individuals, or that he basically agreed my label job needed improvement. Somehow, though, I didn't. It seemed reasonable that if I was going to do it, I should do it properly. I let the idea float out into the air for a moment.

"Well, I guess as my number one or number two purchaser now, I should entertain any suggestions or ideas you may have for me."

He took out another bottle from his drawer and scrutinized it deeply.

"Well, let's see. I like the name. Seems to fit okay. The color scheme is appropriate given your choice. I'm guessing with a word like *American* in it, you could sell this to military guys without a problem. You put a dragon on it. Kind of cliché, but dragons are cool, I guess. Have you thought maybe about giving your dragon some actual muscles? I mean, it is a steroid after all, right?"

"You're calling my dragon a wimp?" I replied jokingly.

"I've seen tougher," he replied coolly.

I paused. "Are muscle dragons a thing? In the gay world? I've heard of musclebears and musclepups. But muscle dragons?"

He laughed at my joke. "Please, don't give them any ideas. If you do, you'll have to end up fucking a guy in a furry costume."

I giggled to myself.

"You got Photoshop?" I asked.

"Somewhere on here," he said as he stood up and motioned to switch places with me. "It's a cracked copy. I can start it if you want to mock-up a design. I don't suppose you have your current design, do you?"

"Nah, I got it from some stock images online, so I'm sure I can find the original source image and redo what I did with minimal effort."

"Be my guest."

I sat down in front of his computer and began to start the image editing software. I was a pretty picky computer user, it being the tool of my legal craft. Ryan's machine was peppy and optimized in a way that only computer professionals can stand. Windows Task Manager was running, along with a billion off-label tools for technological performance enhancement that only geeks like us would find. I enjoyed the ruthless obsession he must have poured into optimizing his machine.

"Hold on," he interrupted.

Ryan took the mouse from me and switched over to an Internet radio station. He increased the volume of the music slightly, then yielded control back over to me before he continued on toward his own projects. He was content zoning out with his creative work, and I was content zoning out with mine.

It was a sweet moment. The square root of two felt like two. I had never been a graphic artist or one to use Photoshop before, but I managed to figure out the basics and get a simple rendering done in little time. It was calming having him putter about in the background while I went to my work. The work of selling confidence.

After a few minutes he stood up and looked at the screen over my shoulder.

"That's not bad. I'd puff out the chest a bit more and maybe focus on the biceps."

"The vanity muscles?" I asked.

"It is a logo, isn't it?"

I looked at Ryan and his muscles. They were beautiful even covered by the tight shirt he wore. Behind him, the rest of the room was really tidying up well. It was a big difference from the original state that I walked in on when I first met him in the flesh.

The doorbell rang. Ryan snapped to attention.

"Shit, that's him. I told him not to ring the fucking doorbell."

He grabbed a tiny bag from drawer number four and headed downstairs.

I returned my focus to the computer and tried to research some odd feature of Photoshop that would accomplish exactly as he suggested. I noticed that Ryan had left his Gmail open. The temptation was far too great.

He had a problem. A shopping problem more than anything. He had no fewer than fifty orders out for various things. Bottles of lube; quotes for drugs from China, Russia, and Europe; random shit from Amazon; and even parts for what looked like a space heater. His inbox was well attended to and sorted brilliantly, with subfolders to represent orders in flight versus completed. It was free of spam. No excess "penis pill solicitations" or "Nigerian lottery schemes." It was a proper filing system that he was working out of.

And, of course, the occasional woof, wink, tap, or like from a gay social networking app.

Some things are just too private. I didn't want to know who found him attractive on a hook-up app. I went back to my logo design work, satisfied that none of the major quotes for drugs involved steroids.

After about ten minutes, Ryan returned. A giant sigh blew from his lips as relief appeared on his face.

"Whew. That's over with. Hooray!"

"All finished with business?" I asked hopefully.

"Nope! Well, I mean I thought I was, but now apparently I have two more people coming over."

"Oh, you really are a busy bee!"

"Yeah, this is the week when I keep the most busy," he said. "Everyone's coming into town so I have orders flying about like crazy."

"Steroids are a much slower business," I replied. "People don't just go out of town and decide to get on a cycle. They aren't the impulse buy your stuff is."

"Actually, funny you say that. I sold some of your stuff, too. Probably."

I was mildly surprised.

"My stuff? Probably? What does that mean?"

"Well, that's these other two guys coming over. They're sweet, you'll like them. One of them, I know, is going to want a basic starter cycle, so I guess that's one more order for you," he explained.

"That's on top of what you already got for me?"

"Yup!"

Damn. This guy really could flip shit. If I had his knack for selling stuff, I'd be a wealthy man. Fuck it, I guess I was going to be a wealthy man anyway. Still, the thought occurred to me that this was an unusual sale. I had never impulse sold or pushed the idea of steroids onto anyone before. Without exception, every buyer I ever had was someone who not only researched the topic but was also heavily invested in the gym with some level of training. My motivation to sell originated with the need to subsidize my own habits, but for Ryan, it was commission on a job well done. Still, I had to trust my distributor to know what's best for his clients.

"That's awesome," I said. "When are they going to come by?"

"Probably in half an hour. Let me double-check with them first before I introduce you, but one of them I know you're going to fall madly in love with."

I was immediately stoked. I loved my night with Ehren, and even Tom the DJ had surprised me. Ryan had great taste in men and I felt he could do no wrong.

The clock on the computer read 3:00 p.m. by the time I had finished my logo design and saved a copy onto my phone for safe keeping. I was in a hurry to meet these new and interesting people. I resumed my place on the bed, eager for what delectable man would come through the door next.

A quiet knock and a turn of the knob revealed this man. Much to my surprise, a relatively average-looking guy in his mid- to upper-thirties came in. He was different than Ehren and Tom. He stood five ten, with dirty blond hair, and a face that showed a certain ruggedness, not from natural beauty but from the wear and tear of a hard life. He was fairly twitchy, already quite wired from pre-partying. His arms were bruised in all the expected places.

"Chris, this is Rick."

I extended my hand and he responded to the introduction with a shake.

"G- g- got a light?" He spoke with the unmistakable stutter induced by an excess of stimulants.

Before I could even answer, Rick had powered off a nearby fan and sat his bag down on the bed. He pulled out a small carrying case and opened it, revealing a pipe, three bags of different colored powders, and a tiny vial.

"Wow," I said, a bit leery, "seems like you're packing quite the mess in there."

"You're welcome to do a line with me," he said with a quiver.

"Nah, I'm good."

I resigned myself to sitting at attention. It seemed to be the wisest and safest thing I could do with my body at that particular point in time.

"I have some G, too, if you want it," Ryan offered to the room.

"No thanks, uh, not for me," I said, unsure of this strange new visitor. I looked at Ryan with a bit of trepidation.

Rick quickly responded. "Y- y- y- yeah, h- hook me up."

He took no time at all digging into his goody bag. He poured a little bit of coke onto the web between his fingers and did a bump, then loaded a meth pipe and took a few quick hits. The pipe shook in his hand as smoke slowly left through the tiny hole on top. He was kind enough to offer to share his with me, but I decided to abstain. Ryan left the room and returned in under a minute, having gained some plastic medicine dosing cups along with a bottle of yellow Gatorade to mix up the GHB.

"I've never taken G, and I'm still pretty over spun from yesterday," I admitted.

"G's all right. It helps take the edge off. Actually, as a top, you'd do really well with it," Ryan explained.

Our guest expressed no particular interest in sexual positions. He lacked Tom's playful and casual banter, or Ehren's need to use chemistry to get out of his shell. Rick was, in my mind, a full-on junkie, not one of the party guys that I had hoped for. In under ten minutes I had seen him do three separate drugs, the last of which was the G that Ryan handed to him.

I looked at his arms. They told a story of desperation and need. While I knew Ryan injected, I saw no such bruising on him. Rick scared me, for lack of a better word. Not in the short-term sense of mortal danger to myself, but more in the longer-term sense that desperate people oftentimes do stupid things.

"Bottom's up," he said as he swigged it down in a single shot.

Rick, satisfied he had reached a certain level of intoxication, started to relax a bit. His quivering and uneasiness began to sedate into more seemingly normal behaviors. Still, he lacked any sense of fine motor control. I hoped against hope that he hadn't driven to get here.

Barring anything else being a socially acceptable topic for conversation, I inquired openly to the room about the chemical regimen I had just witnessed.

"So, G huh? What's it like?"

"It's kind of like booze, only one tenth the price and no hangover," Ryan offered.

"Wow, that's pretty awesome, actually. Is it even FDA scheduled? If so, it'd have to be way on down the list. It has to have a downside," I said with genuine curiosity.

Rick sat quietly, not with a fuming anger, but looking off into space waiting for the chemicals to kick in. I interpreted this as him not wanting to directly engage in any sort of group conversation.

Ryan spoke quietly so our guest could enjoy his high in peace. "It is. Schedule Four or Five, I think. And yeah, it does have a downside. If you dose it right, it's actually less habit-forming and less toxic on the body than booze. The problem is usually centered around purity and knowing your source. There's GHB and GLB, and you actually dose them differently, even though they're both called 'G.' But they're both barbiturates."

"What do you call a normal dose?" I asked honestly.

"Well, that depends on the per—"

Ryan stopped himself. Frozen in his tracks. A glance at his fingers showed them drumming briefly in space. A look of confusion went through his eyes as he grabbed the measuring cup.

"I mean, do you always drink it?"

"Um, yeah . . ." he faltered.

"You seem unsure."

Ryan seemed pensive, lost in thought, staring at the measuring cup in his hand.

Ryan looked at Rick. "Do you normally do one ml or three?"

"One. *Why?*" Rick asked, staring at him with an intensity in his eyes, raising the level of alarm in the room.

"Because I think I may have given you more than you asked for."

"Dammit, Ryan, I don't wanna fall out again!" he said, bringing his knees and hands up toward his head in a near fetal position.

"I'm sorry," Ryan said with contrition. "Maybe I didn't, but I thought I should tell you. I just now thought to check how it was labeled. I'm pretty sure I gave you one ounce."

I interjected. "One ounce or one milliliter?"

Ryan fumbled with the cap. "One . . ."

He looked back at the cup.

He looked back at me.

He looked at Rick.

"We'll find out soon," Ryan said biting his lip. "I'm sure it was somewhere in the middle."

It didn't take long for Rick to start convulsing. It was gentle at first, with some frothing at the mouth and an inability to keep his limbs to himself. But within another five minutes—five minutes of absolute utter hell, mind you—he was having full-on seizures. Both Ryan and I leapt on him and, using all of our muscle, tried to keep him from breaking his skull on cabinets and shit in the room.

"Jesus Christ, Ryan, an ounce!?" I said, audibly upset.

Ryan and I were having a difficult time talking. The wrestling of this man, normally much weaker than us, was wearing us both out. "I'm . . . I'm sorry! I thought I looked at it right. I'm so used to 'one' being milliliters that I didn't even think to check the units."

"Is he going to die?" I asked, avoiding accidental blows from Rick. "How many milliliters are in an ounce anyway?"

Ryan was beginning to show frustration, which was an attribute I had never seen in him before. Still, even in a panic, he managed to keep it under control with a joke. "Well, *darling*, I'm not where I can look it up right now—"

"Have you seen anything like this before?"

"Yes, it's normal. He should be fine," Ryan said, trying to calm me down.

"Normal?!"

If I hadn't been in complete disaster-management mode and trying to keep this man from becoming the bull in Ryan's china shop, I would have beaten Ryan senseless.

"It happens from time to time! It happened to him last week. That's what he meant when he mentioned falling out 'again'."

"How long does this last?"

"Twenty minutes, pretty reliably. Then he'll be out like a light."

We maneuvered Rick so his head was hanging off the bed, away from any hard surface. I sat on the bulk of his body to keep him pinned down. He was stronger than anyone I had ever wrestled or lifted with before. Rick had no control whatsoever of his body. His arms and legs started angling off the side of the bed and Ryan tried to maintain enough control to keep Rick from bouncing me off. The seizing was relentless.

I asked, "Can we even keep him contained for twenty minutes? The guy's strong as hell."

"It's just all of his involuntary muscle movements. After that's done, he'll be quiet."

He was true to his word. After the twenty minutes were up, the man was still.

Dead still.

I felt for a pulse on his wrist. It was still there, though fast and heavy.

I was exhausted and so was Ryan by the look of him. Sweat was on both our bodies.

I stared at him in admonishment. "Holy absolute fuck! How much did you give him?"

"It had to be an ounce instead of a milliliter."

I kept digging. "Do you at least know everything else that he took before he got here?"

"How would I know that? I know what he has on him now, if that's what you're asking."

It wasn't. Still, I was in crisis mode even though Ryan was beginning to calm down.

"What's the LD50 of GHB?"

"What's an LD50?"

I scowled at him, anger pulsating through my veins. Ryan marketed himself as a chemist but wasn't sure what an LD50 is? How was that even fucking possible?

"Goddammit, Ryan. LD50 stands for 'lethal dose' for fifty percent of the population. Look up what the LD50 is for GHB, and then look up how many milliliters are in an ounce."

The word *lethal* pierced through any calm facade Ryan wore. His eyes widened with intensity.

"On it!"

He hopped over to the computer. His fingers blazed away at the keyboard at a speed that seemed impossible.

"Nearly thirty mils to the ounce," he announced, still working away at the computer.

"Fuck, that would be a lot then, wouldn't it?"

"Oh yeah, it is," he said without pausing.

I got off of Rick and turned him over on his side. The last thing I wanted was him to cough up something and choke to death on it. I then stood behind Ryan, looking at Rick intermittently to ensure his state hadn't changed. I stared into the blurring motion of windows opening and closing as quickly as Ryan could manage them.

As calmly as I could, I gave orders. "Go to the heavies—Erowid, Google, Bluelight, anything you can find. If you can find something that can counteract an overdose, I'm on it, too. The guy had way too much shit all at once."

"I've seen him do a lot more and react a lot less."

"Really, Ryan!" I said in astonishment. "You've seen a guy take nearly thirty milliliters of a substance when you asked him if he normally takes one or three? That doesn't make any sense."

Ryan got quiet. Pages whizzed by on his screen as he searched for information.

For lack of anything smarter for me to do, I ended up checking Rick's pulse in multiple locations, even though I knew he had one already. They all showed the same thing—rapid heartbeat. His complexion seemed mostly fine, but I was scared to death he was going to turn blue at any point. His chest heaved with force and his air passage seemed clear. I found a small mirror in his bag, presumably for doing lines of coke off of, and kept it nearby, even using it once to test his breathing. It was a stupid trick from the movies, but the only thing I could think of at that time.

"Found it," Ryan said. "Printing now! A rat study, best I can do."

"Great! Pen?"

He tossed me one along with the sheet as soon as the printer released it from its grasp. I took a book that was lying on the headboard so I would have something to write against. I jotted down the LD50 and began doing unit conversions while he continued his research for treatments.

"What do you think he weighs?" I asked as I pulled out my phone to use as a calculator.

"Probably two hundred."

"Good enough for ballpark," I said, looking at our comatose victim.

I started doing the math. It was the most hellish math I had ever done. The results were going to show us the man's chance of living or dying. And even then, what good are the numbers based on a rat study? Still, I had to know our chances as best I could.

"Just under thirty percent."

"To live?!" he exclaimed.

"No, to die."

"Holy shit!" he said.

"And that's all presuming he didn't take anything other than what we saw him take. Anything on overdose treatment yet?"

"Not really!" he said with despair in his voice. "A few random things."

"Show me!"

I suddenly developed a respect for ER doctors and their ability to diagnose and work with patients who couldn't speak. More than anything, I hoped against hope that I wouldn't be seeing one any time soon.

Ryan found a few articles on overdose treatments. He showed me the list and likelihood that any one could help. The only chemical that I could even recognize was incredibly unexpected.

"Thiamine?" I said with shock in my eyes and voice.

"What's that?"

"Thiamine!" I said with urgency. "Do you have any inject-able B12 solutions?"

"Maybe?" he hedged. "A few from some other juice heads I know."

"Let me see it!"

Thiamine is more commonly known as vitamin B1 and is sometimes included with other B-vitamin concoctions. It was a long shot, but I had to hope that whatever B-vitamin injections Ryan had would include a full B-vitamin complex.

He handed me a bottle and I scanned the ingredients.

Thiamine. Holy fuck it was there.

I quickly reviewed the rest of the list to make sure there was nothing else unusual or problematic in it.

"Get me a three ml syringe and help me pull down his pants."

I loaded up the syringe, well past the labeled notches that it was designed to hold. Once the shot was drawn, we both went back over to Rick, undid his pants, and pulled them down far enough for me to access his hips. I then stuck the needle in the guy and injected him slowly.

"What the fuck is that going to do?" Ryan asked nervously.

"Thiamine is a B-vitamin. It's water soluble, so even if you mainlined a gallon of the shit all that's going to happen is you piss it out. What we're doing shouldn't harm him. I'm giving him an injection of a shitload of B-vitamins and hoping that the thiamine will get to him in enough time to raise his chances of survival."

Ryan was silent, clearly out of his depth. Not that I wasn't. Though everything I'd said was true, it wasn't bulletproof. I didn't have time to research the science better either—if I had, my explanation may have been better.

I discarded the needle in the waste bin, and we watched Rick for what seemed like an eternity. His breathing was steady, which was great, but we still were on pins and needles.

Less than five minutes after the injection, we were startled when he began snoring.

Loudly.

Damned loudly.

"I take that as a good sign," I said, finally allowing the tension in the room to ease.

I had no fucking idea if that was a good sign or not, but corpses don't snore. Ryan looked relieved as well. His shoulders eased and his fingers were no longer the nervous drumming and typing machines they once were. His eyes closed in silent prayer, thankful the results came out the way they did.

Seeing him thank God for mercy left me somewhat upset. It wasn't God's fault the man nearly died, nor was it His practice to spare junkies from the morgue.

I had to stir the pot.

"I could have left, ya know."

He knew I was right. There was no evidence I was there really. Any sensible man wouldn't have implicated himself by adding more drugs to an overdosed junkie.

Ryan's face reflected pain. His eyes drifted down and inward, almost as if to find what part of his soul could make such a foolish mistake. He knew he was responsible for this in more ways than one and, thanks aside, he wasn't in a place where he could ask for forgiveness. It wasn't my forgiveness to give anyway, and forgiveness from the man passed out on his bed was the least of it.

"I'm glad you didn't," he muttered.

"Me, too."

We sat in silence for five minutes, except for Rick's relentless snores.

"Look, Ryan," I said, "I love party boys, don't get me wrong. But, dude, this man is a junkie."

"Yeah, I suppose so."

"You suppose?" I said argumentatively. "Man, how many drugs do you need to be on in order to have a good time? It's one thing to like a drug and enjoy it, but it's another thing to check out from reality entirely. It's escapism, and people who use drugs for that are almost always trouble."

More silence. I was cutting at him, but I felt like I needed to. We were both children of chemistry, yet I had the moral high ground.

Ryan looked deep into nothingness. I scanned his room. Everything he knew or had was drugs. I thought back to our conversation on the Presidio. I knew he didn't mean to hurt Rick or anyone. He was only trying to help by offering the one thing Rick wanted, but he was unable give him the one thing he needed.

Sobriety.

"It's fine," I said in a more peaceful tone. I realized that any further anger from me would be torturous without being helpful. "No harm, no foul. I've never heard of long-term complications because of GHB. Still, you need to reconsider who parties at your place. This could have gone very differently."

"I know," he said with his head hung in shame. "From now on, I'll have someone else dose things like G."

"Or at least have them double-check the dose," I suggested. "And don't trust a guy like Rick to double-check shit. The answer will always be 'More is better.'"

"Agreed," he muttered.

"Just curious," I asked, "how much would it take for me to fall out like this, having never taken it before?"

"Probably about five mls or so."

"So that's the downside. The effective dose and lethal dose are too close together. I was going to say what you described made it sound too good to be true. But I guess he'll learn the lesson one way or another. If nothing else, when he wakes up his ass will hurt like a motherfucker from the B12 injection, and his shoulder is going to be in tremendous pain from the seizure."

Ryan was almost in tears. I needed to be more conciliatory. The damage was done, and our worst fears were averted.

"He'll live."

I reached out to Ryan.

"He'll live," I repeated.

Ryan shook off the stress and looked at me with a weak smile. A smile which widened more and more with Rick's loud snores.

I stood up and tried to lighten the mood by changing the subject.

"Look, I'm exhausted and need to crash. I've had way too much uptime. I think I still need to sleep off some of the craziness from yesterday. This excitement didn't help, either. I'd like to get some sleep, but I don't think I can with this man hogging the bed! Frankly, I don't want to move him any more than we already have. He'll be bruised up enough, I can tell."

"You can take a nap in the garage if you want. I'm sure the roommate won't mind."

"I appreciate it. How long will Rick be out for?"

"Four hours," said Ryan. "It's almost always four hours after falling out. GHB has a really short half-life. Soon as he wakes up, he'll have no memory of what happened."

"There's a perk, I guess."

"Yeah, I'm sure he'll be pissed that he missed all the fun."

"Hardly fun in my book," I said. "But I think it's important that you stay up and watch him. If he gets sick, starts gurgling, or stops breathing, let me know immediately and I'll come up and help. But I don't think anything's going to happen."

Ryan agreed. He was the party planner after all, and Rick was his guest.

I left and went to the bathroom. I stared at myself in the mirror as I washed my face for no reason other than that I felt dirty. Dirty from having to deal with the outcome of Ryan's shit. Dirty from dealing with this junkie and whatever his problems were. There is a difference between those you can trust and those you can depend on. You can trust a loved one to have your interest close to their heart. But that doesn't mean they have sense enough keep you safe from poison.

I went through the kitchen and back down the stairs to the garage. An old, dusty sleeper sofa was in the back far away from the garage door. I laid down on it and watched the light bounce off the dust particles flying through the air. It was an old house, as the ones in the Mission are known to be, and draftiness came with the territory. A warm breeze could be felt even though I was inside.

Thiamine. I'll have to remember that.

God, I'm good.

I didn't just fall asleep—I leapt in with both feet.

THIRTEEN

I WOKE UP REFRESHED BUT still troubled. While I was no longer tired, I could still see Rick's body convulse in my mind's eye. It wasn't every day that I got to witness a violent seizure and, truth be told, I'd be thrilled to never witness one again. Somehow, though, I doubted that would be my last encounter with a poor drug reaction and I could only hope next time would end just as well.

I laid on the couch staring into the dust swirling in the sunlight. Drugs and I had a relationship going way back, and I thought of my first exposure to them. I had gone over to my grandmother's house to water the plants while she was out of town. Upon my arrival, I noticed one of her dogs was violently injured. As much as I had hated that particular animal, I never forgot its terribly sad whimpers and labored breathing as my mother and I rushed it to the veterinarian emergency room.

As we arrived, we were greeted by a kind but unkempt doctor. It was probably around two in the morning, and her long blonde hair wasn't combed or coiffed like the pictures on the wall showed. Instead, a cute pair of penguin pajamas could be seen underneath a white coat. She was more pleasant than I had expected given the short notice for such an emergency call.

As she laid her healing hands on the damned beast, it instantly went nuts. Still thinking it was in a fight for its life, it began wrestling with every ounce of strength it had. Any attempt to come near the thing with clippers to clean the wound were met with intense fighting.

She loved animals, but even her patience was tried in this case. The vet instructed us to hold him down and said, "I have just the cure."

My mother held the dog's upper shoulders, and I, the hips of this ankle biter shih tzu, which was difficult, but we managed. The vet drew liquid into a large syringe then approached the dog. As the needle disappeared into his flesh, she commanded, "Now count to three. One . . ."

Before she finished enunciating the final breath behind the word *one*, all of the fight vanished from the dog. Every bit of its energy was drained. He was spent and forced to lay there while the doctor went about her work.

That was a very powerful moment to me. I didn't care if the dog lived or died, I was more scared than anything around such a mean critter. But I was mesmerized by the powerful magic that the vet performed. The tranquility of that damned dog was infinitely more kind than that of the passed-out junkie I had dealt with moments earlier.

I inhaled the sofa's dusty smell. There was a white peg board and some half-full bottles of engine grease and paint strewn about the garage. Wooden planks and other scraps of projects long forgotten were nearby as well. I got the sense I was in the space of one who actively liked to work on things—or did, at one point. I knew Ryan was the kind of guy to pick up random tweaker projects and toil into all hours of the night, but this seemed more deliberate. There was no evidence of the erratic neurotic behavior that I imagined inside a meth user's garage.

Instead, it felt homey and, despite the violent memories in my mind, relaxing. I was in a space separated from the hustle and bustle of work and the endless barrage of conference calls and remote desktop screen-sharing sessions. Nothing in this garage was virtual. It was concrete and solid, almost like it was the foundation that held up the rest of existence. It felt more real than so many things in my life did.

The wood on the doorframe to the stairs was starting to strip. It was old and dilapidated. I thought how easy it would be to get a splinter from it if I touched it wrong. Like wallpaper and potted plants, doorframes are just items that fade away into the background.

I was deep inside the safety of this garage, hidden behind a large door. I sank into the couch, reveling in being hidden from the world. So little separated me from the madness that was upstairs and from the cacophony of urban sounds right outside.

And I loved it.

I focused then on what I wasn't hearing. The sounds that were obviously missing that I would have expected in a place like this. The houses touched, yet no steps, thuds, or clanks could be heard through the walls.

Even in this relatively quiet and peaceful neighborhood, I felt part of the community. I had a feeling of oneness with the world, while being alone. It was a feeling I never had in the suburbs. I wasn't ever going to know the names of my neighbors and I hated pretending not to see them when I mowed my lawn. But here I sensed less pretense and more harmony because I instinctively knew I was part of an ecosystem.

The suburbs allowed me to pretend that I had complete control of my land. In the city, I never presumed to have control of anything. Nature just flowed.

Suddenly, the door swung open and a very determined Rick stormed through it. I had no desire to interact with him so I faded back into the couch and pretended to be asleep. He left through the garage door, seemingly unaware of my presence.

After he left, I feared for Ryan. His mental state had just calmed when I left, but I wondered if Rick's anger about the incident would have upset him further. Soaking in the last bit of tranquility, I prepared myself to be the positive company I presumed Ryan needed.

I ascended the stairs and swung around the kitchen. I tried to be as quiet as I could to preserve the calm as I entered Ryan's room. He looked up from his computer with a soft but unenergetic smile, one that said, "I'm glad to see you" more than, "I'm happy."

"Hello," I whispered as I closed the door behind me.

"Hello. Rest okay?"

"Yeah. How was Rick?"

"Meh, he'll survive," he said. "I'm sure he'll lay off things for a while."

"Good. I hope he wasn't mad."

"He can be mad all he wants. Doesn't change anything. He's the one who decided to take way too much."

To a degree, I agreed with Ryan. He didn't tell Rick what to take, but he was the one who dosed it. Still, I didn't want to dwell on the past or focus on the negative experience.

"Well, now that I'm caught up on sleep and there isn't going to be more work for the day, why don't we hit up the gym together? You can come with me and it'll help us get out of the house."

"I can't. I have to work," Ryan replied.

"Yeah?"

Ryan seemed a bit flustered. He looked at the clock and at the fourth drawer a few times.

"Yeah, like I said, this is a busy week for me. Everyone's coming into town and I'm going to have a lot of deliveries I need to make tonight."

"That's fine, I understand. Do you have any place you'd recommend?"

"Absolutely. Fitness SF is just down the street. You can take an Uber or jog if that's what you do for cardio. Usually all the hot musclebears and musclepups train there. I'm sure you'll find some eye candy while you work out. Plus, the equipment's in decent shape."

"Fair enough. Well, I think getting out of the house will definitely do me some good, and I'm sure it'll do you some good, as well. If you get a moment, why don't you change your environment and at least go for a walk for a bit? I'm sure you'll feel less 'bleh' after all of—"

He dismissed my final attempt with a wave of the hand while pulling out some powder and a scale from the drawer. "I'm sure I'll figure something out."

"Fair enough. Well, I'll be gone for an hour or so. Maybe more if I shower there. Would you be interested in snagging dinner later? I'm always starving after a good training session."

Ryan began portioning out small bags of a slightly bigger ball. "Maybe. All depends on what my schedule looks like. Not everyone is as punctual as you."

"Ha, I believe that. Hey, do you know what the slowest thing in the world is?"

"What's that?"

"A tweaker in a hurry," I said.

He paused to look at me, then made a rimshot gesture indicating my corny dad-joke landed its mark as intended.

"Okay, well, I'll text you when I'm done and we'll see what's going on from there."

"Sounds great," he smiled.

I paused for a moment.

"You mind if I do a stick of testosterone before I head out?"

"Not at all! Be my guest."

Ryan tossed me a bottle of TNE and a fresh syringe. I performed my normal pre-workout rite to receive the sacrament of the bodybuilding gods. I asked where I could deposit the syringe. He pointed to the waste basket, and I dropped the used rig inside.

The taste of pine needles enveloped the entirety of my mouth. Fresh and familiar pine needles.

Fitness SF was cleaner than many of the shitholes I'd trained in before. The clientele was very different from many of the gyms I had visited. Where the more hardcore gyms advertised to cops, bouncers, and powerlifters, this place catered to gay men and those who were scheduled for photo shoots and beauty pageants. As I walked in, I tried to find the baby powder and chalk stains, or the heavy-grunting strength athletes. Instead, well-manicured bodies in bright retail-like lighting was all I could see. There were even fresh towels available.

I approached the front desk. I gave them my ID and a strange look when I was told the ridiculous price for a day pass. Even gym memberships cost a fortune. One day, maybe I'd appreciate how cheap things were in my hometown. Fuck it. It was worth the price to get out for an evening and enjoy the sweet release that pumping iron gave me when I was stressed.

I had already written off the week as a loss in terms of my normal training schedule. I resigned myself to the vanity lifts—chest and arms. It was going to be all about looking good and feeling better more than sticking to my program. The walk from Ryan's had gotten the blood flowing and the testosterone in my veins was already starting to pump. My veins were already visibly popping in my arms before I even started my warm-up sets.

Music was a necessity so the headphones came out, as did my air of, "Don't fuck with me, I'm lifting." I began playing hard rock, then walked upstairs to the free weight area. After grabbing a pair of sixty-pound dumbbells I went over to an incline bench and started warming up on it.

It didn't take me long to start grunting. I didn't give off the air of a natural lifter but, then again, I didn't want to. I looked around me, unsure who was on chems and who wasn't. Moreover, I wasn't sure who was on *my* chems. The idea turned me on as I went for another set on the bench.

I started to feel good. It was working. I was changing the man in the mirror.

The pace picked up. I began alternating different shoulder movements without rest periods to pre-exhaust my muscles. Bodybuilders call this method supersetting, and it was a favorite in my routine. I liked focusing on my front delts in particular, and fought hard to get as much shelf on my pecs that biology and chemistry could allow. A strong chest and back were the hallmarks of masculinity that I aimed for.

The gym was busy, but not overly so. Most of the patrons were men, and I liked the two-floor concept they used. Most of the cardio equipment was on the lower level, and that meant that the monsters like myself had our own area above and away from those just looking to lose a few pounds. Ryan had been right about the attractive men. There were some older daddy-types talking by the water cooler, younger jocks experimenting with free weights for the first time, and a handful of others also familiar with the weight room around me. Still, as much as I was in my element, this wasn't a place to socialize. The people that I saw were all there for a purpose and seemed more dedicated to training than meeting new friends.

I was well into my routine after about thirty minutes. I noticed I was pacing angrily from machine to machine, nearly frothing at the mouth with aggression. I wasn't upset at any particular person or thing, but I had no patience for interruptions to the rigorous pace and tempo I had established. When another lifter got in my way, I worked around them instead of asking to work in with them. I felt more full of focus than wrath, though both left me feeling in command of the small area of the gym I monopolized.

I felt alive. The sense of control I got from training on testosterone was fantastic. My body had been morphed and modified into a machine for slinging weight. I was giving it exactly what it had been adapted to enjoy. All my energy was directed toward self-hate and manipulating the puppet strings of my body that I had come to master.

Other gym patrons left me alone. When someone needed a machine, I yielded with only a nod or a gesture, and then usually picked another machine or station.

It didn't take long for my mind to wander to sex. And red meat. Steroid-using young males typically think of these two things, and my mouth watered for both. I thought about how great a steak and a blow job would be after my session.

In between sets I pulled out my phone, loaded my favorite hook-up app, and scoped out the area. Ryan had been right about that, too. There were a lot of hot guys mere feet, not miles, away.

Everyone nearby was in the gym, and, as such, had gym-based selfies. All the pictures showed them pumped and the profiles said they were into guys who worked out like they did. I was in a den of muscle worship, and everyone was into exactly that. I concluded every single gay guy in San Francisco was a muscle-bound Adonis in need of my dick.

And I was going to give it to them all!

I was at the cable cross-over machine finishing up my routine when two young guys about my age walked up to me. One was much taller than the other and seemed more dominant. He was white, balding even at a young age, and walked with purpose. Like myself, he wore dark workout attire and seemed to command a presence. I sized him up. I was pretty sure he could've taken me if he wanted. He had a weight class on me and about two or three inches of height and reach. He shared my intense vascularity, and my mouth watered when I saw his veins. His blondish hair was styled after a military buzz cut.

His friend was shorter and leaner, with a slick dark goatee. The individual cuts of muscle in his skin were visible through the stringer tank top he wore, and his complexion was a beautiful mocha color. I guessed him to be Latino or Italian. Either way, combined with the mohawk and tunnel style ear piercing, he had a certain exoticness that I found extremely attractive. Pierced ears and septum also showed his flair for an alternative look.

The taller of the two pushed me on the shoulder, in a way that was both confrontational and assertive.

"Hey, what are you doing?" he asked as I was bumped out of place.

"Hey, yourself!" I shot back. I didn't know if I was about to get in a fight. I let my headphones fall out of my ears and clenched my fists, fearing for the worst.

"You're pretty hot."

I was dumbstruck. I'd been in a lot of gyms and had guys hit on me in unusual ways, but this was different. There was something oddly familiar about him. More importantly, I was incredibly turned on by his approach.

He was a bull I wanted to tango with.

"You too. What you gonna do about it?" I edged close enough to his face to kiss him.

I glanced over to his friend. The shorter mocha one licked his lips in a way that was deliciously inviting. Briefly looking down, I saw his hands in his pockets, not holding a weapon, but beating his hard cock against the fabric.

It was like stepping into a porn.

I looked back to the older one.

"I'm Chris."

"I'm vers."

Fuck. Seriously! He skipped his name and went right to his preference. This guy was more direct than any human being I ever imagined. And I liked it. His friend stayed quiet and seemed along for the ride. Still, they both looked like they wanted to eat me alive.

"I'm all top," I said, "and from out of town. Got a place?"

The gruff one said, "I saw you on the app. And yeah, wanna come over?"

I smiled, almost uncontrollably.

"Sure, though I was hoping to finish my workout."

He stepped back and gave me some space. He reached into his shorts pocket and pulled out a cell phone. Moments later, mine vibrated, and I checked my messages on the app.

It was from him. It was an address.

"I gotta shower anyway. See ya in forty-five minutes?" he asked.

"I can do that."

Then they turned and left as quickly as they showed up. Tall muscles first and the shorter pierced one followed suit. I relished every moment of them walking away.

I liked to think that I was a purist, dedicated and devoted to the skill of bodybuilding like it was a religion. If I was really saintly, though, I wouldn't have cheated myself out of the remaining few sets I had planned. I was no saint. I was just a horny, 'roided-up doofus with the promise of getting my nuts off. I dropped the weight to a bare minimum and threw out a few extra sets in an effort to look like I cared.

After they were well out of sight, I retreated to the relative calmness of the water fountain. I felt more than the regular amount of water dribble out of my mouth as I drank.

Is it going to be just the one? Or both of them?

I went to the showers and rinsed off, scrubbing my genital region and borrowing a spare gym towel to dry myself clean. I hadn't really planned this trip to the gym from Ryan's, so I was forced to wear my original workout clothes after showering. I hoped the sweat didn't offend him and that he was as turned on by the smell of men as much as I was.

While I waited for my Uber I found both guys' profiles on the app and tried to figure out what I was about to get into. Both were into muscle guys and man smells, described themselves as pigs, and were into quite a variety of kink and role play.

It was like winning the lottery.

I screen capped both of them and sent pics to Ryan along with a message reading, "Do you know these guys?" I couldn't contain myself I was so excited.

It didn't take long for the Uber to show up. I gave him the address. I was so worked up, only two things were going through my mind: steak and sex. As far as I was concerned, the bigger guy was steak and the smaller guy was sex. Was what Ryan said true? Were all the hyper-sexed attractive men in existence here in town for this particular week? Was this Dore Alley fair really what it was cracked up to be?

I became so lost in the world of my phone that I didn't notice when the driver pointed me to a large apartment building after we parked. After nudging me out, I stepped onto the sidewalk and gathered my bearings. From what I could tell I was down-town, back toward the financial district. The smaller three-story buildings of Ryan's neighborhood and the Mission were nowhere to be seen. Every direction was obscured by towering skyscrapers, the sky only visible when I looked directly up.

I found the building with the matching address, a large tower carving a place in the sky. As I walked in, I got a response from Ryan.

"It's Richard Steele. Why?"

Richard Steele. The name didn't ring a bell. But that face. I knew I'd seen that face!

Not responding to Ryan, I Googled the name. He was a real porn star. I recognized his face because I'd jacked off to him before. Given his body type and fetishes, probably more than once. I wanted to do more to research, but the elevator was within sight and I rushed to catch it before it closed. I was the only occupant.

I thought about what it must have been like performing in front of a camera like he did. To be able to cum on demand (or, at least, to get hard on command and fuck whoever the direc-tor put in front of him). The idea was appealing but foreign.

I oftentimes dreamt of how wonderful it would be to turn my brain off and lift for a living instead of debugging software problems. Being a porn star was in many ways the same dream, only this man had attained it. There was a certain joy that comes with following one's baser instincts while turning off the cerebral cortex, and he got paid to do so.

"Oh my God!" I was so giddy I was jumping up and down.

I Googled him again. He was HIV-positive, as were many of the actors he worked with.

"Fuck. I hope black market Truvada works. Thank God for Ryan," I thought.

The elevator doors opened and I stepped out. I stood in the hallway for what seemed like ten minutes before I had the courage to approach the door and knock on it. When it opened, I was rewarded with a familiar face. Richard Steele stood there brushing his teeth, wearing only shorts. Dripping wet and fresh from the shower, his booming chest and broad shoulders filled the doorframe in its entirety.

I gave him a casual nod, the kind normally reserved for heterosexual males when passing by on the street. He gestured me in. Once in the living room I saw his friend, stripped down to just a jockstrap. He looked thrilled when I came in.

Richard went into the bathroom and turned on the faucet. The sound of him rinsing could be overheard. I stood near the door, not sure of my bearings or who I should follow. After expectorating the last of the toothpaste, Richard reappeared and spoke from behind a towel he was using to dry his face.

"I'm glad you made it."

"Me, too."

Richard walked up to me, his bravado cooled somewhat, and his assertiveness replaced with sensuality.

"Come in here," he said. His friend, still silent, followed us down the hallway and into a bedroom.

Richard's friend approached me on the right and we started making out. His greedy tongue made a beeline for the back of my throat. Part of me wanted to ask his name, but I preferred not knowing. All that mattered was if he was a top or a bottom and if I could breed him bareback. If he had hopes and dreams that didn't involve me pumping him full of semen, I didn't want to hear them.

Richard undressed himself then got on the floor to my left. He pulled my shoes and shorts off before sucking my dick. It took me no time at all to get hard.

The friend went from kissing my mouth down to kissing my biceps, then shifted to rubbing his nose in my armpits. This friend of his was a muscle worshiper, and his eyes stayed shut as a smile overtook his face in enjoyment. Pleasure flooded him in waves as he took in my sweaty post-gym smell. I let him worship me, flexing intermittently so he could feel the strength in my arms, which he responded to with moans and subtle licks. I took his response to indicate that he was submissive and, in all likelihood, a bottom.

Richard was infinitely more direct. He was not nearly as turned on by these kinks. He didn't look up or moan or give passive groans. He focused entirely on my dick, and as soon as I was hard, he was, too.

We fucked.

I could spell out in elaborate detail how aggressive Richard was but, to be honest, it doesn't really matter. Being scared turned me on more than anything he did. When I thought about it, that was the whole point of the experience in the end anyway. What sexual encounter is both wonderful as well as boring? Fear and risky sex were my kink. I had never knowingly penetrated a guy who was HIV-positive before, much less bareback. I wasn't a regular at the sex clubs and leather bars like some of these men were. I wasn't among the one-in-three HIV-positive males that roamed the streets. I was a total top from a small state and never set specific sexual boundaries with a partner before, and I didn't even know their names. It was thrilling sleeping with someone who just oozed sexuality and who I knew was far more experienced than I was.

No words were spoken and no condoms were used. While I was buried deep inside of Richard and kissing his friend, I kept my eyes open the whole time.

Dumb looks of satisfaction filled our faces when we finally laid on the semen-soaked sheets, exhausted from what passed for the day's cool-down cardio.

Breaking the silence, I asked, "What's your name?" to the mysterious third in the room.

"Ethan."

"Chris," I said, offering a wave, which seemed a happy medium between sucking his dick again and a more formal handshake.

"Nice to meet ya."

Richard got up and went to the bathroom. He lacked the panting, exhausted joy that Ethan and I had on our faces, but his skin shimmered with sweat nonetheless. No names were formally exchanged between us.

I admired his body. He had a certain ruggedness to him that I hadn't noticed before. He had a square and stubbled face, the kind that said he was a construction worker or furniture mover, but he also had a body that was way too beautiful for a hard trade like that.

"Today was unexpected," I muttered. "I can't say I've ever hooked up with a couple of guys from the gym before."

"Us neither," Ethan responded.

"No way, really?!"

Ethan laughed lightly. "Yeah. We saw you online and were both talking about how much we were into you. We figured since you were on the apps and in the gym during Dore, you must be down to fuck. We honestly thought the whole time, 'What if he isn't into us?'"

"I'm glad you didn't give in to your fear."

The sound of running water filled the room again. Richard had turned on the shower and appeared with some towels.

"I'm going to rinse off," he said succinctly, dropping them on the bed before returning back to the bathroom. The door closed quietly behind him.

I was concerned. I asked Ethan, "All rough in the gym, and now he doesn't talk. Did I piss him off?"

Ethan sat next to me on the edge of the bed. "Nah, if you pissed him off, you'd know about it."

"Good. You from around here?"

"No," he responded with a light gesture. "New York actually. Bit of a trip, but so far it's been worth it."

"I can imagine. A lot of sex pigs out there?"

Ethan smiled. "Yeah, a few. Nothing's like Dore though."

I couldn't resist running my hands across his abs. I appreciated his dark muscles and edgy look. He didn't look like a model or a porn star, but his intensity was attractive. I started kissing him again, playing with his piercings as I explored his body.

"Especially if they're muscle freaks like you," he confessed.

He snarled and passionately kissed back, but only briefly before signaling he was spent. The soul was willing, but the body just wasn't in the mood for a third hour of fucking.

"That turn you on, huh? The idea of being a 'roided up freak?" I asked.

"Muscle turns me on," he replied.

"I can tell. What about steroids?" I asked.

He looked lost at the question. We were birds of a feather, but not quite the same species. The running water came to an abrupt halt.

"I don't know about that," he said with some doubt.

"I juice. Makes the gym more fun. What about you?"

Richard walked into the room, drying himself off.

"I do, he doesn't," Richard volunteered.

"Nice," I said. My attention shifted toward him. "What are you running?"

"I'm cruising on what the doc prescribes me right now. About 200 mgs of test per week. Occasionally I like to blast with deca and a few others." He nodded for Ethan to head off to the shower, who diligently obeyed.

"I can hook you up if you want," I offered.

He paused then glanced upward toward the ceiling as if he was admiring the ridiculousness of my offer.

"That's a first," he replied.

"What is?"

"To be offered steroids during a hookup. Usually it's things like ice or some such."

"Steroids can be a great party if you want them to be," I argued. "Add enough TNE and you'll fuck like an animal."

"TNE, huh? I guess I can see that. Still, I try to only do that stuff on special occasions."

"Like Dore?" I said with a smile.

"Yeah."

Richard's voice had become almost monotone. Ethan was right—he wasn't upset, he just sounded bored. Perhaps it was presumptuous to make that leap based on his voice or the way he seemed distant in the conversation, but he wanted something more. I imagined that a porn star like him had hooked up thousands of times and had a thousand loads and it just wasn't interesting anymore. Perhaps he was caught in an endless loop: showering in between sex in between showering again.

He got exactly what he wanted. A life dedicated to life's baser instincts filled with never-ending sexual experiences. The city wasn't going to run out of horny gay men, yet all of them couldn't satisfy him. Whatever it was he wanted in life wasn't in that room. Nor was it something I could put in a baggie or bottle. I believed he understood drugs and Ryan's scene, and no doubt had run into it at some point in his career as a sexual object. But still, I believed he was looking for something more fulfilling.

So I responded with the closest thing I had to offer. Honest friendship.

"Well, the next time you want to train for something big or have a goal, hit me up. I'll leave my phone number in the app so you can reach out to me. I'd love to talk about your training goals and things some time. I really do enjoy the gym as more than a meat locker. Meeting guys there for hot sweaty sex is fun, but I want more from life, myself."

He turned to me and listened. He warmed up instantly when I expressed interest in his dreams and goals, and it was a privilege to see that side of him. For the first time, I saw him show curiosity and not just aggression or apathy. Inside that beefy body of his was a mind with gears and a heart with strings. I may not have touched any part of them, but I was glad to see them. I concluded few could see him as anything other than a penis that ejaculated or a hole that needed filling. I wanted him to know that I saw more.

"I appreciate that. I might do that. You local?" he asked.

"Nah, Oklahoma. Out in the middle of nowhere."

"Shame," he said genuinely. "I used to live here, but now I'm on the East Coast."

"With Ethan?"

"DC, actually. Ethan and I just met."

"Well, aren't we all just a bunch of social butterflies," I joked.

"Eating ass is how I say hello," he replied wryly.

Ethan returned, drying his hair in his towel. It was my turn to rinse off.

"Well, you can say hi to me anytime you like. I'll be brief and head out soon."

I grabbed my shorts and a clean towel from the bed as I headed into the shower.

While the warm refreshing water washed over me, I pondered both the beauty of my spontaneous adventure and the world I lived in. I had just traveled halfway across the most powerful country in the world, spent some time working on my body, met two guys who wanted nothing more than to exchange carnal pleasure, and went twenty stories up to perform the ungodly act of sodomy before I was supposed to head back to my employer-paid hotel room.

I took fewer than five minutes to rinse, then stepped out and laughed quietly at my reflection in the fogged-up bathroom mirror before turning off the water. Drying was done as hastily as the rinse job. Afterward, I retreated back to my sweaty gym clothes and socks, which gave me a shudder. Before I left the bathroom, I pulled out my phone and messaged them both my number.

I had no idea how to end our tryst. A handshake? A kiss? "Good game, sport!" and a slap on the ass?

I went back into the bedroom and just went for it.

"Well, I had fun guys. I'll be in town until Sunday. Sadly, I have to leave shortly after the fair picks up."

"Cool," Ethan said. "I'll be in town until Monday morning. Richard leaves Monday night."

"Very cool. I wish I could've stayed longer, but I guess that's what I get for my first Dore."

"See you at the fair?" Richard asked.

"Absolutely! Wouldn't miss it for the world."

I hugged them both separately. Two small pats each on their thick muscular backs.

With that, I left the apartment. As soon as the elevator doors shut behind me, I instantly texted Ryan.

"You're not going to believe this!"

FOURTEEN

ARRIVED AT RYAN'S PLACE almost an hour later. I was excited to see him and had a feeling of great joy when I opened the door to his room. Beaming, I couldn't contain myself for more than an instant.

"Best. Hookup. Ever!"

Ryan looked up inquisitively from his computer. He was browsing the web, at his normal pace of a million tabs per minute. All three monitors were in use.

"I was wondering about that. I thought you said you needed to get away for a bit?"

"I did. Then, eh, the city happened, I guess."

"Impossible things do tend to happen here," Ryan said.

"Do you want to hear about it?" I implored, crawling on his bed and hugging a pillow.

He chuckled. I could tell he didn't, as he seemed preoccupied with his work. But he indulged me. I felt that any story I could tell (true or otherwise) would be more entertaining than anything he was shopping for online. He agreed with his simple, "Sure."

I sprawled out on his bed and began talking with my hands. I regaled him with my tale of overpriced gym passes, supersets with amazing chest pumps, and my unexpected sexual encounter with two strapping musclebulls. He seemed warm to my emotions, though he lacked the luster for the details as

I shared them. My passionate narration was being met with a cool sterility, tempering the flame of my story.

"Isn't that crazy?" I asked, almost begging to elicit some emotion from him.

"It was certainly unexpected," he said matter-of-factly. "Though, to be honest, it's actually not the first time I've heard of people hooking up with a porn star."

"Well, it's the first time *I* have."

He chuckled. "Yeah, I'm glad you got your cherry popped. You'll get another one tomorrow."

He seemed underwhelmed by my story. He turned back to his computer and put on some music, softer than the house and trance beat I heard earlier, and a bit darker. There was a different mood in the room. The lighting seemed whiter than it did before.

"Did you redecorate or something? Everything seems . . . off. Are you okay?"

"Yeah, sorry. I had the room in 'leave me alone' mode. Let me fix things."

He pulled out his phone and adjusted some settings. Soon, the room's hue turned softer, with hints of turquoise. It was still bright enough to see, but infinitely more inviting. The music, which seemed foreign before, blended to match and a general vibe of calmness swept over.

"While you were out," he explained, "I had to meet up with a few people. I use Philips Hue LED lights and sometimes set subtle clues to get rid of people. Drugs aren't the only way to alter someone's mood. I figured you were coming back over and wanted to make sure we had the place together, just the two of us. Most people can't stand that setting for more than half an hour."

"Oh, interesting. I guess I never thought about how you Silicon Valley types have to have an app for everything. In Oklahoma, all you can find is The Clapper and touch lamps."

He moved to the bed and sat next to me.

"Cute," he muttered. He sprawled out facing me. We were close, only an intimate distance between us.

"So, if the sterile florescent white was 'leave me alone' mode, what do you call this?" I asked.

"This is warm, friendly mode. Makes the feng more shui."

"Those your only two modes?"

"Oh, no. I have several. All sorted by mood. You might also enjoy this."

He pressed a few buttons on the phone. Soon, the room was plunged into a deep sultry red, the kind that screams primal lust or rage. His eyes took on a demonic glow due to the lighting change. I immediately imagined them dilated. Even though I knew only kindness was in them, my gut churned with a visceral feeling.

"Whoa!" I said, almost startled.

"Yeah. That's a favorite."

"Bathhouse mode, eh?"

"Great for sex parties," he said with a smile.

He pressed another button and the friendly blue returned, feeling even softer than before.

"It must be nice to be able to set your mood with the touch of a button."

"It's actually more nice to be able to change other people's moods at the touch of a button."

I glanced over at the clock by the nightstand. With the excitement of porn stars, gym training, dealing with G'd out junkies, and seeing the city, I had lost track of time. It was approaching nine o'clock and I had to be at the convention the next morning.

"What's wrong?" he asked.

"I just now realized how late it is. I'm still two hours ahead but it doesn't feel like it's that late."

"Busy day, huh?"

"Yeah."

I let silence fall as I looked back up to him.

Your eyes are kind, I thought but didn't say.

Maybe it was a lighting gimmick. Maybe it was the music. Or maybe it was one of a million other subtle tricks that he played in the environment to change the social dynamics, but I had never even considered that I would find someone like me—someone who thought and dreamt like I did.

"You know," I said, after an appropriate amount of silence had passed, "if I had to change someone else's mood, I would probably use something more powerful than music and lighting."

"What would you use?" he asked. "A selective serotonin reuptake inhibitor, perhaps?" he mocked.

"Maybe," I said. A slight tear came to my eye.

"Well, lighting and music tend to be more instant. And you don't have to slip them into someone's drink."

I laughed. He looked at me deeply and I stopped. His eyes were tired but soft, with red lines visible from them. Every line in his beautiful face was clear. I focused on them so deeply and wondered about the story behind each of them. As my mind raced, I noticed the room gained a slight haze to it. My eyes were watering. I was crying.

"Uh oh, what happened?" Ryan asked, surprised.

"I don't know," I said. "I just . . . I'm so . . . Sad? Happy? I don't know."

He reached over and dried a tear.

"I think someone's testosterone aromatized all the way to estrogen. You're probably just crashing and going through a man-period."

I felt so close to him in his understanding. No one else would have known the chemistry behind my feelings, but it was a well-known phenomenon for bodybuilders. The human body likes to operate in homeostasis, and if you pound enough testosterone and male steroids eventually it rebels. Hard. The net effect is a very emotional bodybuilder who wants to eat chocolate and watch reruns of *The Golden Girls*.

I wanted to say something like, "Maybe, but I'm honestly not sure that's it." I wanted him to ask, "What is it then?" And I wanted to respond with a soft touch or a gentle kiss.

But he was already in my head. And I was in his. There was no need for any of those words, and he wiped away my tears before we kissed. It was a romantic, nonsexual kiss. The kind all little girls watch in Disney movies and all little boys struggle to figure out how to perform.

Even when our kiss was over, I pulled him toward me as I whispered into his ear, "How do you do it?"

"Do what?" he said kindly, running his hands through my hair.

"You're all alone. On the edge of the world. You gave up everything you had just to pursue a dream. A fucked up dream, but a dream nonetheless."

"I'm not alone. I have a lot of people."

"But you're alone," I insisted.

He smiled meekly. He knew I was right on some level. It wasn't that he was single and living the life of a meth dealer. It wasn't that he did so without a financial safety net, or an emotional confidante, or, hell, even a best friend. He was the only one of his kind. A drug dealer with a worn-out soul. A lonely creature in a lonely world.

"I'm not alone. I have you," he whispered back, kissing me on the forehead.

The words stabbed me like a knife. Only I didn't bleed blood, I just bled more tears.

"You can't keep burning the candle at both ends," I sobbed.

"I know," he said. He put his arm around me, comforting me even as I held him close. "I'm working on it."

"I've never met anyone who thinks like me. And I know you aren't used to finding people who think like you. I had to go to the edge of the fucking world to find you, and it's terrible. I know it's always going to be worse than you let on, and all the more terrifying that you're alone."

He said nothing, just kept holding onto me. His breath was heavy, each breath comforting me only slightly.

"I'm here right now, aren't I?"

"For now. But I know what happens when the candle's out. What happens when you can't feel happiness anymore? When you can't enjoy your blue room that you made?"

My comments were silly and I knew it. I didn't give two shits about the blue room. I just wanted him to be able to enjoy the regular day-to-day things that bring people joy. But I didn't need to tell him that. He knew exactly what I was talking about.

I began rambling. "No one dies from a meth overdose. Well, very few. Cocaine, sure, but not meth. Meth is so much more sublime than that. People just quit feeling happiness until all that's left is bleak existence."

Ryan pulled away from me. He gazed into my eyes.

"Find what you love," he said, "and let it kill you."

"That's it, huh?"

"That's happiness," he said plainly.

"That's sad," I said trying to pull away.

"There's nothing that could be less sad," he said confidently. "What more to life could there possibly be than doing what you love?"

I wanted to ask, "But is that really your happiness?" and for him to say, "No, but what's yours?" I wanted us to follow it up with a kiss. But again we didn't need to speak. He kissed me anyway and there was no need to exchange words.

"You're my happiness," I whispered.

"And you give me the confidence to keep going. But just because I'm your happiness doesn't mean you should let me kill you."

"I'm not," I lied. I teared up again. "But, goddamn, you're good at it."

I pulled away and rolled over so I was staring straight up. I focused on the popcorn ceiling. He did likewise and together we stared up at the would-be stars. The distance from him gave me composure that I was sorely missing.

"I'm good at a few things," he admitted.

"Seriously, though, how are you doing? And I don't mean in that stupid way only native English speakers use where they mean it as a passing greeting. I mean, sincerely, how are you approaching this and how is it working?" I asked, unable to look him in the eyes.

"I'm working on quitting. Frankly, it cuts into my profits, so there's that. It's a cheap drug, so it's not that it costs me a lot of money, but no one wants to buy from the geeked-out guy. I can't just stop cold turkey. I mean, physically I could since there's nothing that stops me, but when you use like I do, it's best to nurse yourself off of it."

"How much and how often?"

"I'm down to twenty cents most days. More on some."

"I have no idea if that's a lot or a little. I've never shot it."

"It's a lot lower than it could be, but higher than it should be. If you did that much, you wouldn't sleep for two days," he confessed.

"I'm always here if you want to talk about it. Obviously, I don't judge on these things."

"I know you don't."

"But I also know how it ends up. Meth-induced psychosis is the worst thing. I mean, you'll end up deranged before your body gives up. I've talked to more than my fair share of people who were perma-fried."

"I know," he said, getting onto his side and propping his head against his hand. "You either burn up or burn out. And I'm hoping I burn out of it before I get anywhere near that point. In a lot of ways, I already am. You were telling me about this amazing sex adventure, and in the back of my mind I was just thinking, 'Yeah, I've heard it a dozen times.'"

"Yeah?"

He rested his free hand on my chest. Occasionally I could feel his fingers drum on me like they did on the dash of that old car.

"More or less. People come from all over the world to see sex fairs and leather events, and yet so many of them are blind. They either don't see the dealer in the background or are so naive as to pretend he doesn't exist. Sure, there are those saintly few, but they're the minority. Usually the ones cast out by our society. It's just too easy to blind a new guy with glitz and glamor—throw a porn star and a rig his way and send him to la la land."

"I'd hope you don't exploit people like that."

"I don't. I'm the guy they call when they get fucked up and need help. And I certainly couldn't exploit you like that. Hell, you're the first person I've ever run into that gets this kind of excitement without me."

"Funny," I laughed quietly, "I'm the guy they call when they want their hormones fixed because they already fucked them up to kingdom come."

"Ironic that I'm the junkie and you're so off on your estrogen you're a weeping willow."

"Yeah, funny how life works, isn't it?"

I positioned myself onto my side so I could look at him. Our hands clasped each other's. For that moment, we weren't alone.

"My biggest fear," he admitted, "is that one day I'll get so high I won't come back down."

I felt he wanted me to say, "My biggest fear is losing you." I felt he wanted me to hold onto him so he wouldn't slip away into darkness and never return. But there was no need for such words. I just held his hand tighter and he responded in kind.

"My hotel's on the other side of town but, if it's okay with you, I'd like to stay the night."

"I'd like that very much."

I got up to undress. My enthusiastic energy when I entered the room was completely replaced by a somber, sober quietness. Ryan also got undressed, then he shut off the music and turned down the lights. A soft glow from the street drifted in through the window, along with the sounds of a city that never slept. We got in bed and held each other closely in the night. We were at the edge of the world, in a small Victorian house, nestled in a thriving city. Quietly and peacefully, we surrendered to a dream-filled sleep.

Together.

FIFTEEN

ALWAYS RESPONSIBLE ME FORGOT to set my alarm. When my eyes drifted open they landed on Ryan, who was already dressed and working at his computer.

"I guess I'm going to be late," I said.

"Meh, like you've never been to a work convention before. You're welcome to a protein shake if you're in a hurry."

"Yeah, I could use one."

My sweaty gym clothes from the other night were washed and folded on the bed ready for me.

"Thanks for doing the laundry. I don't suppose you have something more appropriate for me to wear for work, would you?"

Ryan looked over at me and then went to his closet. He pulled out an old T-shirt. While he didn't have any pants that would fit me because of our height difference, the shirt at least looked better than my tank top. I tried it on and figured it'd at least be passable.

"At least it's Friday," I said, "so the rest of the weekend is fun time."

"Got any plans tonight?"

"Not really."

"Well, there's a bear dance party this evening. Bears by the Bay. There will be some good musclebears there. I'm sure you'll have fun, if I've guessed your type correctly."

He had. He was it.

"Yeah, that sounds great. When does it start?"

Ryan took his seat in front of the computer again. "Nine, but you don't want to be the first person there. Fashionably late is on time."

"Awesome. Maybe we can get dinner before?"

He looked at me for a moment. His eyebrows were flat above his still-tired eyes, and he was worn out. I had presumed he was asking me on a date.

"I have to do some things first. I'm not sure I'll be able to go myself."

"I really would like to see you there. It'd mean a lot to me. We haven't really gone out together, I mean, somewhere."

I watched him while the logistical part of his brain was churning, attempting to carve out some time in his day. His fingers drummed lightly on the keyboard in front of him. He had to make deliveries, pick-ups, and God knows whatever other errands someone of his lifestyle had to make.

He finally settled softly on his answer.

"Okay, I'll see what I can do. No promises I can make it though."

"Awesome!"

I finished styling my hair and gave him a kiss before heading out the door. I swung by the kitchen, searched for a few moments, then grabbed a protein shaker from above the refrigerator. After mixing the water and powder, I shook it. I watched the hydrolyzed whey product homogenize into some sort of palatable liquid so it could be ingested with minimal taste. Marginally successful in the mixing, I chugged it.

I licked the top of the lid to get the last drop of protein. I never left protein in the bottle. Those were future gains.

Afterward, I pulled out my phone and requested an Uber. While waiting, I took the time to admire the kitchen, not in a covetous way, but in an attempt to take in the full atmosphere and feeling. This must be where he cooked breakfast every morning. Or where he planned his grocery shopping or the needs of the house. A small table, worn by the sun, was off to the side. A standard chef's block and bowl mixer were on it. That could have been where he prepared his meals. The window had a small crack in it, though, given the climate of the area, I was sure it would not have made much of a difference in his utility costs. Finally, I noticed the chip in a part of the tile flooring near the stove. I guessed a heavy object, maybe a cast iron pot, had dropped and damaged it in just the same wrong way that makes toast land butter side down.

There were flaws, but they were beautiful flaws.

With a few minutes to spare, I headed down the stairs and out the garage to get my Uber.

The ride was uneventful and I arrived at the convention in better time than I had hoped. I was greeted by thousands of people carrying swag, badges, laptops, and all of the other accouterments that are standard for these places. I stood out as an oddball, having only my badge on me and wearing gym shorts. No fancy tech or tools, and I lacked the suit and trimmings that the executives had. I made a conscious effort, this being the last day, to go to as many training sessions as I could. I was forced to take notes on my phone, but at least it was something I could study later.

Building some sort of professional network (that didn't involve drugs) seemed useful. I followed the crowd, looking for people like me—or as close as I could find, given the venue.

I had the unique curse of standing out, regardless. During a discussion on network security policy, the point of "good" and "bad" guys came up. Malicious hackers versus vigilant IT staff. Large muscles, in a room full of twigs and fat middle-aged white guys, made me an easy target to peg as a "bad" guy. The analogy of digital security being like physical security was the context.

The speaker regaled us about a job he did for a bank where, after it was infiltrated by a group of hackers, they used it as a launch point for attacks on other organizations. All the while, they were unaware that they were doing so from within a bank that had hundreds of millions of dollars in it.

"This strategy will keep out most would-be attackers, and most attackers are not sophisticated in their attacks. They don't know they're in a bank, all they know is they own an IP address," the speaker went on. "And just as you wouldn't want a big brute like this gentleman," he gestured in my direction, "to show up and break things in a physical store, you wouldn't want a brute inside your corporate network. No offense, of course, sir!"

I didn't mind the comment. In fact, I kind of liked being referred to as a "brute." The image of being the proverbial bull in a china shop seemed quite attractive, actually.

I smiled and quietly mouthed, "None at all."

The speaker went on with his topic without public comment. This was an audience I could easily command, but chose not to. I decided in this particular case it was more fun to be in the middle of it and allow the speaker the full stage.

The rest of the sessions completed without issue. Many of the attendees voiced excitement about the closing party before I looked up the event poster for Bears by the Bay. It looked more like my kind of event.

I texted Ryan around four o'clock to let him know that I was free and looking for dinner plans. Ideally something low-key. I chatted with some of the remaining vendors who were packing up and getting ready to leave while I waited to hear back from Ryan. A few who were local suggested I check out the Haight if I wanted dinner plans outside of downtown. After twenty minutes and being among only a handful of people left, I decided to go out on my own.

I took an Uber over to Haight and Ashbury.

It took a while to get to, but seemed to fit the vibe I was looking for quite nicely—plenty of shops, but without the hustle and bustle of downtown or the apparent density and overt gayness of the Mission or Castro. There were no rainbow flags, but plenty of tie-dye. The smell of pot filled the air, though the sun was still firmly in the sky. I was surrounded by old-school liberals and hippies who refused to become baby boomers. The dreamers who never woke. The Haight was a small town in a huge city. Head shops, tattoo parlors that offered body suspension, and niche diners with inviting smells that overflowed into the street dotted the neighborhood. My overly casual but dark clothing looked wrong in the sea of Bob Marley and Che Guevara shirts. But I didn't feel unwelcome.

There was a genuine friendliness about the area. When I stuck my head into a random shop, I was welcomed sincerely, as if I were entering someone's home. Once inside, I was surprised that the rich colors of the city extended throughout each store as well. Tie-dye dresses filled shelves where each article was unique. Hand-stitched shirts elegantly filled the display cases.

"Each item is handmade, and a portion of our profits go to environmental sustainability," the shopkeeper mentioned.

I looked inside cases and across the racks. Prices were higher, but the quality better, than at home. Each item had a "Made in the USA" sticker attached to it.

After spending a few minutes browsing the racks, I selected a shirt which was more appropriate than the plain one Ryan leant me. It was Hawaiian–style, with rich yellow and purple plumeria flowers on it. The shopkeeper thanked me graciously as I paid cash.

"I'm from out of town. Any place good to grab something to eat?" I asked.

"Absolutely," he said, pointing the way. "Though you may want some entertainment first. Stop by that bookstore across the street. A hungry stomach makes for an open mind. Then try the diner on the corner."

"Sure, um, thanks! I'll give it a try," I replied.

I thought about how hungry I was as I crossed the street toward the bookstore. Some of the city's homeless were sitting on the corner holding signs, and I thought of the odd way the shopkeeper offered the suggestion of a book first. I decided to give it a go as he suggested. The store's sign indicated that it specialized in banned books and forbidden topics.

When I walked in, I saw an older gentleman with a harried professor look. He wore a plaid shirt and worn jeans. If someone told me he had read every title in the store, I would have believed them without question.

"Welcome, let me know if there's anything I can help you find. We sort the books by banned topic, generally, but there's a few that cross topics. If there's something in particular you need, I'd love to help you find it."

I glanced around the store. The organization was chaotic, but oddly sensical. Most of the titles I recognized were forbidden in various public schools or third world countries. While most bookstores have fiction, nonfiction, and biographical texts, this one had sections like "government coups," "human sexuality," "underground spirituality," and "crimes against the environment."

Many of the authors eluded me, but I wasn't a regular reader. My time was spent slurping up technical documents as fast as I could. The last time I picked up a book that wasn't in PDF format seemed to be a lifetime ago. Yet, I felt these books weren't the kind that I'd find through an online service or by buying a Nook or Kindle. They were bespoke texts, each one conveying unique ideas as one-of-a-kind as the shops in the city. They lacked the regurgitated sameness of the chain stores or formula romance novels I expected in a used bookstore. Instead, each volume represented a heretical idea about how the world should work, and the more antithetical a book was to another only brought them closer to each other on the shelves.

I wandered the aisles, examining the sections one at a time looking for my favorite flavor of heresy before giving up and asking the owner for help.

"Sure, um . . . Do you have anything on drugs?"

He didn't hesitate.

"Try the third shelf on the left wall."

I was pleasantly surprised that a section existed. The spines of the various volumes were new, or as close to new as I could have expected from such a boutique collection. I picked up and leafed through a few of them, where occasional highlights or circled words would show up. A few pot titles still lingered, though most of the volumes focused on the heavier drugs. Some dealt with the topic of drug use in accordance with religious rituals and the like. A few were biographical accounts of what I could only take to be terrible stories. A single copy of *The Secrets of Methamphetamine Manufacture* was present. Seeing it made me think of Ehren and how he was thinking of going into cooking. A brief smile ran across my face as I thought of how it could be both a great gag gift and a way to make a new business partner.

I stared at the titles for the longest time. Nothing seemed to fit me. Was I really the only one in the steroid game? Were there no bodybuilders willing and capable of writing books?

My frustration must have been visible, because the shop-keeper came over and asked, "Not finding what you're looking for?"

"Apparently not. I was hoping there were some titles related to anabolic steroids."

He gave me a once over. It was the genie that I couldn't put back into the bottle. The illusion of having muscles and looking like a model is fantastic, but whenever I let out the *S* word, I damned myself to being viewed like a construction. I anticipated the knowing look on his face that would show me that my humanity had been replaced with a golem fabricated entirely out of spare parts. I expected pure criticism or a comment like, "It figures." Instead, he just smiled and scanned the shelves with me.

It took him a moment, then he said, "That's because they aren't here."

"So nothing on the topic then, huh?"

"Well, I didn't say that. Come with me."

He led me over to a tiny corner of the store in a much larger queer and gender studies section, which focused on transgender identity.

"You might find favor with this one," he said, handing me a copy of *Testo Junkie* by Beatriz Preciado. "It has some good stories about personal use of steroids and the like. It focuses on the social and biological impacts of such use. I also have this one."

I followed him to another shelf, the section label on which was worn almost beyond reading. It was handwritten on faded paper. Most of the spines on the books were tattered, too. I assumed these were truly the forgotten titles—the black sheep among black sheep.

He selected a book. "This is a very used copy. It's been out of print for a while, but occasionally I find myself with a rare gem—a book that just needs the proper reader."

He handed me a paperback, much smaller than the first: *Underground Steroid Handbook* by Dan Duchaine.

"As you can see, it's more of a reference book than anything else. Not really a personal account, per se. Perhaps there's a few things you can learn from it."

I never felt so wonderful being in a bookstore before. The idea that I wasn't alone in my mad obsession to remake myself was powerful. Other people had taken the time to share their knowledge, and I was speechless with the realization. I truly felt like I was the reader these books needed to find. When he handed me the title, I held it with a certain degree of fear for hurting the knowledge I had been entrusted with.

"Or learn from both," I said meekly.

"Great! I'll ring them up."

We walked to the front counter where he pulled out an old-style invoice pad. He jotted down the titles and amounts on the ticket and I paid with cash. I was afraid to ask if he took credit cards. I thought it would somehow defeat the purpose to buy books on banned subjects through trackable electronic means. I walked out of the store satisfied that, somewhere out there, was a group of people like myself.

Ryan texted me as I ordered my ride home.

Sorry, was busy. Still going to BbtB?

Yeah, though, what should I wear?

Get a leather harness yet?

Nope.

**Fuck, well, you can borrow
one of mine if you can make
it here. We'll take you to
Mr. S later.**

Cool, I'll head over.

When I got back to Ryan's, I entered his room quietly. Inside was a small gaggle of gays. Three of them. Each was young, chatty, and held in some trance by Ryan and his mystique. So much so they didn't notice my entrance. Ryan was holding court, dynamically talking with his hands. When he moved or talked, the other three got quiet. A glass pipe was circling among them, though when it was offered to Ryan, he just passed it on to the next without missing a beat in his story. They were all clothed. It was a casual, and non-sexual, affair.

"Hey, look who's here! How's it going?" Ryan asked shortly after I entered. He squeezed by his guests to hug me. We kissed lightly on the lips, in that polite gentle way that gay men like to do. The pipe was offered to me, but I declined.

"Sorry it took so long," I said, offering my newly purchased items for inspection. "I was in the Haight. Bought some books and stuff."

"Very fun! I like the new shirt! I'm glad you're getting to see the city."

One of the guests looked at my haul. The Duchaine book on steroids was the most prevalent. His mind, accelerated by the meth, jumped directly to a conclusion I hadn't understood. His jaw dropped.

"Holy shit! You're Oklahoma!"

"Uh, I'm from there, yeah," I said dumbly. I had no idea who he was or what else he knew about me.

"Is this really him?" he asked Ryan, almost in awe.

"Yeah, Zach, that's him," he said with a smile.

"Fuck me! Seriously, how much do I have to get to look like him?"

I laughed. The idea that someone just pumps their body full of steroids and gets to look like me without serious work was comical. And yet, I got asked that question all the time. It was exhausting. The fact was, he was trying to both ask a serious question and give a compliment. The only way I have found to deal with such a socially awkward predicament was to laugh.

Ryan stepped in. "Told you he has good stuff. He'll be a real crowd killer tonight."

"Yeah, where's he going?" a second asked.

"Bears by the Bay. He's just here to borrow a spare harness."

Not wanting to miss the opportunity to show off, I stripped off my newly purchased shirt. Zach and the guys each gave a "wow" while Ryan pulled a wad of leather out of his closet. It was his bulldog harness. As I put my clothing and books down on the bed, Ryan untangled the leather and helped me into it by undoing one of the straps. I put it on like a winter jacket. Zach started massaging my abs and I smiled at him flirtatiously as if to say, "Yeah, I know you want it."

"Now, come on, you could just stay with us instead," one of them said. Ryan started fitting the harness tightly to my chest in an effort to make my pecs pop, adjusting each buckle one at a time.

"I'd love to, gents, but I really do wanna see how you California guys like to party."

As if on cue, they all looked at the pipe then back at me and laughed.

Zach finally said, "So, how does this work? Can I just pay you for stuff now, or—"

Ryan cut him off. "Everything goes through me, guys. You know the prices."

Suddenly, the three tweakers pulled out their wallets and started counting cash. I looked at Ryan in awe. Ryan looked back, smiled, and said nothing.

"What's the lead time?" Zach asked.

"For smaller orders, I can get you started right away. What would you say, Oklahoma? Three weeks?" Ryan deferred.

"Sure," I said with no actual confidence behind the answer, really hoping that by "smaller orders" he meant bottles and not barrels. I wasn't Costco.

The guys threw wads of money on the bed. Ryan nudged me out the door of his room where we spoke quietly in the hall.

"You're amazing. I really hope you like the party," he said.

"Holy shit, that's a lot of cash. How much do they want?" I exclaimed quietly.

"We'll figure it out. Anything you can't do I can source somewhere else and put your label on it. I'll try to make it to the party tonight, but I have a few other people I need to meet up with still and I can't make promises."

It felt like the "family" part of "family business." I wasn't sure if he was calling me amazing because of my look or my ability to sell stuff for him. As he ran his hands across the leather on my chest, I thought about the pride he must take in his work of making me look good, and I felt a similar pride in helping him close a few sales. Perhaps we were both just using each other, but it felt so right.

"I kind of like being called Oklahoma."

"Well, you know what they say: Never divulge a source. They don't know your real name and they don't need to. I'll take care of your books and such. Just go out and have fun tonight."

We looked at each other in the eyes. Until that point in my life, anyone who looked at me saw either an IT nerd in a husk of a body or a dumb slab of muscle. Ryan saw past both. I honestly felt he saw the person who wanted to define himself by his own means, whatever they may be. I wanted to see him later more than anything, and to enjoy a night in the city with him. No one had ever given me the gift of being mysterious before. It was something I treasured.

I kissed Ryan goodbye and put my shirt back on as I ran downstairs.

SIXTEEN

THE UBER DRIVER DROPPED me off in SOMA near the bar. As I approached, I saw a line had already formed and could hear the music pound from outside the club. There's a party for everyone in San Francisco, and in my mind, this particular party was for me. The guys were all masculine (or hyper-masculine) and eager to latch onto the largest source of man-meat they could find. Having had the affirmation of my previous encounter, I took my role as a dealer in such things quite literally.

I may have been wearing a harness, but at this convention, I was the suit.

Still, being from out of town and relatively unknown meant paying full price for admission. After paying the cover and walking inside, I found myself in front of a giant dance floor.

The scene was more than I could have hoped for.

Two floors of thumping progressive house music filled the spaces where light did not. What I took to be an abandoned warehouse on the outside was completely outfitted as a recreation hall on the inside, complete with DJ booth, dancing stage, and a light show that I could only dream of. The bartenders were more delicious than a forty-dollar buffet, and I would have gladly eaten my dinner off of them given the opportunity.

Moreover, the other attendees were all incredibly attractive—bearded, rugged, most of them muscular or otherwise brawny, and all nearly naked. This was exactly what I had pictured a proper party should be and unlike what home offered. Harnesses were all around, and some even glowed in the dark. The strong scent of man permeated the space.

"This must be why gay men travel so much," I thought. "They are chasing this exact moment from city to city."

I stopped by the bar and got in line to order my favorite drink, a sugar-free Red Bull and vodka.

An intriguing sign behind the bartender read, "No Nudity on the First Floor," which begged the question, "What can I do on the second?" I was curious to find out.

While waiting in line, I noticed my ass was getting played with. Instead of turning around and confronting the man, I let it happen. What better way to advertise than to let people get their hands on the product?

After grabbing my drink, I waited for my molester to order his. He was attractive as well, a bit more otter than I normally went for, but a guy who looked like he was up to no good. He had dark captivating eyes, and slicked back hair, and wore a collar around his neck. He didn't appear to be with anyone, so I presumed the collar indicated a look and style more than a relationship status.

After he got his order, I grabbed him by the arm and led him to the dance floor. The beat pounded away with my heart. I was fueled by whatever was left over in the air of Ryan's bedroom and tempered by my favorite beverage. In record time we had our drinks devoured, glasses disposed of, and hands all over each other. After making out for a few minutes we parted ways, disappearing into different sections of the club, never to see each other again.

That dance of meeting, making out, and parting ways repeated like the house music that was being played—all chorus, with no definite start or end. Both musical and social themes repeated for what seemed to be a good two hours.

After having worked a sufficient amount of the first floor and feeling I'd exhausted the pond of its fish, I retreated to the stairs. A nearby sign read, "Clothing check, $3." I wasn't wearing a coat and figured no one else would be either. A guy at the front of the line stripped down to just a jockstrap and his harness, and I got in line behind him. I tried to remember how stylish my underwear were. I wasn't wearing a pair of the fashionable brands that were popular at the time, like Nasty Pig or Andrew Christian, but on my body they still looked good. I determined them passable at least. They were no jockstrap, athletic or fetish, but a mainstream pair of men's bikini briefs, which beautifully straddled the line between gay and straight men's fashion.

Three dollars got me a cheap plastic bag, a claim ticket I stuffed in my shoe, and a show for those waiting in line behind me. My shorts, shirt, shoes, and phone, were all checked with the bag and left with the attendant.

Where downstairs was Gomorrah, upstairs was Sodom. Indeed, there was plenty of sodomy going about. The music, set to a more intense beat, filled the room. The crowd raged with it. Activities ranged from the routine handsy make-out sessions all the way to group fucking. Bodies in small groups heaved with the music and sweat filled the air. The room was cast in a dark hue of red, much like Ryan's room was earlier, but flashing brightly in such a way as to make continuous motion imperceptible.

I saw Ryan's possessed demonic eyes in some of the other partygoers, and it was easy for me to tell by look and smell who dabbled with chemistry. The DJ, a beautifully built tall Latino man, was slaying the crowd. His face was overcome with the look of sadistic pleasure as he matched the tempo of the beat with the sexual thralls of the dancers. He was so attractive in my eyes that I felt disappointed he wasn't in the mix as well.

It took a few minutes to work my way into the middle of the dance floor, being tossed to and fro with the pulse of the music. Interactions ranging from kissing to groping were more transient than downstairs, and lasted only a few seconds in some cases. Eventually, I was enveloped in the collective body heat of the group. Then my dick was removed from my underwear.

Seconds later, I was getting sucked off by a thirsty fag. He was a little older than my usual type, late thirties perhaps, but he was in it to win it. He sucked cock with an enthusiasm that too many of the individuals I trained in the gym lacked. He strove for depth on each pulse of the music. In no time at all, my flag was raised to full staff.

Being just as fluid as the downstairs interactions were, upstairs was standing room only and impossible to stay attached to one person for too long. I felt as though my dick got handed around from person to person, and occasionally inserted into a hot sweaty hole whenever the opportunity arose. I caught myself making out and fucking to the music, almost organically, and the more I thought about it the less I wanted to. My cerebral cortex shut down and I moved on instinct alone. I purged my mind of all thoughts but one.

I'm getting exactly what I want.

I couldn't avoid focusing on the chem guys. They were the hungriest. The red lights made it impossible to ignore their demons. I guessed a third of them were possessed by some drug or another. The collective body heat from both floors made the room hotter than a sauna.

The heat eventually broke me and I had to go out and get some air. I swam the sea of people, moving to the beat to take advantage of their natural sways, and found myself on a small landing overlooking the first floor.

A small group of otters were also resting and recuperating from their sexual escapades, bottles of water in hand.

"This is great!" one of them said to me. I smiled and agreed.

I was exhausted, sweating and drained from all the dancing and fucking. I borrowed a bit of water from him and then turned to overlook the first floor. I had never seen anything like this party. It was beautiful and unapologetically human. Moreover, *it was mine.*

I began to feel a terrible longing to share this feeling with someone.

I went back downstairs to the coat check area and grabbed my things. I went to text Ryan before I put on my clothes, but he'd already texted me.

I'm here.

I looked around. Unable to spot him, I climbed halfway up the stairs to gain a better vantage point. The lights flashed with the beat, and I took advantage of the heavy bass to locate him. Finally, there he was. He didn't have a drink in his hand, and instead of dancing, appeared to be looking around for me, using his hands to shield his eyes from the overbearing pulse of the lights.

"Ryan!" I called. He couldn't hear me from the crowd.

I descended the staircase, pushing bears, otters, and other wildlife off to the side in a mad rush for him. I was madly, hopelessly, and foolishly in love. As the gay waters parted, there at the end, was Ryan. And when he saw me, he smiled.

"I'm glad you're still here!" he screamed in my ear above the music.

"I was just upstairs."

"What'd you think?" he asked, though he didn't need to. He knew exactly what went on upstairs and how I felt about it.

"It was amazing!"

"I know."

He pointed over to a sign that I had failed to notice previously: "Leather required for upstairs entry."

I looked back toward him. He smiled and touched my face with his hands. I wanted to say, "Thank you for letting me borrow the harness." I felt he wanted to say, "You're welcome," but we didn't need to exchange the words. We both were in each other's minds.

He broke the romantic silence first. "I have something for you, Chris, but you have to come to the bathroom."

"Okay."

I followed him over to the bathroom. A fairly sizable line was ahead of us, but it was moving quickly. It was far enough away from the madness of the dance floor and the busyness of the bar that, while we couldn't talk in complete privacy, we could at least hear each other speak without screaming. I began putting the rest of my clothes back on as we were in line.

"This is yours, though I suggest we get out of here soon," he said as he passed me an envelope. It was sealed but padded full. I didn't need to open it to know it contained a shitload of cash.

"Goddamn, Ryan! What's this for?" I quietly screamed, trying to prevent others from hearing.

"It's for the orders you have waiting in your inbox. Double-check my math, of course. I rounded down to the nearest hundred. The guys really want your stuff bad. I hope you can fill it all. It's not too exotic."

I pocketed the envelope as far down as I could to make it harder to pick my pocket.

I looked back at him. This man. This impossible man. He gave me his entire world and paid me for the privilege.

"Why?" I asked.

"Because you sell it. Look at you, you're amazing."

"No, I don't mean *how*. I mean why?"

"It's what I do well. My curse, remember? Don't get me wrong. I'm marking this shit way the fuck up! You made my rent for a few months and in San Francisco, that's not bad at all!"

We reached the bathroom and I went in, stood in front of the urinal, and pretended to take a piss while staring dumbfounded at a white wall.

I learned a long time ago to never fall in love with your dealer. It's the first lesson you learn as a drug user. The guy selling you crack isn't there to be your friend. If he asks you to suck his dick, it's because he's trying to make sure you're not a cop. But there weren't any rules for when it's the dealer of *your* drugs.

Ryan was living on the lam. I had more money in my pocket than I ventured many on that dance floor made in a month. At any moment, Ryan's dominoes could come tumbling down. What would happen when he got caught? Or didn't make rent one month? Being a drug dealer is great when you're surrounded by stability, but that stability is largely in place by not being a drug dealer. Bad decisions, like good ones, take a while to mature into results.

Was it just business between us? Was it just a chance encounter and a random occurrence that we happened to meet? Did he just get on gay apps looking for clandestine opportunities? He was from the world that invented Twitter and Facebook, but was Grindr his personal version of LinkedIn? It couldn't be.

I had never thought of myself as a drug manufacturer and certainly not as a poster boy for steroid use, despite my seventeen-inch arms, model chin, and vascularity only bodybuilders and IV drug users could admire. How had I suddenly become an integral part of the circuit party scene with a man I had only met a few days ago?

Did he love me, too?

I flushed, my mind still racing. I washed my hands, as did Ryan next to me. We looked at each other in the mirror and both grinned. He followed me out and put his hand on the small of my back. It was not a gesture I was used to.

"Let's get out of here," he said.

"Did you really pay a cover charge to get into a club just to drop off an envelope?"

Ryan paused, which made me pause as well. He leaned into my ear and kissed me on the cheek.

"You really think I pay cover charges to get into places like this?" he muttered.

I looked him straight in the eyes. He smiled and I cried. Not a lot, just a little. I was so helpless, drowning in a sea of people and drugs, money and adventure, mysterious places and shady characters. He was at the center of it all—a man who was burning his candle from both ends, who knew his time was short, yet wanted to share his light with me before it was extinguished. He had the whole city on strings and plucked any one I wanted just so I could hear the music.

"Could we . . . Could we dance? Just for a bit. Together?"

"Sure. But just for a bit."

He led me back toward the dance floor. I was surrounded by countless masculine men and full of more testosterone than most guys will make in their lifetimes, but I never felt more like Cinderella at the ball. We were the life of the party. And the death. One of us was losing his heart while the other was losing his soul.

Both our candles burning brighter than the sun.

SEVENTEEN

THE PARTY WASN'T DONE, though we both were. Ryan signaled it was time, and I felt my Prince Charming's urgency to leave. He had other business to attend to and I wasn't going to have any fun without him. He gave me more than just the night. He also gave me a sense of adventure, and I needed to follow him. We both went outside. I dried my tears off my face, still unsure if they were of happiness or sadness.

"How'd you get here?" I asked.

"I had someone drop me off."

"Need me to hail an Uber? Work's paying for them all."

He looked over and grinned. "You've been getting free rides all this time? No wonder you use Uber so much!"

I pulled out my phone and started hailing a ride. "Cheaper than a rental car or taxi, so work's thrilled. And they can't tell the difference between going Uber Black and Lyft Line. Going back to your place?"

The toll on Ryan was becoming quite visible. His eyes were drained, with deep black bags under them. He looked like he hadn't slept in days. He gestured briefly toward his pocket. "Yes, but I have a few deliveries I need to make. Unexpected orders."

"When was the last time you slept?" I asked, concerned.

"Hard to say. I get little naps in, but probably five or six days since I've had a full night."

"Wow, okay. Well, do you want me to come with you? I don't want you to be on your own."

"No, it'd be best if not. This crowd is particularly intense. Plus, I know you don't like Rick, and this is all of his friends. If it gets too bad, I'll just crash at home before making this run."

Reality tumbled down on my most romantic evening.

"I understand."

"What are you doing tomorrow?" he asked. "Last full day of freedom?"

"Yeah, I fly back Sunday right after the fair. Actually, I don't even think I can see the fair for too long."

Ryan was depleted. His breathing was starting to whistle due to the extreme dehydration he was undergoing.

"How about this: I'll take you to the leather store tomorrow and we'll pick something out. It'll need to be after noon or so. I do actually need to sleep some. Fuck, I'm the last person who gets what they need. There's a party tomorrow night, which I'm sure you'll love. It's a few older guys, very laid back and chill. I told them you were in town and I figured you wouldn't mind."

"You inviting me on a date?" I asked hopefully.

He seemed too exhausted to be romantic, his voice more matter of fact than anything else.

"Just a party. There'll be some play, of course. But if that's what you call a date, then I suppose so."

"Then I gladly accept."

Our ride arrived.

We both got in the back seat and rode away from the night that was still raging on. Bars were still packed with all sorts of patrons. I told the driver we had two separate destinations, and she said it wouldn't be a problem.

I turned my gaze back to Ryan. His eyes were staring at the stars, or rather, where the stars would have been if the city wasn't full of nightlife. The haze of the city seemed to make everything in the night sky but the nearest planets a wash. I could almost see a younger version of him riding in the back seat of his parents' car somewhere in rural Nebraska. I imagined him sitting in the bed of a pick-up truck, woefully upset about being stuck in the middle of nowhere. I could see him railing about how they couldn't even get pizza delivery in his hometown while the Internet revolution was happening, only to leave for the big city on his own.

In my mind, the older him longed for the simpler life he left behind, which he'd replaced with his current dimming existence. Somewhere, inside, he hated it. But hating something and being good at it aren't guaranteed to go together.

I reached over and touched his hand. He glanced downward at mine, then up back toward my face.

"How many people come out for Dore?" I asked.

"I don't know. Thousands?"

"What do you think they come for?"

He thought about it for a moment. "To meet people, I'd reckon."

Reckon. Such a delightfully Midwestern word. I hadn't heard him use words like that before.

"I think they come for us," I suggested.

"Us?"

"Yes. Confidence and happiness."

He looked over to the driver. She was zoned out, navigating the weekend's traffic up and down the hills.

He smiled. "Maybe so."

San Francisco was ours. Even if just for that week, it was all fucking ours. We had become one of the city's major institutions. We didn't sell our happiness or confidence to high school kids, nor did we push it on the weak-minded. We were both moral in our own ways. I had seen him interact with his users like I did with my trainees. We both treated drugs as a prescription to a problem, a means to an end. But we were also the people you called when you needed something.

After all, who do you trust? I knew he didn't have another hookup for steroids. Not one he could put a face to, at least. If he was buying from someone else, then he was doing so from some random guy on the Internet or overseas somewhere. I felt he wanted out of the meth game, but I had no idea how far into it he was. Certainly it was deep, deep enough to scare me. It was eating him alive.

The driver dropped him off first. He leaned over and kissed me before leaving.

"See you tomorrow?"

"Bet your life on it," I said.

I watched him W-O-O-F himself in. I didn't break my gaze from the house until it dropped out of the distance.

"You got it bad, man," the driver said looking at me in the rearview mirror.

"You can tell, huh?" I said, looking back at her.

"Oh, yeah. Going to a hotel I see. Long distance romance?"

"Something like that," I responded.

"Well, hopefully it won't always be that way," she said optimistically.

"May be the only way it'll work. You can't expect a ring from one like him."

She chuckled. "You made my night, deary. You made my night."

"He's like fire and ice that one," I explained. "More ice than fire some days. Beautiful to look at, but he'll get out of hand and burn me one day."

"Well, hopefully your burns don't scar," she said as we pulled up to my hotel.

I thanked her for her words and the lift, then exited the car. I made my way lazily to my hotel room. My bags, still mostly packed from my arrival, were sitting on the floor. The bed my work paid for was largely unslept in. Parc 55 was a luxury hotel, and so many of the city's homeless would have killed for a single night's stay indoors. Yet I hadn't spent much time in the hotel at all.

I got into bed. It was much nicer than Ryan's, with bedding that was quite fluffier. The room had a beautiful view of the city's downtown. The only sound was the faint mechanical humming of air conditioning in the background. I was surrounded by every creature comfort I could hope for, down to a room service menu on the desk. Yet I was overcome with sadness. I would have gladly traded all of it for another night next to Ryan in his small room.

One final night was all that was left.

The sands of time were slipping through my fingers.

EIGHTEEN

WOKE UP LATE AND just stared at the ceiling, reminiscing about the previous night's events. Most of all, I thought of Ryan. I was excited for our day together and the leather store. As much as I wanted to pester him, I knew he would be exhausted. I needed to let him sleep a bit more.

I lazily got up and brushed my teeth, staring at my unkempt self in the mirror while the shower ran. I was tired, but not to the hellish degree Ryan was the other night. My eyes still had sleep in them, though lacked the extreme dehydration I had expected. My beard was coming in thick and fast (a side benefit of testosterone usage) and desperately needed a trim. My naturally oily hair retained an element of bar smell. I had a funk about me, not in that super-hot man-smell kind of way, but in that I-need-to-take-care-of-myself-better kind of way.

I rinsed and properly scrubbed. After my shower, I reviewed my itinerary. It was Saturday morning and the fair was Sunday around noon. My flight left around 4:00 p.m., which left only enough time to enjoy an hour or so of the fair. No matter. Who cared about a damned fair when I had a wonderful man waiting for me in this city?

I texted Ryan. Just to let him know I was up.

While I waited for a reply, I leafed through the hotel tourist guide: Alcatraz, Golden Gate, the art museum, countless dining tours, and the iconic cable cars. They all seemed fun, but way too mainstream. Any one of those events would have been great to pass time with, but I didn't want to pass time as much as invest it. I had to drain every drop of beauty out of the city before I left. Plus, it was the weekend! Every bar gets busy on weekends, but the inner socialite in me craved being at the right party. And I was sure Ryan wasn't going to let me down.

I called him. I figured he was likely up by then. I wasn't mistaken.

"Just finishing up breakfast," he said when I asked what he was up to. "How about yourself?"

"Ready to check out Mr. S if you are."

"Yeah, how about you meet me there?"

"Sure, does half an hour work for you?" I replied.

"Yeah, I'll be there."

I hung up the phone and quickly finished dressing and grooming. Once outside, the morning sun was bright even though an intense fog engulfed the city. The air was brisk yet energizing. Cars were humming along, and it seemed traffic didn't really care if it was the weekend or not.

The walls of the buildings gave away that San Francisco was real. Worn concrete and gum on the sidewalks were beautiful to me because they were so authentic. Oklahoma City's downtown was only used for nightlife and it lacked tiny necessities like barber shops and pharmacies. Musicians here played the streets because they were hungry, not because they were hired by an event planning firm. As I turned a corner, I saw some spray paint tagging on the side of the alleyway. It read, "Graffiti is just art they don't want you to see."

The homeless people were as ubiquitous as the fog. Tent cities were all around, and indigent people were passed out in the shade of mighty skyscrapers. Their faces were absent perceivable emotion, and even lacked the smiles that I had noticed when I first arrived. As I walked by, I wished them dreams more pleasant than their waking realities.

Not all were asleep, though. Plenty of the obviously homeless had gone mad. Many muttered to themselves, expressing multitudes of emotions within single incomprehensible sentences. I could see a few rocking back and forth, a common sign of heroin abuse, or manically rearranging worthless trash near their hovels of cardboard. Some panhandled for change outside of luxury stores, where shoppers did their best to ignore them as they bought high-priced imported items.

The buildings got smaller and smaller as I approached the outer portion of the downtown area. I was still deep in the heart of the city, but any glimmer of prosperity was behind me. A small unassuming retail sign indicated the leather store ahead of me. A line of hundreds of guys waited in queue. Could this place really be worth the wait?

My heart felt lighter at my first glance of Ryan in line. He had beaten me there and, fortunately, was already toward the front. He was wearing aviator sunglasses, shorts, and a long-sleeve thermal. His outfit looked peculiar on him, more concealing than a man with his beauty would normally select, but he seemed comfortable.

"Hey!" I said as I tapped him on the shoulder.

"Oh, hey!"

We kissed, in that nonchalant "We're both gay men and it's totally not romantic" kind of way. It felt appropriate given the venue.

"This is where all the leather comes from," Ryan explained, waving his hands at the store.

"I figured. Are they usually this busy?"

"On Saturday during the fair, absolutely. Though, sadly, it's one of those things you'll have to pay full price at. I curry no favor here."

I got the gist of what he was saying. No amount of little baggies was going to get us VIP treatment at an establishment like this. I took in the atmosphere. A group of leather daddies and sirs were in front of the store. True to life, they looked like they were ripped out of Tom of Finland's artwork. I saw so many happy faces leave the place, oftentimes in groups of two or three.

Everyone had a sizable shopping bag. People of all builds and personalities were in line, all with the machismo and force of personality commensurate with attending a sex fair. It wasn't for the faint of heart. But this was more than a leather sex store—it was a microcosm of the city and a nexus of activity. It was a social event, as well attended as any nightclub could hope for during the evening.

But unlike at the mall or similar stores, the sound of people getting flogged emanated from inside.

"So, do you know what colors you want?" Ryan asked.

"Colors?"

"Like, which colors you flag? You know the leather hanky codes, right?"

In times gone by, gay men used to use colors to signal what they were into. I didn't know all of the codes, but I was familiar with the common ones. I relied on things like apps to broadcast my tastes more than antiquated charts.

"Yeah, I know most of the big ones. Blue and white are for lame guys, just fucking and jacking off. Yellow is piss play, that's obvious. Green is—"

Ryan interjected. "There's several greens, actually."

I was stumped. I knew there was a list somewhere, but I couldn't remember them all.

"It means you like daddies."

A young twink behind us chimed in. His lisp was overpowering and his voice was filled with contempt. He seemed to delight in proving he knew something we didn't.

We both turned around to face him. Ryan tugged down his sunglasses and exposed his tired eyes. Eyes that were too tired to be corrected at this time in the morning. The kid had all the markings of a tourist. He was wearing a rainbow flag shirt and pink flip flops, both available for purchase from any window in any store in any town on the gay strip. He was openly effeminate, with a twist of his wrists that, if left to their own devices, likely doubled as nunchucks at a drag show.

Every inch of him said, "I'm a fag who loves musicals." He couldn't have been older than nineteen, and was as barefaced as someone much younger. Ryan and I gave an understanding look to each other. We both concluded that the kid was too ignorant to understand life. He likely couldn't comprehend how to use half of the sex toys in this store, and his intrusion into our conversation wasn't welcome. Smugness was not something Ryan or I found enchanting. Moreover, even in his exhausted state, Ryan could bench this kid two dozen times on the street and call it a warm-up.

"It does! That's right!" A loud, over-exaggerated and sarcastic Ryan chanted. His hands waved in the air to draw attention to himself before he reached into his back pocket. I saw the orange cap of an insulin syringe back there. Without removing the syringe, he popped the orange cap off and showed it to our interloper.

"Thank you, I nearly forgot! Maybe you can tell me what this means, too?"

The poor boy was in over his depth. He stared at it for a minute, not sure what he was even looking at. "Orange means you're into everything. I know my colors."

"Yeah," said Ryan. "Something like that."

He threw the cap on the ground and turned to face forward. A few older guys ahead of us saw what happened, got eerily quiet, and backed away. What this young pup seemed to miss was obvious to them. When someone is that brazen and experienced ahead of you, three times your size, and possibly under the influence, the best course of action is to shut your fucking mouth.

"Be my guest, sirs," one of the gruff older guys ahead of us said. The line was progressing forward, and he yielded his spot for us to cut ahead. He seemed confident and assertive but didn't want to be caught near a short-tempered meth head. Putting some space between us and this kid was a wise way to avoid trouble.

"Thank you, dear," Ryan said politely, pulling me by the hand into the store. As the line disappeared from view, the last I saw of the confused twink was the older gentleman explaining that he shouldn't play sir or teacher when he has much to learn himself.

After we were fully in the store, Ryan apologized.

"I'm sorry about that. I *really* hate 'Internet gays.' These queens are taking over the entire weekend. It's like these guys think they can read a color chart and understand what half my life means."

I laughed. "Oh, I get it. He may know his colors but he needs to work on his shapes."

Ryan tried to change the topic. He took me to the back section reserved for harnesses and began leafing through the racks.

"So, let's get you into your first harness! I'm thinking a bull dog or a cross over would be the best. It'll make your chest pop more. Orange isn't quite you, so perhaps we stick with something more conservative. We can let your muscles do the talking. You don't need a bunch of color to distract."

"Can't go wrong with black on black."

"Exactly. I was thinking the same thing."

All around me, men were getting naked as they tried on items. I looked at the price tags on some of the pieces. Basic harnesses started around $250. I didn't think of the price as bad, especially given my recent windfall and the obvious quality presented, but as I listened in to the crowd, I could tell others were pooling their money. Some were in groups and occasionally mentioned that they owned similar pieces or would let their friends borrow them to save cash. The few veteran shoppers who knew the layout of the store already wore significant pieces and were generally in their mid-thirties or older. It was quite the contrast to the younger twink or beginner title holder which seemed to dot the space.

I looked at the models in the pictures. Ryan and I looked better than most of them, given my bias for muscle, of course. I smiled when I saw Richard Steele's picture among them.

"What else are we getting?" I asked.

"Anything you want."

We tried on everything. Leather shirts. Hats. Pants. Vests. Body suspension suits. Athletic gear. Jockstraps. He picked most of the items, and I liked the same ones he did. The only reason I didn't ask for prices on the sex furniture was because packing it on the plane would have been a bitch.

And they had a helluva selection, some much more intense than I cared for. Dildos as big as my leg, fuck machines, floggers and paddles, and electro play. They even had a few chemistry items I took interest in (mostly centered around hot/cold/ and numbing sensations). The creativity of sexual deviants was overwhelming, and I could feel gears turn in my head as I was exposed to new concepts.

"J-Lube? Powder to make your own lube?" I said questioningly. "I wonder what I could add to the formula when I compound it?"

Ryan's ears perked up. "Woof! Now we're talking!"

It was an amazing shopping date, and I enjoyed being Ryan's Ken doll. Price didn't matter. I just wanted to look good for him. About $1,200 later we danced out of the store, our bags fuller than most, and jotted down the street.

"So, what did you think?" he asked.

"I think that was the most fun I've had shopping in a long time."

"Told you it was great. There's a BDSM-themed coffee shop on the way back to my place if you want to peek in."

"How could I say no to an offer like that?"

Wicked Grounds was its name, going by its modest but well-crafted signage. We peaked in without entering. Some of the patrons were drinking out of doggy bowls while others gave flogging demonstrations.

I laughed. "It's more surreal than sexual to me. Back home, I can't even get a smoothie from 7-Eleven without a shirt on."

We continued walking down the street.

"I know, right? Welcome to San Francisco," he shouted to the world. In the distance, unseen by the eye, his call was responded to with a "woo-hoo" and light cheering.

"You really like it here that much, don't you?"

"Of course I do! It's my city!"

I felt scared of the answer but had to ask him.

"Would you ever consider going back home? Or getting back into IT? I mean, I know you have the skills. You were great at what you did. And I could get you hired in no time at all."

"No, it's not for me."

"And dealing is?" I asked cautiously.

We paused walking for a bit. He thought for a while. He looked pensive, not in the way that he did when evaluating new thoughts, but the way he did when he was trying to explain something he understood well. He didn't need to drum his fingers at all.

"Why do you coach people in sport?" he asked.

"Because I can make a difference."

"That's why I do what I do. Nothing in IT matters, you know that. Every line of code you will ever write, every server you will rack, and every user you will ever educate means nothing. All will be deleted, overwritten, or replaced in time. If it's still around after that, then it's considered legacy and a liability, and that means holding up whatever progress people need now. I prefer working with people. I live for the here and now."

I liked his answer. Perhaps too much. It was hard for me to advocate getting into an industry that I myself hated, even if I was good at it. The fact he was just as skilled meant as little to him as it did to me. I did love working with Ryan, too, and thought fondly of doing so on an aboveboard project. Something that wasn't illegal sounded like an adventure worth pursuing.

Before I could continue my thought, his phone vibrated.

Business.

"Wow, they really are early this morning," he said.

"Duty calls?"

"Yeah. After the fair things will calm down, and I am so ready for it. You're welcome to come back to my place for a bit. I have to get a lot done tonight if we're going to make the party, but there's enough time to hang out if you want."

"Sure."

As we walked back toward Ryan's house, our philosophy discussion continued.

"I bet you're measured on how many trouble tickets you close, aren't you?" he asked.

"That's one of the things, sure."

"Don't you think that's like measuring the value of a spouse by how much laundry they do? Sure, it's a nice thing to have, but wouldn't you rather have something meaningful instead?"

"Like what?" I asked.

"Like how many times you need to change clothes to go to once-in-a-lifetime events? I mean, if your goal is to feed the machine that is your laundry, then be my guest, but I'd rather sample all of life and throw away a shirt or two to keep going."

Maybe he made sense because I lived in the same rut that he did. The IT industry felt like a sausage factory sometimes. The big dreamers like him never sat in front of a terminal and churned through e-mail. Inventors belonged in the lab, not attached to digital leashes. Professionally speaking, IT killed souls. It killed his for damned sure, and was wearing on mine. Still, a 401(k) certainly sounded a lot better than any sort of retirement plan he had in the works. And I worried for him.

As we turned into his neighborhood, surrounded by the familiar houses in the Mission, I agreed with him.

"I suppose you're right. You know who you remind me of sometimes? The way you talk? The caterpillar from Alice in Wonderland."

He smiled and sang lightly. "I like that. 'One pill makes you larger, and one pill makes you small.'"

When we got back to Ryan's room it looked like a circus had been there the previous night, complete with rampaging elephants. He'd been busy since I had last been there, doing what I wasn't sure. Things that were previously on shelves were now on the floor. The bedding was almost completely off the bed. Glasses and dishware were everywhere.

A set of tools I recognized from the garage was on the headboard, and a few bottles of lube I didn't recognize were around as well. It looked like an arts and crafts night had coincided with a sexual romp.

"Oh, yeah, pardon the mess. Had a few people over yesterday as you can see."

"It's fine. Hey, do you still have those books and my shirt?"

"Yeah, over there in the corner."

I gathered my things neatly, almost as if to force the rest of the room into order. I took my place on the bed and tried to stay out of his way as best as I could. Ryan began picking things up, starting near his computer desk.

After he had the largest things organized, he pulled out a small zip-up organizer, the kind usually reserved for pencils and school supplies. Inside it, instead of the normal paper pad and pen was a collection of insulin syringes and a baggie of meth as large as a Kennedy dollar. He pulled out a tiny scale and a set of tiny baggies and began portioning it out. I opened the Duchaine book and started giving it my first read.

After a while, he interrupted my reading.

"There's something I think you should know," he blurted.

"Oh?"

"Yeah. You've given me quite a bit of advice about your business, and I think it's only appropriate that I share something with you about mine."

I laughed. "Well, I appreciate it, but I'm not interested in a profession change."

"No, I mean as far as keeping your stuff safe."

"Yeah?" I responded, confused.

"Yeah. Obviously, with my stuff the markup is in piecing it out. Acquiring it has a fixed risk cost. People who sell typically buy in bulk and sell in smaller, higher-priced portions. Like, a lot. So, whenever someone says they need something, I always show them this organizer and they can watch me portion out their cut of an 8-ball, or whatever. The thing is, if I fall out or am not around and my shit gets stolen, they always go for this organizer."

He pointed toward his bookshelf, specifically to a computer networking reference guide. It was outdated and thick. "Hand me that book over there."

I got up and fetched it. It was deceptively light. I handed it to him.

He opened it up. Inside, was a compartment which contained more meth than I had ever seen in my life.

"Jesus Christ!" I exclaimed.

"Calm down."

"Ho— Holy . . . Fuck, how much is that?" I asked, concerned.

"I don't know. I don't have a scale that will weigh it properly."

"That's all real?"

"You've been smoking it so you tell me."

I couldn't believe my eyes. "How much is that worth?"

"Parted out? Jeez, I don't know. Thirty, forty thousand dollars, maybe? I have more, but this is all I keep here."

I was in awe. I had never seen that much dope before. Even when I was in college and using fairly regularly, I never had more than two hundred buck's worth of shit at any given point. While some of my supplies at home were expensive, nothing was in that ball park.

"Are you really moving that much stuff?"

"I can. I actually got this on consignment. There's not a lot of people in the city who move more than I do."

"I would hope so," I said with a slight tremble, "or we'd all be dead!"

This wasn't advice he was giving me. It was a confession. No one shows the most valuable thing in their home to a stranger, even as quickly as we built our relationship up. His voice was casual, but he spoke with the same tone when he got the dosage wrong with Rick. Behind his false bravado and his tired eyes was a man who begged for understanding and a rescue. He seemed more concerned about my response than expecting thanks for a tip. He was in deep and he wanted out. I feared what possible ramifications could exist for not paying back "a consignment" of that size. Still, he didn't take the IT lifeline I offered earlier. There had to be another option to save him.

"You know, if it's that hard to make rent here, I'll buy you a ticket to Nebraska. Or even Oklahoma City. I know you love this place, but you can't keep doing this. The chickens come home to roost eventually, you know?"

"I know," he said quietly. "But I'm not there yet. Close, but not yet. When I am, sure, I want to do something different. I've seen the sex parties and the big city. It's fun until it's not. But

I'm not in a place where I can jumpstart my next big change yet."

"What would that take?" I asked, willing to do anything for it.

"I don't know. Make a million dollars in Bitcoin? Invent a new sex product and have everyone else sell it for me? I just can't go back home the way I left."

He had the tremble of fear in his voice. Fear of the future or the past I wasn't sure. I didn't know what he meant by "the way I left," but I wasn't going to pry much deeper. He was feeling exposed and vulnerable. And I didn't want to push him back to the hair trigger he'd been on earlier in line at the store.

"I just want to make sure you're safe. Goddamn, you know I don't judge. Hell, you wouldn't believe how much equipoise I can make at home. I have enough for you, me, and the entire Kentucky Derby. But you have a lifeline if you choose to use it. Because that is a shitload of crack and people don't come back from that lifestyle beyond a certain point!"

He closed the book and handed it to me without saying a word. I deposited it safely back on the shelf. I couldn't look at it anymore. He took out his organizer again, removed a few syringes, and started prepping shots. Grabbing a bottle of drinking water off of his desk, he back-loaded each rig, then replaced it carefully in the organizer.

I hated watching him at "work." He was a slave to the machine that he built, and it was obvious he was no longer in control. I was desperate to change the subject.

"So, this party. When and where is it?"

"About twenty minutes from here. We'll probably show up around ten-ish. You'll like these guys. Everyone calls them The Pit Bulls."

"Interesting nickname."

Ryan explained. "Yeah, they're both short. They're not on the apps. Adorable older couple, but not too old. They usually throw a nice get-together. Very tame compared to what all is out there, and kind of the opposite of Rick. I think you'll enjoy it."

"Well, that gives us a lot of time. Do you want to get out of the house and explore around town with me?"

"No, I'm going to be busy up until then," he said, not looking up from his work.

"Okay. Well, do you need me out of your hair?"

He thought about it for a bit, cocking his head to the side. "Well, I don't think you want to tag along and, honestly, I don't even know where I'm going until I start getting texts. But it's the weekend and there's plenty going on. How about we plan on meeting up closer to ten?"

I agreed, both with not wanting to tag along and with meeting up later in the evening. It hurt to see him distressed and so enslaved to his work. I'm sure it was the same pity he felt for me knowing I had to return home soon. I understood that he had to get out there and move ice. That was how he kept the roof above his head and the food in his belly. I got up from the bed, gave him a hug which he returned only because he felt obligated to, and then I left.

NINETEEN

I SPENT A COUPLE MORE hours exploring the city before heading back to the hotel for a recharging nap. When I woke, it was dark. The city seemed to burst with life, much more so than the nights before. Even the homeless people seemed livelier, energized by the collective heartbeat of the city. Booze, I figured, lubricated the wheels of all this social interaction.

Ryan sent me an address and told me to meet him there around ten. Fashionably late may have been on time, but I didn't want to miss any fun. I locked it into Google maps, and made my way there quickly.

I took my time walking up to the house. It was complete with an attached garage and a tiny yard. There was a wrought iron gate which led to a small garden, and past that a small walkway to the entrance. The natural incline of the land ended at a porch step. It was both welcoming and foreboding.

My clothes were decently uncomfortable. I wore my new harness I bought from Mr. S and a custom jock underneath my normal clothes. While the leather looked great and was durable enough for even the roughest play, it felt somewhat confining. It hugged my muscles closely and made them pop from under my shirt. I thought about how ironic it was that looking good and feeling good were so antithetical to each other. The only people who understood that did porn, bodybuilding, or fashion.

A homey porch light lit the area. I rang the buzzer while pondering what excuse to give if it were the wrong house. I always had a slight paranoia going up to houses I didn't know. Where I was from, you could get shot for that type of thing. I guessed every millennial had that problem though. My friends who used GPS for directions inevitably checked it every two minutes, even when fully on track. The need to be vindicated that I was in the right place, at the right time, was powerful.

A man in his mid-fifties fumbled with the lock then opened the front door of the house. He was wearing nothing but a white terry cloth bathrobe, which covered a strong muscular frame. He was short, maybe five feet three, tops, and seemed just as wide. His stance made him appear infinitely more humble and warm than I would have imagined a moniker like "The Pit Bull" would entail. When I thought about pit bulls, I thought of aggression, and their fierce bite. This guy was a lapdog by comparison and seemed excited to see me. Beneath the robe, he possessed a tinge of femininity without being over the top.

"Is Ryan here?"

"Of course, sweetheart," he said, making no other introduction. The unmistakable quiver of stimulants could be heard in his voice, but he seemed lucid enough.

He stepped back and motioned for me to follow him. Before I did, I took one last look at the yard through the gate. The garden was well-manicured, and I imagined beautifully green when lit by the morning sun. In the background was a tiny fountain, dry, accompanied by some Japanese–inspired statues which established logical, well-framed borders. These statues were small, and more upscale than the typical lawn gnomes I had seen adorn more familiar suburban landscapes. I thought of how tranquil and deliberate the whole scene looked compared to the chaos I was stepping into.

I decided homicidal maniacs or drug freaks don't hire a landscaper.

I looked back to him. Two steps were all that separated this seemingly well-to-do regular home from the bacchanalian scene I knew went on inside.

Step. Step.

As I followed him through the front door, I was greeted by exotic art. Gigantic oil paintings filled the entryway. Each one encapsulated Asian and eastern styles and gave the room a spacious feel. It was very much the antithesis of Ryan's cramped room, full of projects and random Amazon purchases. There is a difference between wealth and class, and this home seemed to have both in noticeable amounts. The entryway felt like a formal gallery dedicated to oriental artists. It made me feel small and, possibly, my host, larger.

A spacious ceiling opened up to where the second (and perhaps third) floors would have been.

Music was playing in a far-off room. It was electronica and mirrored the same bounce that I had felt earlier at the dance party. I had become numb to such music, though my attention was captured when the volume suddenly increased. A door opened and a naked man, about my age and also fit, walked across the hallway to a bathroom on the other side. The music returned to its previous volume, all the while my host smiled as I caught the eye-candy traversing across.

"We're in the back. Would you like me to get you anything?"

"No, I'm fine. Thanks."

He led me to the room with the music. The volume turned down quite a bit as I approached, and I could hear a few people bickering about what to play and how far to turn it down. The door opened. Six guys, almost all in their mid-twenties to mid-thirties were there, sitting on or around a large L-shaped sofa. Their builds varied, but they were wholesomely attractive. Only a few were wearing pants, none had shirts, and all were socializing. Their voices rattled with joyful laughter and rapid enthusiasm as their hands alternated between resting on the legs of their partners and stroking their cocks. A seventh was adjusting the music downward on his phone. Music, which was piped into a very expensive sound system, eventually settled at a reasonable volume and blended perfectly into the room.

The seventh captivated my eye as much as he captivated my heart. Ryan. His face lit up when I walked in.

"Chris! You made it."

"Of course! Where else would I go?"

I entered the room without acknowledging the others and greeted him with a kiss. When we finished, I took stock of the rest of the room. A few torch lighters were on a high-end, glass-top coffee table. A couple of pipes joined them, off to the side, and the guys were taking turns passing one around. Their hands shook a little as they brought it to their mouths, lit the bowl for a few seconds, and rocked it to and fro. My host approached the only other man similar to his age on the couch and grabbed a pipe from him. The pipe, still warm, took no time to let off white cloudy wisps, which blended seamlessly into the paint and color of his bathrobe.

I took the man who gave the pipe to be my host's husband or partner. He was naked and, after giving the pipe, started receiving head from an eager otter at his side. The robed host went to reload the pipe, and in doing so exposed his partner's cock to me in full view. It was girthy to the point of inducing some fear and made mine look modest in comparison.

This man could never be straight. His cock is just too impressive.

I focused on the otter and admired his hunger for the older man. He was in his mid-twenties and happily engaged in unhinging his jaw. After a moment, he opened his eyes. Realizing we both saw each other was energizing. Without losing his rhythm, he lifted his head, removed the man's penis from his mouth, and smiled at me before closing his eyes and resuming again. The older man didn't seem to notice or care about this small break. Of all of the individuals in the room, none exuded sexuality like he did. His eyes were as dark as his hair, and just as devilish. Ehren had a humanizing companion in his dog Ruffles, Ryan had his wit and his way outside of the bedroom, but this nameless otter became burned into my memory with both precum and a smile on his face.

"You have good timing. I was just talking about you," Ryan said. From what I could tell, he was sober and relatively well rested.

"Yeah, he was," another said. His hands reached into his pants to pull out his hard dick. "And he wasn't exaggerating!"

"Anything he said was either all good or all true," I responded.

I pulled off my shirt to expose my new harness. Not many individuals were wearing leather, leaving me feeling somewhat overdressed for the occasion. Still, my willingness to outperform the others trumped any inhibitions I had. My muscles were accentuated by the leather and I took comfort in knowing I looked better than most.

My admirer's eyes flared open and his cock throbbed. He was excited. Excited and high. What a great combination. Even though I figured they knew my name through whatever conversation I had missed, I had no idea of theirs. But I didn't want to. I went to take a seat by the sofa but was interrupted by the person to my side who started removing my jeans. He struggled with pulling my pants past my beefy thick quads, but his eagerness paid off in the end when he won out.

A pipe, which I took for being passed clockwise, was handed to me. It was a treat and an invitation to get more comfortable. I took it gratefully and ignited the torch lighter which came with it. The rocks inside were already melted to a thick slab of chemical goop at the bottom. It ignited almost instantaneously. There was much more in there than I would have loaded myself but, to be honest, I had never smoked with this many people before. The smoke filled the bowl then escaped through the tiny misshaped hole in the top. As I exhaled, billowing clouds flooded the room, then rose to the top and slowly faded from view and into the ether.

It took no time to make it from my lungs to my head. The taste had the same overly pure quality I remembered from Ethan's place. I immediately wanted more but forced myself to pause as I didn't want to cheat the rotation.

Ryan interrupted the silence instilled by my breath.

"Anyone wanna do some G?" he asked the group.

"Oh my God, you have some?" the guy to my left said, as if it was a wholly unexpected invitation.

"Whatever you need. Who else?"

The man to my right, looking dazed, fell gently off the couch and started sucking my cock. He was sloppy but into it, and spent most of his time playing with my head. He was a bit fuzzier than my normal type, and brawny. I remembered him as one of the go-go dancers from Bears by the Bay. While he wasn't the kind of guy I normally picked up in clubs, the fact he was paid to dance nearly naked made it worthwhile.

At first, only a few hands went up, but quickly more joined them. For the briefest of moments, all sexual activity in the room paused. Seizing the opportunity but still wary from my earlier experience, mine joined them.

"Can you dose mine in half?"

I wasn't afraid of trying new things, but I felt asking would at least remind Ryan to double-check all of the dosages. Ryan nodded to me silently while counting the hands.

He walked across the room to the bar on the far wall. A mini-fridge was inside a cabinet, along with even more Japanese shit. He pulled out a large Gatorade bottle and some shot glasses then began measuring things out. A small bundle of syringes sat on the bar, identifiable by their trademark orange caps. All were pre-loaded and ready for use.

"Your feng is very shui," I said to my hosts, gesturing toward the art while sneaking in a second puff. My comment broke the spell of silence, and sexual contact seemed to resume almost instantly across the room. It felt oddly appropriate to converse about things that weren't sexual in nature, even while my cock was getting sucked.

"I'm glad you like it. We collect," Beer Can Cock said over the gurgles of his friend, who then decided to get up, go to the next man who had his dick out, and start sucking him.

Ryan returned with shot glasses in hand, all filled with what appeared to be yellow Gatorade. Mine, at his left index finger, was given out first. In my experience, the party-and-play crowd never judged participants for wimping out on dosages. I wasn't a sissy for taking the weak shot, and if someone had the fleeting thought that I was, all I had to do was call them a junkie to shut them up.

Plus, it was just hard to call me a sissy while I was getting my dick sucked.

After everyone had their drinks, I gathered everyone's attention for a toast.

"To hedonism?" I said questioningly, raising my libation.

We all guzzled the drinks down while giggling at the awkwardness of it all. I didn't need to tell them this was my first shot of GHB, certainly that much was known. Still, it inspired a chuckle that I enjoyed while relishing the moment where I stole the center of attention from the drugs. I listened to them and smiled as they commented on the foul taste. Years of diet and training allowed me to focus on function over flavor. A feeling of superiority overcame me as I realized these guys couldn't handle half the protein powders I drank daily, while I ignored the irony of me handling half their routine dosage.

I passed the pipe to Ryan, who looked at me graciously and smiled. He passed it to another, refusing the smoke as always, and then downed his drink.

I tried to relax and focus on my partner. He was enjoying the taste of precum from milking my member. Occasionally, he'd greet me with a devilish smirk. I couldn't help but put my hands around his head and thrust on occasion. He felt good, and the dope enhanced the experience. The outer part of my brain melted into self-indulgent pleasure. Sex was becoming more mechanical all around, and I could feel my upper brain functions suspend as my rawer urges took over.

Someone tapped me on the shoulder, and I noticed part of the group stood up. People were walking off toward a backroom. I motioned for the go-go bear to stop. After he slowly limbered up, I got up to join him and followed the rest of the group.

They call it California king for a reason. After a certain number of people, even a regular king just isn't big enough. We had pushed that envelope before all of us could sit down on the enormous bed. I made a point to sit next to the cock-hungry otter with insatiable thirst, as there was something in his eyes that attracted me. Someone pulled out a wet rag and the pipe then set them both down by the nightstand. It was only a moment before another individual picked it back up and began hitting it again with the lighter. Someone commented that it should cool. A small cloud was pulled from the bowl then a hand wrapped it in the wet rag with a slight hiss.

Ryan looked over at one of the other guys, then they both disappeared from main view. After what seemed like only a couple of minutes, slight coughing came from their general direction. When they emerged, they were both wide eyed and intense looking. Their pupils had dilated significantly, though it was hard to tell because they almost refused to stand still. They had shared in a ritual that the rest of the group didn't want to partake in and pretended didn't exist. Ryan then placed two empty syringes in a nearby waste basket, before they all but disappeared around a corner, barely still in view. While I couldn't see the top's face, I had full view of Ryan's head and upper half as he got into a nearby sling. Given how quickly he began rocking, the other took no time at all to penetrate him.

The energy was certainly different on their side of the room. I knew Ryan injected, and while I had plenty of experience with meth, I had never seen anything like this before. He appeared lost in his own body. His arms flailed somewhat wildly, but he kept the one I believed he injected into above his head for optimal blood flow. Doing so seemed to facilitate as much circulation into his brain as his body could stand. He seized regularly in pleasure, as a smile, cruel and satanic, filled his face. He looked up fiercely at his unseen partner. The two fucked, hard. The intensity could be described more as violent than rough. A few of the others, including my go-go dancing friend, watched from the relative safety of the bed. They jacked off while taking pleasure from seeing the fruits of that forbidden tree.

If ever there was such a thing as perversion, this was likely it. The drug and its effects were as much a turn-on as the sex. And for some in that room, likely more so.

I focused on my partner, the cute otter, who had done enough speed before I arrived to not be distracted by such things. We kissed and fondled each other with an almost joyous playful sense. Our intensity, mild in comparison, was still rigorous as we smiled in delight with every touch. We both filled each other with sensations, relishing each nuzzle and lick as the rest of the room faded away. I took the intermittent chance to hit a pipe, but mostly enjoyed the spontaneity of it all. After fifteen minutes, a sudden drunkenness hit my mind.

The GHB had kicked in.

It hit suddenly, like a freight train, with the strength of a pillow. Ryan was right, it was similar to booze. I was instantly at the equivalent point of a few hours of celebratory drinking. I felt relaxed but also turned on. My cock got harder, almost abnormally hard, in fact, and I could feel myself almost cum. I was experiencing all the pleasure of a full orgasm but without the costly bodily expense of physically shooting my load. My partner appeared to sense my high and redoubled his efforts to bring me to climax. I enjoyed every moment of the ecstasy as he rubbed his fingers over my chest and around my ass. Occasionally, he'd bite my nipples, playfully but intensely, yet not so intense as to cause alarm.

I turned him over to his stomach. I explored every orifice of his body that I could find, taking the time to feel the separations in his muscles. He loved it when I pushed deep and hard into his flesh, and I used my knowledge of anatomy to my advantage. He enjoyed when I pressed into his lats or ate out his hole. The smell of sweat, from me and others, filled the room. More importantly, perspiration coated our bodies, creating the most sensual lube imaginable and enabling me to easily penetrate him. I massaged his scalp as I buried his face in a pillow.

He grunted, exposing his desire to be manhandled. I pressed my cock deeply into him, feeling myself leak cum into his innermost guts. His thin frame made it easy to abuse him, and an occasional whiff of a nearby bottle of poppers enabled him to receive as much cock as I could give.

He got back up, exposing large puddles of sweat on the bed, and began using its slickness and the firmness of my harness to maintain whatever position seemed to suit him at the time. He was as rough as I liked and didn't show weakness or fear of demanding what he wanted. He was a bottom who was exacting.

I felt myself get dizzy from the pleasure, and looked over to the nightstand. Time had passed in the manner of a dream. I was either enjoying myself too much to note the time or maybe I passed out, I don't know. I didn't recall losing consciousness or falling asleep, but the bed had become less occupied. I could hear fucking and occasional laughter from the room with the couch in it. A few glasses, presumably of water, were on the nightstand where the pipe used to be. I could only assume that the rest were tiring of the cottonmouth and chemical smoke which filled their lungs and the room, or that we had monopolized the scene. By my senses, time had slowed down more than I sped up. I was hardly the most inebriated in the room, yet I began to feel like I was the most thirsty.

I excused myself from my playmate, who honestly seemed glad for the break.

"I think I should lie down for a bit," he said, pulling himself up and lying in the bed naturally. He threw a nearby overstuffed pillow under his head and grabbed a drink. Not trusting any of the glasses around, I got up to fetch my own.

I found an empty glass by the bar, filled it with tap water, and drank it heartily before filling it up a second time.

"Did you cum yet?" My playmate had followed me.

"No," I said, still hard as hell from the GHB.

"Woof! Take a break then, because I want your load."

I ignored him and walked back into the bedroom where I positioned myself across the bed. Ryan was still in the sling. His playmate had disappeared and been cycled out for another. Given how much time had passed, I had no idea how many partners he claimed that night. The hardy angry fucking sounds were replaced with much more calm ones. The shot they did earlier had run most of its course. He was still very intensely sexual, but more lucid now.

I was enamored by watching him get what he wanted.

So enamored, even, that I didn't notice The Pit Bulls come back in the room to spectate as well. Both men held each other in a romantic warm embrace. They didn't wear wedding bands or those dog collars some gay men wore. Instead, they wore each other, deeply and affectionately, around their necks and hearts. They were kindred spirits, higher than the moon, but in orbit with each other.

"Happy Dore, sweetheart," one whispered, lost in his lover's eyes.

"Happy anniversary, babe."

They kissed. Passionately. Affectionately. I could see the exhaustion in their eyes. It was a celebration of life these two were sharing, even though they were killing themselves doing it.

I wondered what circumstances caused them to meet. Was it at a previous Dore? How old was this damned leather festival, anyway? Maybe their love forged the first one? Was there some great Book of Life that "Gay Saint Peter" kept up in "Gay Heaven"? Was this a romantic vacation at a friend's house or how they normally were? Maybe it was a milestone for them, like a twenty-year anniversary. Or thirty? Perhaps they weren't a couple and just lifelong friends with benefits. Maybe they were bullied together in their younger years based on their size. Perhaps they were rich socialites who had more money than morals and this was their way of escaping it all.

My mind raced with possibilities, accelerated by chemistry. I badly wanted to ask them what the real story was. More so, however, I wanted to keep it a secret. A secret only the two of them could share. Away from me and the rest of the spun-up boys.

Someone had to preserve the romance in the midst of the misery.

They were in each other's minds and we weren't invited.

My legs began cramping from a lack of electrolytes. Not severely, but enough to be uncomfortable. I needed to move and get some blood flowing. I went over to the sling with Ryan.

The person topping him sensed my presence and went into the room with the couch.

I stood at the sling. Ryan looked up at me with his wild, dilated eyes. The glint in them, his soul, still shined as brightly as when I first met him. His candle was burning at both ends while he grabbed the straps of the sling firmly. He was tired, but happy, and he wanted me inside of him. He bit his lip, pushed his cheeks out slightly, and smiled. I didn't say a word as I penetrated him. He was very wet, with lube, sweat, and cum. I had enough GHB and crystal in me to have kept going for quite a while. Moreover, there was enough sexual desire and lust in me to have torn him in two. I had basically practiced all night for this main event, and had been enabled by the fluffing of numerous strangers in an environment where casual sex was considered appropriate and normal.

But I couldn't do it.

The only bodily fluid I could produce for him was a single tear down my cheek. It was too much. Whatever aggression or anger I could inflict onto other men, I just couldn't bring to him. I fucked so many and never wanted to even know their names, but this one I wanted to make love to. I wanted him as a person, not like the rest of this hedonistic orgy. My upper brain functions won out completely over the rest of my mind. I felt my erection lose its rigor as I leaned over (as though to fuck him deeply), kissed him softly, and whispered.

"I'm sorry."

"It's okay," he said, returning the token. I stood up, regained my distance from him, and walked out of the room, drying my eyes as discretely as I could.

Outside the bedroom the lights were brighter. Stealing a look in a mirror by the bar, my eyes were dilated widely and intensely. Several hours had passed since the party started, though it was hard to tell. A few of the guys who were undressed previously had put their clothes back on, and the mood became a lot more casual than sexual. I found my pants, put them on, and entered the conversation when appropriate. A few people were telling jokes and commenting about their hometowns. Even the topic of sports came up at one point, though it was quickly changed since too few people could keep the conversation going.

Eventually, the previously robed Pitbull re-entered the room with a cheese tray and some grapes. He was ever the host even as the party was winding down. It was a polite gesture, but it changed the dynamic of the room yet again. It seemed to indicate it was time to disband.

Ryan eventually entered the room as well, also with his pants on. He used a hand towel to dry the sweat from his brow and chest. He was a mess, dehydrated and drained, and didn't have much gusto left. He went over by the bar, reached around the mini-fridge, and grabbed his bag. It didn't take me long to guess he had brought the drugs. Putting the bag behind the fridge made it awkward enough that to reach for it would have broadcast an attempt to steal something. He pulled a glass from the bar, filled it with water, splashed his face a bit, and snapped back to attention.

"Happy Dore, guys," he said to the room.

"Happy Dore!" everyone replied, somewhere between excitement and exhaustion.

"Can I talk to you for a bit, Chris?"

I got up. I didn't say anything while I followed Ryan back into the bedroom. I wondered what he would say, or if he was upset at me for showing emotion earlier. I braced myself for getting chewed out for potentially killing the party. He pulled a small cloth rag out of his bag and then went over to the night-stand. He picked up the pipe that was sitting on it and handed it to me.

"Is everything okay?" I asked cautiously.

"Yeah, I just want you to help me pick some things up because you're the only one I can trust with my shit."

"Oh, okay."

I stood there relieved yet empty and powerless in front of him. I was the king of confidence, with nothing in the tank.

"It happens to the best of us, you know," he said with an understanding tone.

"What?"

"Crystal dick. It happens."

I looked at him. Deeply into him. "Yeah, I know. It's not that," I confessed.

"Well, what is it?"

I just looked into him. My hands weakly held on to the side of his pants.

"I . . . hmm . . . I just want . . . I want tonight to last forever."

He looked back into me. Not at me. Into me. We were wandering about in each other's minds, and both knew what the other knew. We felt the torturous pain that only love brings, and the cost of paying to get it. Together we had amazing acceleration but no goddamned brakes and we were headed for the cliff. He wasn't stupid, and I knew he sensed the body heat pulsating from my chest. I wanted to feel the same in him so badly. In that moment, I had nothing else to give. My heart was already in his hands, and I had no idea what he'd do with it.

Without breaking the distance between us, he grabbed the pipe from me. Speechless, he reached into his bag and pulled out a cheap lighter. I stared as he sparked it to life. He brought the flame to the pipe where it began to smoke.

He then put the pipe to his mouth, filled his lungs in deep, and kissed me.

The breath from his lungs filled mine. He was so dehydrated, yet he gave me every remaining drop of moisture he had left. The warm embrace of smoke escaped from our lips and circled above us as we enjoyed this final kiss. The world was on pause. No other sound, feeling, or emotion could enter the room. The drug offered me no energy, nor him. It was as solemn, sad, and beautiful of an exchange as any that two lovers ever experienced. We burned both our candles at that moment. And he was burning his out for me.

He took the rag from me, cooled the pipe, put it back in his bag, and then we left.

TWENTY

I WANT TO SAY THAT we woke up together, blissfully in each other's arms after a night of tranquil slumber. The reality was actually far from the truth. I stayed at his place, in his bed, but couldn't sleep a wink. My waking hours were so fantastic that sleep seemed to be a terrible punishment. Most type A people like ourselves looked at sleep as a waste of time, and time was too precious to sleep through.

His roommate could be heard making noises in the kitchen. After all this time, at the end of the weekend, he finally made a proper appearance. I eventually introduced myself in the form of a brief and wordless nod. I wondered where he spent all his time but, ultimately, didn't care enough to ask. I'd had my fill of social experiences from the previous night, and I was going to be in somewhat of a hurry for these last few hours. I retreated to the bathroom and started a shower.

After a good, hard, deep scrub, most of the chemical smell was removed. I felt clean and comfortable in my own skin again, but still dehydrated in the way that only meth could make me. My skin was somewhat red to show it, and my eyes had small bags under them. Regardless of how I looked, I felt great. I did a mental self-check to determine if I was still high from the night before, but, honestly, was unable to really determine. Normally when I looked this worn down I felt like shit, but I had never experienced a romantic week like this before, either. I eventually settled on just being in a good mood, a natural conclusion to an amazing trip.

When I got out of the shower, Ryan had breakfast waiting for me. Apparently, he had convinced his roommate to make a third plate of eggs and waffles. I devoured them quickly while Ryan took his turn washing away the previous night's sins. The food was good, and while it was by all objective accounts the worst meal I had on the entire trip, it was the first one that qualified as a home cooked meal.

Feeling both refreshed and absolved of the night before, we started anew.

"When do you need to be at the airport?" he asked.

"My flight leaves around 4:00 p.m., so I guess I can't stay too long at the fair. I'll have to check out of the hotel as well."

"Well, you'll at least get the vibe," he said. "If you haven't figured it out yet, all the fun happens beforehand anyway. You should wear your new harness, too."

"To the airport or to the fair?" I asked, honestly unsure.

He laughed. "The fair, silly! Though I'm sure TSA would appreciate the pat down opportunity."

We left as soon as breakfast was done. Together, Ryan and I took a final departure out the garage door. We hailed an Uber and within a short amount of time, were there.

Folsom Street was cordoned off with road blockades. Traffic was backing up so we decided to abandon the Uber early and take a brief walk. The weather was perfect—upper sixties with a calm breeze. I had a hard time determining if the people pointing our way were police or private security guards, but they smiled as though they were glad to be there. The whole place seemed unnavigable without their assistance.

As we approached the entrance, I could see other fairgoers walking with us. Men were pulling off their shirts, putting on harnesses, and lathering themselves up with sun tan lotion. I overheard conversations from people as they walked near us. Many were sex tourists from out of town, asking the way from others. Some volunteered that they were from Los Angeles or San Jose, just up for a day trip. There were even a few women in attendance, though not many, and of course the real possibility floated in my mind that what appeared to be a woman may not have been.

We passed the entrance where a man with a fabulous beard and enchanting green eyes dressed as a nun greeted us. He was taking money. I pulled out my wallet and gave him a twenty. He said he was from the Sisters of Perpetual Indulgence, an organization I had never heard of. But with a name like that, how could I resist contributing a few dollars?

"Preach, sister!" someone exclaimed, much too excitedly for anything going on at eleven in the morning.

Ryan explained. "The Sisters are a great group. They do a lot of volunteerism in the community and make for great social commentary on religion while they're at it."

"Looks like it. They look like a group that can have fun. You know, I've thought about what my drag name would be."

Ryan looked off-put almost. "I so can't picture you in drag. You're way too masculine for that!"

"That's why my name would be *Anna Bolic*."

Ryan looked impressed. "Wow, yeah, that could work, actually. Clever."

We went up to the coat check, though I figured it made more sense to stuff my shirt in my pocket instead. Being only able to enjoy an hour or so made the idea of waiting in line to dress and undress seem kind of silly. I did linger around long enough to enjoy watching other men strip down, sometimes to absolute nothingness, and then go about the fair. Most people wore clothes of some type, though. Shorts and a harness were the equivalent of jeans and a T-shirt, with people adjusting their fashion up and down from there.

The second-most-popular clothing item was pup hoods. As one person wearing one walked by me, I tried to pass out a compliment.

"That's a beautiful mask."

No response came my way.

"Don't call it a mask. It's a hood. Masks are for hiding who you are. You won't find anything like that here," Ryan explained.

He was right. Farther along the path I saw an area where nearly a dozen individuals wearing pup hoods were crawling around on all fours, some taking the opportunity to sniff each other's butts or otherwise emulate playful canine behavior.

On the more extreme end of this cosplay, and by far my favorite, were those in dark fantasy attire. A few people were dressed head-to-toe in leather and latex suits, and showed themselves as ponies or other wild mythical beasts. One such pony, less adorned than the others, took the role very seriously. He was shirtless, decently well built, and pulling his mistress on a tiny chariot. Around his head was proper horse tack, custom fit for a human head. He, like everyone else, took great pride in showing off his attire. His mistress, for added flair, would occasionally whip him for excitement, mostly for show more than an actual insistence that he go faster.

"Wow! You don't see that in Oklahoma."

"I know, right? The ponies are pretty fun."

"So much better than the pups, I think. Why would anyone want to be a pup? Everyone's a pup now, and when I hear gay guys tell me they're pups I usually take that as 'I have issues and need someone to take care of me.'"

"Probably true."

"Plus, if everyone you know does it, I guess it's not really a kink, now is it?"

Ryan didn't respond. He didn't need to. Instead, he pointed out some of the must-see places.

"There's Powerhouse. And Hole in the Wall. Those are usually some of the better ones to go to if you want to get your dick wet. They cater to the hardcore crowd that you like. Plus, plenty of the travelers just walk from nearby hotels, so if you had time I'd say pick up something you like."

"That's convenient. Shop around, walk a quarter mile for a fuck, then come back for more, huh?"

He feigned fatigue and strife, raising the back of his palm to his forehead. "I know, life here is just so hard!"

Vendors filled the street representing nearly all possible aspects of the adult entertainment and sex industry. There were those who sold the classic must-have items such as lube companies, porn producers, and sex toy manufacturers. The fair was designed to cater to leathermen and kinksters specifically, so individuals selling paddles and harnesses were the bulk of the booths.

And, of course, like more commonplace events, plenty of these vendors were giving live demonstrations of their products. One sex furniture vendor had someone tied up to a Saint Andrews Cross while another patron got to sample a flogger on their partner. Such demonstrations gathered sizable crowds, usually eager with money in hand to purchase items.

Food was also a large part of the fair, as was the drink. The beer lines were quite long, and the aroma of trans fats and cholesterol filled the street from sidewalk to sidewalk. Those not indulging in food were oftentimes sampling life's other pleasures. Some were enjoying live music, others were meeting old friends, and a few individuals were getting fucked or blown.

"Obviously, the rules are you shouldn't be fucking in the street. You should go inside a club for that. But that doesn't stop the adventurous types," Ryan pointed out.

"That's awesome!" I said, entranced at the brazen attitude of it all.

I thought about how fun it would be to fuck someone on a public street in front of all these people. Sadly, though, time didn't allow for it.

Goddamned motherfucking time.

"If only I had more of it," I said.

"More of what?"

"Time."

He looked at me. He knew exactly what I meant. He smiled, but kept on showing me things. He was doing his best to fill every moment with pleasure and I could tell.

"And here, they do naked Twister every year!"

Indeed, there were a few guys I recognized from posters at Mr. S and from various porn movies doing just that. It was comical more than sexual, and the crowd was enjoying the show. Music played loudly on a nearby stage and while it was really good, the spectacle was in the sights more than the sounds.

"I love the sense of humor everyone has about sex," I commented.

I then saw Ehren about forty feet from me. He was there with a few other people, walking up the street.

"Oh, wow, it's Ehren! Hey! Hey! How's it going!"

I waved. He smiled and waved politely back but continued walking. I felt somewhat betrayed that he didn't come and say hi.

Ryan could sense my disappointment. I whispered under my breath, "Was I that bad?"

"Nah, he's just busy. He told me he had a blast with you. That's the thing with sex out here. It's just another way of saying hello. Friends with benefits is really more benefits with friends. You fuck, find out if you click, and if you do, socialize afterward. It's how the gay man 'do.' If you were here another weekend, I'm sure he'd be begging for that dick of yours again."

"Well, who cares about him when I have you?"

Ryan smiled back. I suspected he didn't feel the same way about me that I did for him, and I was coming to terms with it. Before it could turn into too much of a squishy moment, he said, "Hey, if you want, I can wait in line and get you a beer while you check things out."

"No, I'd rather just walk around with you if that's okay."

He paused. "Okay, that's understandable."

We continued on. A few minutes later some people I didn't know waved at Ryan. He, in like kind, waved back but didn't seem to stop or spend much time with them.

"Happy Dore!" they'd say.

"You too, babe! Call me sometime!" he'd respond.

This happened a few times before I finally had to say something.

"You really do know everyone out here, don't you?"

"Me?" he responded, somewhat surprised. "No, not at all. I don't even remember the last guy's name. Everyone knows me, though."

"Yeah, I'm that way back home, I guess."

"Not a bad thing, to be well known."

"True. It has its perks. I also can't get over the greeting, 'Happy Dore!' Like, it's more of a holiday than Presidents Day and Martin Luther King Day, isn't it? After all, no one says, 'Happy MLK Day!'"

He thought about it for a moment, cocking his head to the side. "True, but you don't get laid because it's Martin Luther King Day. But, yeah, now that you mention it, I don't know where the greeting came from. It's just what people say."

I figured I had to try it out. I found a random stranger and enthusiastically said, "Happy Dore!"

He seemed confused, but hugged me anyway before going on his way. "Happy Dore!" he returned, somewhat cautiously.

The fair was starting to get pretty packed. At this point, we were almost shoulder-to-shoulder, pushing ourselves through the crowd with some difficulty.

"Damn, it's more like Mardi Gras than Pride."

"Yeah, well, Pride has all the political gays. This just has the ones who like sex. Tends to attract more people when they realize they don't have to do anything but bust a nut," Ryan responded.

I grabbed his hand to avoid getting lost in the shuffle. In the stream of people, I recognized a large number of faces. Many were at Bears by the Bay (some of which I was sure I made out with or danced alongside). Others I recognized from my walk in the Mission or from shopping at the leather store. It was a beautiful microcosm of the city—our city—and I felt a closer kinship with these people than I did with those I lived near and had known for far longer.

Even the damned twink Ryan got angry with could be seen in the distance. He took no time pretending he didn't see us.

The faces passed by us like the sands of time, each one carrying with them a precious memory or the potential to make a new friend. When the familiar faces were exhausted, we were on the other side of the pack, walking onto the sidewalk off a small street. My heart fell in my chest suddenly. I was speechless.

"It's beautiful," I finally said solemnly.

"You think so?"

"No one's ever given me a whole city before."

"Yeah, well, it's a good start."

I looked at Ryan and teared up. He truly was incredible. My fishbowl must have seemed so tiny compared to his ocean, which still wasn't enough to satisfy him. He wanted the whole world and was just starting at this edge. I felt he didn't want it to himself but, rather, to share it with me. That meant more than I could ever give him in return. What drug could ever replace that? No chemical can make you unlonely. No formula can grant companionship.

He gave up the life I was going back to, and while he was lonely, he didn't regret it. Just the same way I didn't regret going back home. It was the right thing to do, not in a moral sense, but in the correct sense. We both were getting exactly what we wanted. It wasn't happiness in that breath, it was companionship. Even if it was for a short period of time.

The now-familiar San Francisco fog lingered in the distance. In my mind, the collective clouds and companionship were wrapped around the city like they were wrapped around us the previous night.

"It's time."

TWENTY-ONE

MADE IT TO THE airport on time. I didn't have much to spare, which, in my mind, was the most optimal of all situations. It meant none was wasted earlier when it was most precious.

Airport time is, of course, worth absolutely nothing. It is simply waiting for other people to do things so that I can do the things I want to do. Or to be at the places I want to be, with the people I want to be with. What I wanted was to be with Ryan, in some fashion, but it wasn't in the cards.

So I did the thing anyone in an airport does when they can't be with someone they want to be with, in the place they want to be at.

I cried.

A lot.

I knew I wouldn't get to see him again and, if I did, it wouldn't be under the same circumstances for sure. The odds of someone in his situation making it out alive (and sane and healthy) were slim at best. Just how many impossible things could someone wish for before karma decided the bill was due? I tried to pull my composure together by boarding time and for the most part succeeded. Upon takeoff though, I lost it again. My heart sank as the plane ascended with a steep incline, and I'm pretty sure it's still there, sitting on the runway in that city at the edge of the world. My tears became more gentle as the distance grew, but my sadness remained.

The next few weeks were pretty rough. My work suffered. A broken heart tends to break other things one loves, and I certainly wasn't kind to the customers. Or to my co-workers, for that matter. "Respectful but not friendly" would have been the best way to describe my demeanor and attitude. I debriefed Donald and lauded the technologies that the convention focused on. I brought up specific recommendations that we could undertake as a company. None of my recommendations were actualized into reality.

People asked several questions about my time.

"Did you get to swim in the ocean?" they'd ask.

"I didn't get around to it," I'd respond.

"How could you go to San Francisco and not tour Alcatraz?" another would say.

"How could you go to San Francisco and that be the first thing you do?" I'd say back.

Whatever was going through their heads, wasn't going through mine. And wherever Ryan was, I knew it wouldn't be going through his, either.

My business relationship with Ryan did take off for a while. He placed a few big orders with me, and was always respectful of when I needed to take time off to focus on training and other personal things. He wasn't always on time with the cash, but he was predictable. I tended to offer him credit when it made sense and we always squared up later.

His preferred payment method was cash, sent in greeting cards and other packages. He'd usually scrawl some friendly note in the card and I looked forward to seeing his handwriting more than the money. Sometimes he'd text me about hooking up with a porn star or going to the bathhouse, but on the whole we kept it to business as much as it made sense to. Occasionally he'd mail me a bottle of something: Truvada sometimes, other times Viagra, which made me smile. His regular brand of happiness wasn't what I wanted and he knew it. Instead, he substituted other things which made me smile, usually with the comment, "Go out and get laid."

We continued like this for the better part of a year. The social calls and even the orders got fewer and farther between. He started becoming less responsive and I found myself eventually texting Ehren to find out what was going on. Ehren told me Ryan was starting to lose friends and was becoming a bit unstable and reclusive. He had gotten kicked out of the house when he quit paying rent. Even with all the money he mailed me and deals he was making, his profits went to the city's incredible cost of living or up his arm. A few months later, Ehren also became unresponsive and disappeared. We had shared a fun night, but he had other things to do with his life than keep in touch with me.

Ryan's decline in sales led to mine, and I decided it was time to retire the steroid gig. His lack of a permanent address made it impossible for me to ship supplies to him anyway. Sure, the money was great while it lasted, but the long arm of the law tends to catch up with you in the end. I feared for Ryan and he talked about too many close calls with the police for me to tempt fate anymore. Dylan and I still dabbled from time to time, but the longer our relationship bloomed, the less about drugs and bodybuilding it became. He started dating a wonderful girl, and I rededicated myself to the career in an effort to find meaning in it.

I called Ryan to ask if there was anything I could do to help. He refused to take a hand-out and said he was going back home to Nebraska. His parents were going to take him in as long as he went to rehab. Even a thousand miles away, it didn't take them long to figure out something had broken in their son. He didn't want to do it, but being a homeless drug dealer was the alternative and it just wasn't viable. He explained that his customers and former friends didn't want their dealer moving in with them. I offered him a plane ticket to Oklahoma if he wanted to try and start over here, but he declined.

My love affair with the West Coast is still a very real thing. Each year, I make a point to go out there. Sometimes to San Francisco, sometimes to other cities. It's hard to think of myself as a drug cook or kingpin or whatever people would label me as. Life's too short to limit myself to one life experience, though life wouldn't be the same if I was denied any experience I ever had. Not every vacation is a sexcation, and regardless of who I travel with, I make a point to get something out of it. Something to take home that isn't a shot glass or tie-dye shirt. Something that is more personal and meaningful to myself and my identity. As I heard a close friend of mine say once, "I am not as good as I once was, but I was once as good as I ever was."

Whatever the fuck that's supposed to mean.

My last trip took me out to Oregon.

I was alone enjoying some coffee when my phone rang. It was Ryan. I asked how he was doing and he said, "Not well."

He had been a passenger in a car with a small group of his friends. They were all smoking meth and getting spun when they got pulled over for speeding. Ironic, right? While only the driver was arrested on the spot, the cop let Ryan go after taking his information. Ryan had to take a court-ordered drug test and wanted my help. It was important that he passed it. There was only one person on earth he trusted with this habit who knew anything about chemistry, and I was the lucky guy.

It was hard listening to his story. The hope, beauty, and passion that made me fall in love with him had faded, but the love was still there. Just like the stairs to his house, or his messy room, it was so easy to ignore the blemishes while I was caught up in the moment. The journey was meaningful, even if it was taken on a broken road.

I couldn't deny him my emotions when he told me what had happened. Even though we had flipped positions, with him being in flyover country and me on the West Coast, I still felt close to him. I felt sadness when he felt sadness and no time apart numbed that. If anything, it amplified it. Yet I couldn't help but see it through the prism of fact. His reality was falling apart. He lost his career, his friends, his home, and soon—unless I helped him—his freedom. He asked me what he could do to make this go away, and I wrestled with the answer unlike I've wrestled with any before.

The pharmacology of how meth breaks down wasn't new to me. It is processed by the kidneys, which, as luck would have it, are also in charge of manipulating the body's pH levels through the careful regulation of electrolytes. If you massively manipulate the pH of the body toward alkalinity (non-acid), you can lower the amount of meth that is detectable in urine.

Baking soda and antacids would set Ryan free. He'd have to drink so much that his stomach would feel like a volcano, but he'd pass the test. He'd end up back on the streets, lost and without hope, but he'd have his freedom.

But even though I knew the answer, I struggled with his question.

Sometimes what we ask for isn't what we need.

He was hurting. He was in pain. I remembered his confession and him toiling away in his room prepping shot after shot, many for himself and many to sell. He wasn't at a point in his life where he wanted to be, and he had no North Star to guide him. I was the only one he felt comfortable with getting him back on track, but his pride wouldn't let him ask me directly.

I decided to answer his question with the truth, and his query with a lie.

"Orange juice," I lied. "The acid will get what you need."

We talked for a bit longer. He sent me pictures of him and I sent pictures of me. He looked beat up. Meth had damaged his skin in terrible ways and he was rarely smiling in the pictures. He was still my love, and always will be, but the candle had been burned pretty badly in the journey—a journey that wasn't ending in a happy way or a sad way, just ending with him getting what he wanted. It had a completeness to it. I knew that whatever he would face by failing the drug test was going to be better than the path he was on.

He would have continued harming himself. He would have continued beating up the one body he was given, and one that I loved so much.

He would have burned up completely. I was greedy and had to keep his fire alive just a little longer.

I hung up and thought about what I did. I think about it every day. Every. God. Damned. Day.

I want to say now, "I'm sorry, Ryan, if it hurt you. I love you very much. You mean the world to me and I would give anything to have you back as I remember you." He is still in my head. I hope that he can hear my thoughts. I'd give anything to hear his.

I drank my coffee and looked out over the forest. For the first time in too long, I let my senses and feelings overflow my body. I felt my heart pound from the stimulants in the coffee and from breaking over Ryan. Even in the woods, I had stimulants. I focused on the sounds of nature, letting them echo in my brain like so much dance music had before. The countless birds reminded me of people I saw at Dore, dancing at the far edge of the world.

I found myself in the smell of pine needles.

AFTERWORD

I'VE OFTENTIMES SAID THAT for a joke to be funny, it has to be strictly between zero and a hundred percent true. Things that are self-evident are never funny. Neither are outright lies. Whether it's a stereotype or a punchline, humor requires an element of play-with-the-truth in order to be effectual.

In writing *American Dragon*, I found the same to be true for fiction.

In 2015, I was found guilty in a court of law for the manufacture of anabolic steroids. I had always lived a privileged life, and am an accomplished IT engineer. I consider myself a good person who contributes time and money to various charities and my community when I can. Making steroids was to me, like so many others, a natural way to afford a personal habit which got me in the best shape of my life.

To be quite honest, I felt the court system didn't know how to handle me very well. It had been a good half decade since anyone in Oklahoma had been busted for steroid manufacturing and would be at least another three years before someone would be caught with them after me. When people think "drugs," they don't think "steroids." In jail, I spent my time with DUI and other low-level drug offenders for lack of a better place to put me.

My time in jail was brief, but valuable. It allowed me to reflect on the condition of Oklahoma's criminal justice system and the work that we need to do as a state. Many of these reflections you see in the novel. Moreover, though, it afforded me the opportunity to meet remarkable individuals. One of my cellmates, who I will refer to simply as Justin, was dying from Hepatitis C. He was no older than thirty and was an IV drug user. At night I watched him cry himself to sleep as he had very little to look forward to outside of jail or prison. I still remember his face and his cries to this day.

Conversely, I was a fairly affluent individual who had countless opportunities waiting for me upon my release.

Shortly after getting out, I discovered one of my first romantic partners, Shawn, had died a few years back. We had been out of touch for some time, and while we never formally "dated," he was someone I always held dear to my heart. Like Justin, Shawn was an IV meth user and paid the ultimate price for his addiction. Shawn's favorite song was "Bless the Broken Road" and the words described our relationship perfectly. I miss him greatly, and would do anything to have him back.

Like many bisexual and gay men, this is just a small sampling of the lives I've lost to drugs. Justin's and Shawn's deaths could have been prevented if they chose not to use. By no means is that a false statement, and sobriety is the correct answer for the majority of the population. Sadly, though, drug use is a problem we don't know how to solve yet as a society. However, I feel it is the responsibility of the majority to provide help to our fellow men (and women) where it is sensible to do so.

Their deaths could also have been prevented if Oklahoma (and other states) were to adopt common-sense guidelines for handling IV drug users, most notably, implementing sterile syringe exchange programs. Let's be honest with ourselves: criminalizing drug use hasn't reduced the number of users, it's only filled our prisons. However you feel about drugs morally, the ability to spread diseases like Hep. C to the rest of the population is a concern for all of us.

Our nation's drug policy problems don't stop with illicit substances. Too many people who need drugs can't afford them, and we can't even get "good" drugs to "good" people who need them because of high prices. The criminalization of drugs has created a plethora of moral arbitrage conditions where black market is oftentimes cheaper than white market, and quality or speed to access is sometimes better. Solving one of these problems will greatly help in assisting with the other, and too few of our politicians discuss or consider policy in this light.

No system should ever force people to choose between illegal-but-effective care versus legal-but-dangerous care. That isn't justice. It's assault, battery, and sometimes even murder.

As of today, the pharmacology of drugs plays no part in the legal scheduling by the FDA, nor does the situation of the individual user. FDA scheduling is done instead by an archaic interpretation of the word *abuse*, which has been patched by decades of political manipulations. It is for this reason that the most lethal dangerous drugs are Schedule III while marijuana is considered Schedule I. Furthermore, there is no legal safety value for compassionate use, or for those like myself who find certain drugs (steroids) provide more positives than negatives.

When our drug policy becomes more harmful than the conditions drugs can cure (or damage they can cause), the policy itself is flawed.

As a reader, you may notice the contrasts between California and Oklahoma are quite over the top. It is my hope that this novel inspires conversations about these contrasts. We should look objectively at quality (and length) of life as an indicator of what is the right thing to do, not our inner sense of what we feel is "moral." Being "right" while a population struggles and dies is not a good foundation for ethics, nor does it create stable governments.

Is a poorly performing doctor better than a world class drug chemist? What role do "lifestyle" drugs like Viagra, Lipitor, testosterone, or Truvada play in our society? How do we rationalize the desire to achieve peak human performance while refusing ourselves access to our own biochemistry? Does drug control even make sense in a twenty-first-century world where legality is just a matter of where you domicile a corporation or host a webserver?

These are all good questions. But, politics aside, I want this novel to serve as a human story.

I have always loved people, saints and sinners both. Bodybuilding taught me that life is too short to make all of my own mistakes, and sharing in the stories of others is the best way to learn and grow as an individual. Ryan, Ehren, and the other characters were inspired by the countless people I've met through the years. Not representing a single individual, they are emblematic of every drug user and dealer I've ever met. The truth is simply that I have loved getting to meet and interview every user I have for this book. I hope that I meaningfully represented your character, values, and subculture honestly and correctly.

Thank you for your stories. I love you all.

While the plot and story line are fictional, every character has an element of truth to them. In this way, it's almost hard for me to call this fiction, simply because I feel I could run into you all at any point in time, and likely do routinely, without knowing it.

All drug users, abusers, and addicts fall in love at some point on drugs. Oftentimes, this love is with themselves. I was no different myself. These love stories are rarely told because of the cultural taboo that drugs have. The parallels between Ryan and Chris's characters are there for this reason. Whether it's the reprieve from pain that opioids bring, the sexual energy and excitement of meth, or the aesthetic beauty of steroids, drugs are a fantastic way of getting what you want—temporarily. This love affair with drugs, like Chris and Ryan's, is short and powerful.

If you are a user, then you know that love affairs like these are sacred. They are something to be cherished all your life. Try with all of your might to let the word *addict* reflect respect for the positives along with the negatives. Remember the good times you had on the drug as well as the bad, for they are inseparable. The life experience you gained from it is as much a part of your identity as anything else. Resolve to keep as much of the positive in your life as possible without the negatives, and be ruthlessly creative and persistent in the pursuit of this. My experience is that those who do so find untold potential as sober individuals with happy lives.

I further encourage you to seek professional help in tandem with sharing stories with those who have successfully eliminated or reduced their usage. If your drug counselor has never had a substance problem personally, fire them and find one who has. Just as you would take on any skill, goal, or task, don't settle for so-called experts. Find someone you look up to who has accomplished what you need done. If all of your heroes and idols have a habit (or abstain from one), you will mirror them, too.

Alternatively, if you have a loved one who uses substances (or has other addiction problems, such as gambling), the worst thing you can do is judge them. The second worst thing you can do is label them with words like *addict* and *loser*. Focus instead on understanding them as people and exactly what role their drug use plays in their lives.

Every drug has a pharmacological use and, similarly, its own culture. It may be uncomfortable to talk about, but the darkest saddest stories of drug use involve drugs serving as a substitute or symbol for something else. All drug use is self-medicated use, and the root cause of the "disease" lies in the effects of the drug, the environment it's used in, and what the user temporarily gains from it. The best thing you can do is provide your loved one a meaningful alternative to achieve their goals.

Dragons aren't easy to slay, but they're not invincible.